Time X 2

Time X 2
ISBN: 9798612267133
Copyright: U. S. Gov. TXu 2-169-238
Cover design by: D. L. Hammond
Cover photo: No copyright infringement intended
Contact: dianna.hammond90@gmail.com

Acknowledgements

I would like to thank Mary Ann Howard Matesich for her dedication and help while I edited this book. Your encouragement was invaluable.

All my thanks to my son Alex Fontana, for all your help and support.

My family, Kim Hays, Valerie Gernazian, Dorian Harwood, Arthur and Beverly Hammond for your support and love.

All my beta readers and friends who read the draft and gave their honest heartfelt opinions. John Pronos, Brooke French, Amada Schaefer, Sue Erickson, Tracy Campbell. If I have forgotten anyone please forgive and know I appreciate your help.

Dedicated to

Alex and Ali Fontana

I hope your lives are full of laughter and love

Chapter 1

"Living is easy with eyes closed, misunderstanding all you see."

Emily hit the pavement hard. Getting up slowly, she cursed under her breath as she dusted herself off. She had to talk to Sam about these rough landings. She expected to break a leg soon. For as long as she had been time traveling, the landings were always a jolt.

It was quiet on the street as she had anticipated at this hour. She was making this jump hoping to save Paul McCartney's life. The time of his death was recorded at 5:00 am. Glancing at her watch, she had 45 minutes to convince him she was telling the truth. She had to be careful how she appeared to him, she didn't want him thinking she was a crazed fan looking for his attention. Coming around the corner eyeing the door of the studio, her heart skipped a beat, realizing she was about to meet one of the most famous men in the world.

This jump was the first she had insisted on doing. She thought that being closer to Paul's age would be an advantage. Sam, her supervisor, had been against the jump to begin with, not seeing the end game. Her analysis and a nod from the director convinced him to let her try.

She knew Paul's replacement would help the band achieve landmarks in music as never before. But she felt that Paul deserved to live even if it meant a different path for The Beatles. Their influence had led a generation. She believed that it was still possible but with a slightly altered journey.

She looked up at the door, he would be coming out soon. He would be upset having just had a fight with Brian, their manager. It may be hard to get his attention, but she believed she would be able to convince him she was telling him the truth. Emily saw the door open. Paul stood with his back to her as he continued to argue with Brian. He was wearing jeans and a blue sweater with a black jacket swung over his shoulder. He kept running his fingers through his hair in frustration. She heard their raised voices but not the words. She knew why they were arguing. Brian had just told him he needed to write six more songs for the next album. Paul was too tired to think, let alone write. John was in Spain filming a movie he had a small part in, and without him there, Paul didn't have the energy or will to write without him.

2

John and Paul met when they were young, 16 and 15, roughly around the time they had each gotten their first guitars. They have been close ever since. People often said that they were soulmates and once they met, they were complete. John was a lost child at times, but Paul knew what John needed when he got out of hand. Paul became his brother, friend, confidant and savior. They were the Nerk Twins, a name Paul's cousin gave them when they would strike out hitchhiking on holiday.

Paul and John had both lost their mothers at a young age, giving them a bond that could not be broken. Emily knew that without Paul, John would be lost forever, searching for that closeness in everyone and anyone. Paul's father, Jim, often told him to stay away from John, that he would only lead Paul into trouble. There are times when the child knows best.

Emily prepared for the assignment by spending hours watching interviews of the band. One thing she noticed was how protective they were of each other.

Especially when John would make broad, outrageous statements in those endless interviews. Paul would always be the one to explain it away. In one interview, it was obvious that Paul was not feeling well. The concern from John was palpable as he whispered to Paul, "Are you alright?"

In another, Paul plainly protecting John when the interviewer began questioning them about their mothers. Then there was the photo she saw of a quite distressed John walking in front of Paul, while Paul hid under his coat after they had to cancel a show due to him being ill. They are one half of each other. They are brothers. As the band grew and musical differences developed, they would have disagreements and fights. At the end of the day, John would pull his glasses down, look Paul in the eye and say, "It's just me."

Reading about the time the band spent in Hamburg, Germany, well before they hit it big, she saw that they were no angels. Paul and another band member got into a fistfight on stage, as the others kept playing. Performing seven or eight hours at a time, barely sleeping or eating, they popped Preludin daily to keep going. The image of them that was later created with their matching suits and long hair was a far cry from the black leather pants and the Elvis style hair they flaunted in Hamburg. Things in Germany were raw and gritty. There, they became a cohesive unit in order to survive their grueling existence.

Jarred out of her thoughts, she watched him as he stood for a moment at the top of the stairs. As he slowly began taking the steps down to the street she calmly moved closer to him. He must have seen her out of the corner of his eye, as he reached the bottom step he turned to face her.

He looked at her uneasily, as if maybe she had been part of his dreams. He quietly asked, "Is it you?"

She looked up at him, haltingly she said, "Paul, I'm Emily and I've come here to help you." He smiled slightly as she noticed he was taking her in, her clothes, her hair, her composure. "Is that right, Emily?" He asked coolly, "And how are you going to help me?"

Leaning closer to him, her lips brushed his cheek as she whispered in his ear, "I am going to free you from your dreams." He drew back sharply, his eyes filled simultaneously with terror, confusion, and hope. Emily touched his arm lightly and whispered, "I know about your dreams, I know you are scared, and I know how to help you if you'll listen to me."

Stunned, his eyes widened as he asked cautiously, "How is it, Emily, that you know about me dreams?" He looked at her more closely noticing she was different from other women, but he couldn't put his finger on it. She was beautiful and had the air of someone wiser than her years. He was wary. So many women had tried to be with him because he sang a good song. The constant parade of fans and gold diggers, although amusing at first, quickly became tiresome to him. The other three had already married, but he hadn't been lucky enough to find 'the one' yet. He had recently come to realize that his latest relationship was not as he had hoped. He had told a friend, 'I don't have easy relationships with women, I never have. I talk too much truth.'

"If I told you, it would be hard for you to believe, so I'd like to show you instead," she said firmly. He stood there bemused, his frustration and anger began fading away. He smiled at her seriousness waiting to see the treasures she had. Although he was tired and had a massive headache, he waited. A shock went through him as she touched his arm to guide him to the bench across the street.

She sensed the tension and weariness in him. "Well now, Emily, you have me undivided attention. What have you got there?" He asked as he sat down on the bench with a sigh. He was carrying a large notebook, he placed it on his lap, laying his hand over it protectively. She smiled, hoping to ease his mind. Paul noticed her bright green eyes, the way her skin glowed under the flickering light of the lamppost, and her dimples when she smiled. She began by pulling out two pictures side by side, one of him and one of his replacement looking quite a bit like him. Drawing in her breath, she laid it gently in his hands. He watched her face for a brief second longer before looking at what she had handed him.

His hands trembled as he lifted it closer, using the street light to see it better. She was worried that he would be disturbed enough to get up and walk away, he didn't. Instead he stared at it closely, looking back at her with questioning eyes. He flinched slightly as the picture took him by surprise. He had seen that face before, in his dreams. Then, when he came face to face with him at a party a few weeks ago, it had unnerved him so badly he had to leave.

Next, she pulled out a coin she had in her pocket. It was newly minted, she handed it to him calmly saying, "Look at the date." He looked at her inquisitively before squinting to see the coin in the dim light,

"What in the bloody hell, it says 2019. What is this?" he demanded as he drew farther away from her. Emily said, "Paul, I am here to help you."

"How is this helping me?" he asked with his voice slightly raised when she didn't answer immediately, he asked, "And again, how?" He moved to rise, but she touched his arm and said, "Paul, please try to understand, I've traveled through time to save your life."

He slumped down on the bench, shaken and confused. He reminded her of a helpless little boy with his messy hair and huge brown eyes. He began laughing, almost uncontrollably. He wanted to run. He wanted to get into his car and drive away from her, from himself. Looking at her closely, he implored, "Why are you doing this to me?" He was the lost one now, not John. Taken aback by the vulnerability she saw in his eyes. "I'm not trying to hurt you, Paul. I'm trying to save you," she said.

She knew this last item might put him over the edge. It was official documentation proving he had been replaced by another. She waited as he scanned it. She said, "I know you are finding all of this inconceivable but..." He stopped her with a sharp wave of his hand, he clutched the article to his chest he bent over and began to softly weep.

For a moment she didn't know how to continue. Then he looked at her with a tear-streaked face, "God, I don't want to die, Emily. Please help me." With urgency in her voice she began, "Do you see the date on the article? That is today, minutes from now, you will die in a horrible accident. We need to keep you away from your car. Is there somewhere we can walk?"

He stood and held out his hand to her. He started leading her down the street. He explained, "We can take the trolley to me place. Come this way." They walked swiftly to the stop and waited. Wiping his tear-stained face with the back of his hand, trying to hide his embarrassment, he asked, "So Emily, do they know who The Beatles are in 2019?" She began laughing, he looked at her a bit confused, "Well?" he asked.

At that moment, she heard a car screeching around the corner, he heard it too. They looked up at the same time in near panic. It was coming straight at them. As she reached out to Paul, she got her hand in her pocket and pushed the transponder urgently over and over again. The car was inches from where they had been standing when they jumped.

Chapter 2

Emily and Paul hit the floor of her office hard. His leg had been grazed by the bumper of the car and both were shaken by the close call. Out of breath, Paul gasped, "What in the bloody hell happened?" He was completely bewildered. "I had to get us out of there. We are in Atlanta," pausing for a moment as she turned towards him and said, "In 2019."

His eyes widened in shock as he leaned down to pick up the notebook that had fallen from his hands when they hit the floor. She opened the door of her office and peeked outside, glancing at her watch, she realized no one would be here and asked, "Are you alright? "I'm fine," he said, his voice a bit shaky and low. "We have to leave here and get to my house," she said as she waved him towards the door.

The drive to her place was uneasy. Dazed by all that had happened he looked out the window seeing things he had never seen before. He would occasionally glance over at Emily. She was a beauty, he thought to himself. When she had whispered in his ear that she would save him from his dreams, he felt an electric shock run through him that he had never felt before. He didn't know whether it was what she had said or that she had touched him somewhere deep inside. He believed it was the latter.

She made a quick stop at a gas station as she knew he would need cigarettes. Paul always seemed to be pictured with a cigarette in his hand. He glanced over at her as she got back in the car. "Thank you," he said softly as she handed them to him along with a lighter. He drew one out of the pack and lit it exhaling slowly as he tried to calm himself.

As she drove her mind was racing trying to figure out what was next. This is not how it was supposed to happen. She knew she would have to keep him away from any news and certainly the deaths of John and George, and a million other things that would change the matrix of his life. As they pulled into her driveway, the sensor lights came on. Paul took in a sharp breath and looked at her. Emily smiled saying, "It's a safety invention, it senses motion and turns the lights on. There will be a lot of things you will find hard to understand."

Once inside, she wanted to make him as comfortable as she could and asked, "Would you like something to eat or drink?" Slowly looking around her living room and then back at her, "Yes indeed, Emily, I'd fancy a strong drink if you don't mind," he said.

Limping to the couch, he carefully lowered himself down as she turned to the liquor cabinet. "What's your pleasure?" Emily asked. "I'll have a scotch if you've got it," he said weakly. She poured him a glass and asked if he needed ice. "No, no, straight up is fine. Thank you," he replied. Emily grabbed a wine glass and went to the kitchen to pour herself a drink, handing him the scotch as she passed by. "Emily, excuse me, have you got something for a headache?" he asked. She smiled at him, "Yes, I'll be right back."

As he sipped the drink she noticed his hand trembling, yet he lifted it to her and toasted her silently. After downing it in a few minutes, he asked for another. "Would you mind?" he asked, raising his glass to her. "Of course not," she responded. She picked up the bottle and placed it on the coffee table in front of him. "Help yourself," she said. He poured more into his glass as he looked around the room.

"What is that thing there?" he asked, pointing to the TV above the fireplace. "It's a television," she replied with a smile. "They are thinner and quite a bit bigger

13

than they were in 1966." He rose and went to look at it as it hung on the wall, shaking his head in amazement.

He stood for a moment taking in the room. Looking back at Emily, he asked, "Do you live here alone?" She nodded as she answered, "Yes, I do. I bought this house a few years ago." He was impressed, saying, "I suppose leaping through time pays you well then." Emily laughed, "It does."

He had many questions, most of which she firmly said she would not answer. "You didn't have a chance to answer me, did The Beatles make a mark?" She looked up at him and simply said, "Yes." He smiled and asked, "Well, how much of one?" She laughed and said, "I can't tell you." He continued asking all sorts of questions. She knew she had to be careful with her answers. The slightest awareness of his future could put him in a paradoxical situation.

Cocking his head sideways he looked at her from under his lush eyelashes, "Dear Emily, are you expecting me to accept all of this with no answers to me questions?" He said with a look of confusion. "I understand you're curious, but it would be dangerous for you to know certain things," she replied. She hoped her even tone would help him see that knowing what the future holds would change everything in a second once he gets back home.

"What is that?" she asked, pointing to the notebook. He picked it up from the coffee table. "It's me songs," he said quietly as he patted it. She smiled at him tenderly, "I see, can I put it somewhere safe for you?" He hesitated for a moment, "No, I'd like to keep it near me if you don't mind," he said quietly. She nodded with a small smile, "Of course," she responded.

"You must be exhausted," she said, "Sometimes jumping through time can make people extremely fatigued." "Are there others that know I am here?" he abruptly asked with a look of concern. "I'll have to tell them in the morning, but for now don't worry," she responded. "I'm not certain I can sleep," he said with a sigh as he set his glass down.

He limped to the bookshelf. He was amused that she had some of the same books he had read and loved. It calmed him. Turning to Emily as he smiled realizing that some things hadn't changed all that much. Returning his smile, she noticed he had an aura about him that belied his success. Certainly not what she had

15

anticipated from someone thrust into unimaginable fame and wealth at such a young age. It was a touch of innocence and humility. Something few men she had ever known possessed. Paul was only twenty-four years old, but Emily saw in his eyes someone older and wiser.

He stood there for a moment, running his fingers through his hair as he let out a long breath. Emily felt a shock as he turned and smiled at her again. She brushed her hair back from her face nervously as she quickly rose from the couch, trying to calm her heart as it pounded in her chest. She hadn't thought she would be attracted to him. She was startled at the effect he seemed to have on her. She haltingly said, "Let me show you to the guest room." He slowly followed her down the hallway.

Leaning against the doorway he watched her as she busied herself, pulling the covers back on the bed and looking in the dresser for something for him to sleep in. If this whole situation wasn't as strange as it were, he would turn on his charm with her. She is so different from any other woman he had ever known. He walked to the bed and sat down believing he could sleep for days. He placed the notebook on the nightstand. She looked over at him, he seemed so tired and dejected, yet he had a smoldering look in his eyes that threw her off guard.

"Here. Put your clothes outside and I'll wash them for you," she said as she handed him a pair of flannels that her ex-boyfriend had left behind. He opened his mouth to say something as she stood in front of him. But she crouched down putting her hands on his knees and looked up into his questioning face, "Everything will be alright. I promise," she whispered. She paused then brushed the top of his head with a kiss and said goodnight. "Emily," Paul called to her as she reached the door. "Thank you," he said quietly.

He laid down and stared at the moonlight reflecting on the wall. He was beyond confused and scared. Emily seemed kind enough, but he had been through so much lately that he wasn't sure who he should or could trust any longer. Aside from the dreams he had been having he was being watched by people who had on a few occasions taken to threatening and beating him.

He had been trying to keep it all to himself, but he had to confess when the others noticed his swollen jaw and the cuts on his brow. His tooth had been broken and there was no way to hide that. John seemed to think it was just some obsessed fan or a jealous boyfriend. He had tried to explain how very real it was but none of them seemed to comprehend how terrifying it had become. Brian quickly put out a statement that he had been in a small accident on a motorbike.

He didn't understand what was happening to him and then the dreams began. They were horrific and very real. He would wake in a sweat, screaming as he pulled himself back into reality. His housekeeper woke during one of the dreams and came knocking on his door. He was such a kind man. Paul didn't want to upset him and tried to laugh it off as a childish nightmare.

After throwing his clothes in the washer, she sat down at her computer. Pulling up Paul's file, she scoured it for answers. She knew they could take him back in the afternoon of the same day and that his memory would keep him from getting in his car later that night. But there was nothing there about what happened tonight. She had a sinking feeling that the car that tried to hit them was no accident. Her gut instinct told her it was Ramsgate. When she did the analysis for the jump the director let Sam know that Ramsgate had their fingerprints on The Beatles. He had warned both Sam and Emily to be cautious. She closed her computer. After finishing his laundry and putting it in his bathroom as quietly as she could, she laid down on the couch to try to rest.

Opening his eyes slowly he rolled over and looked at the window as the sun rose to fill the room with light. He blinked as he tried to clear the sleep from his mind.

Still a bit shaken from all that had happened he tried to remember if it was just another dream. Getting out of bed his leg was aching badly. He had no doubt this was not a dream, this was real, and he was waking up 53 years later. He went to the bathroom to take a shower. It took him a few minutes to figure out how the tap worked. Emily had washed his clothes and they were hanging on the door.

After a hot shower he dressed slowly noting his leg was bruised badly and very sore. He sat on the end of the bed wondering what would happen next. He hadn't slept that well since he started having his dreams. He went to go find Emily and hopefully a cup of coffee or tea.

Emily woke with a start, hearing the water running in his bath, she walked to her own room and she took a shower. She put on a pair of jeans and a green sweater, brushed her hair and added a little makeup before heading to the kitchen.

She stopped short when she saw him standing in the living room examining her cell phone. He looked up sheepishly when he saw her. "This thing here was jiggling away and making funny noises," he said. She smiled as she went to take it from him. "It's my phone. They've also gotten smaller since 1966," she laughed. "Did you sleep well?" Paul handed her the phone and answered, "I did. A night of dreamless sleep for once, and you?" She answered, "I fell asleep on the couch so I must have been tired."

"Hungry?" she asked. He nodded. "Coffee or tea," she asked as she headed to the kitchen. "Coffee please," he replied. "Coming up," she said. She noticed he was still limping and asked, "Is your leg hurting?" "'Tis a wee bit sore," he responded.

She grabbed the bottle of ibuprofen from the cabinet and put a couple in his hand while handing him a glass of water. "Do you want me to look at it?" she asked. He pulled back in mock horror. "Are you trying to get

20

fresh with me Emily?" he laughed. "No, it's a bit bruised. I'll be fine." She blushed and smiled as she turned to make the coffee.

Fascinated, he leaned against the counter as he watched her prepare the coffee. She explained that the coffee maker can be set to start even before you wake up. He shook his head in disbelief commenting, "That's marvelous."

As she set his plate of bacon and eggs on the table she poured her coffee and put his mug in front of him as her phone began ringing. "Shit," she whispered under her breath. It was Sam. She let the call go to voicemail. Paul looked up in feigned surprise, hearing her curse. "Emily! Such language!" he laughed. She blushed slightly thinking that maybe back in 1966 women didn't curse as freely as they do now.

Paul had begun eating as she sat down to sip her coffee. Looking at him over the rim of her cup. "What?" he asked as he caught her staring at him. "I was thinking about how strange all of this must be for you." Lifting his mug to his lips, he tipped it slightly towards her and said, "It's rather like a very long LSD trip I should imagine." Emily looked back at him as she placed her mug down on the table. "Paul, I'm just happy we got you here safely last night." He sipped his coffee looking at her over the rim, "Ah yes, indeed, but what now?"

They both jumped when her phone rang. She answered holding her finger to her lips to hush him. He had a glimmer in his eyes as he nodded in agreement but started drumming on the side of his coffee cup. She turned away trying not to laugh. Sam on the other end, "What happened Em? Where are you? Where is McCartney?"

"He is here with me," she answered. "I ran into an unpredicted event and we had to jump back," she answered then, a pause, "Yes, yes he is," looking back at Paul she smiled sheepishly as she continued to answer Sam's questions.

"Sam, my supervisor is coming over. He wants to explain to you the process of getting you back home," Emily said as she put the phone down on the table between them. "What if I don't fancy going back?" he said so low she didn't think she heard him correctly. "Paul, why wouldn't you want to go back? You're safe now, we stopped the accident last night."

"Emily, in me dreams I died and was replaced by someone, you see. Maybe he's the one they need now," he said, his voice filled with resignation and sadness. "Perhaps you shouldn't have come to save me, maybe it would have been best to let me die." She began to protest again, but he continued. "In one of me dreams I was floating above the others in the studio, John said my name, and the other fellow answered. Then I heard a voice behind me say, 'Paul, this is the future,' It was quite unnerving. Then you showed me a picture of him last night as if it was meant to be," he said slowly.

She started to say something, but he hushed her with a wave of his hand as he continued, "I've had these dreams for a long time Emily, and each one gets a bit clearer and more meaningful. I have been trying to get Brian and the rest to take me seriously, but I haven't been able to convince them they are real."

He stopped for a moment, thinking, then continued, "I even wrote a song about how I wanted them to believe me and work on finding someone who could step in."

"What song is that?" she asked. "We Can Work It Out,' if you listen to the words, not as a love song, but in the context of me dreams, you will see what I mean," he continued. "I was trying to get John and the rest to listen to me, to believe me," he explained.

Emily sat back in her chair and watched him. "Me Da says I am making meself sick with worry and if I don't stop I will make me dreams come true. It's a drag that me own Da doesn't believe me," he finished. She wanted to take him in her arms and tell him everything would be alright. She reached for him as he clasped his hands in front of himself. He looked at her as she touched his arm, hesitating he said, "I'm sorry, I shouldn't burden you with all of this."

"It's not a burden, I'm sure it's been horrible for you," she said kindly. She wanted to cry as she looked into his eyes. She could see the sadness that came from deep inside. She touched his cheek as she said, "This whole situation has taken its toll on you. I hope you'll feel better after we explain everything." She reached out and stroked his hair. As she did he caught her hand and held it briefly before letting go. She asked, "Would you like more coffee?"

"Please," he said softly. Watching her, he thought again how she was so unlike the other women he knew. Her long brown hair with golden highlights framed her heart-shaped face, and he had a hard time stopping himself from getting lost in her lovely green eyes. He couldn't recall being affected by a woman like this before.

As she turned back to him with the coffee pot in her hand she almost let it slip as the intense look in his eyes unnerved her. Pouring the coffee into his mug her hand shook. He looked up at her asking, "Are you alright?"

"I'm fine. Why do you ask?" she responded. "Your hand is shaking, Emily," he answered. Embarrassed that he noticed, she quickly turned to the counter and placed the pot down. "I'm just tired I suppose," she answered. She wasn't about to let him know how he made her feel.

She had watched so many interviews of The Beatles, but she hadn't realized how appealing his speaking voice is. It was warm and deeper than she would have thought by looking at him. Shaking her head, she admonished herself for being so taken with him.

"Tell me how you came to do this sort of work. When did people begin scampering about through time and space?" he asked. She paused for a moment to answer as she sat back down. "I began right after I graduated. Time travel has always been possible, but we had to learn how to manipulate gravity to make it safe to do so," she explained. "Once we did that, we could fold space, therefore time. When Sam gets here we will answer as many of your questions as we can." He looked at her and shook his head, "I don't understand, but as long as you do that's what matters," he said with a crooked smile.

Sam rang the front doorbell instead of using the kitchen door as he usually did. He stood waiting, tapping his foot and running his fingers through his hair, feeling slightly anxious. He had been a huge Beatles fan since he first heard them. He even picked up a guitar as a result. He and some friends would practice until one or another lost interest, but he never did, and in the end, he became pretty proficient at it. Now he plays to entertain his young boys Stephen and Zak.

When the door swung open Emily stood there looking beautiful as usual, but with a slight blush on her cheeks and a sparkle in her eye that he rarely saw. He handed her a bag of clothes and other things she had requested he bring for Paul. Sam looked toward the kitchen where Paul stood leaning against the doorway with a cautious look.

Walking across the room he reached out his hand and introduced himself, "I'm Paul. It's a pleasure to meet you Sam. Emily tells me you're the man to talk to," he said. Sam answered, "No, Paul, the pleasure is mine, really." They all settled in to make sense of all that had happened. Sam and Emily explained to Paul the process whereby he would be returned to 1966.

"The jump will take place hours before the original accident is to occur," Sam began. Emily spoke up and said something to Sam that Paul didn't grasp. It had to do with a paradox. He took it all in. Every once in a while asking a question as he tried to comprehend the entirety of the situation.

Sam explained that they would have to wait eight days. "Time travel is dependent on different variables," Sam began, "Sometimes we are free to do several jumps within a short period, but more often than not we have to wait for portals to become synchronized with each other."

Paul laughed as he explained, "I think I'm catching on. I barely passed my A-levels. John and I were always sagging off school to practice at me house while me Da was at work." Sam responded with a wink, "Thank God." Paul looked at him with a slightly confused expression.

After finishing their talk Sam rose saying he had to get to the office. Turning to Paul he said, "I'll be in touch with Emily. Please let me know if you have any concerns or any more questions. We will make your stay here as comfortable as possible." Paul looked down for a moment and then asked the question he had been holding back. "Sam, Emily, I would like to be able to see what became of us, The Beatles. Is that possible?"

Looking at Emily and then back at Sam, Paul continued, "I'm entitled to know about me own life. You would want to know, wouldn't you?"

Emily reached over and touched his arm. Paul looked at her flashing a hopeful look. Sam noticed a closeness between them already. It worried him for a moment but then remembered that Emily was the most professional woman he had ever worked with and trusted her not to complicate an already complicated situation. "Paul, Emily has very good judgment and she'll determine what you can be shown. Oh! I have

28

something for you. I'll get it out of my car." He came back in with a guitar case. "I bought this after I heard The Beatles for the very first time. I thought it would help you pass the time here." Paul's face lit up like a child on Christmas morning. "Thank you Sam, really, this means a lot to me," Paul said with a huge grin. "No problem, enjoy," Sam replied. Emily smiled at Paul's excitement.

Sam was thrilled that he was pleased. He knew that Paul and the rest were never far from their guitars or a piano in case inspiration came upon them. Neither John nor Paul wrote or read music, so when a melody popped into their heads they used whatever was handy to get the tune down in their minds.

As Sam drove back to the office, he thought about the obvious fascination between Emily and Paul. He understood the attraction that many women had to Paul, and he hoped Emily wouldn't fall under the spell of his charms. He knew from history Paul was quite the ladies' man and was never at a loss for the company of women while on the road. Emily is beautiful, warm and kind. Her long brown hair and lovely figure along with her intellect would be hard for any man to resist. He made a note to himself to check in with Emily tomorrow. He didn't want to seem overbearing, but he didn't want Emily to get hurt either.

After Sam left, Emily began emptying the bag he had brought. Not only were there clothes for Paul, but a carton of cigarettes and a bag of marijuana, all of which he was thrilled with.

She sat across from him, watching his fingers effortlessly strumming the guitar Sam had brought for him to use. Smiling to herself as she thought about how many women back in 1966 would have done anything for a private concert by Paul.

"Emily, Emily," he said. He brought Emily out of her thoughts as he called her name. She loved his Liverpudlian accent and the way he said her name. "I'm sorry, do you need something?" she said. He wondered, "Can we take a walk or something to get some fresh air?" She was hesitant to go out in public with him, although it wasn't likely, she didn't want to take the chance of him being recognized. "Let's take a walk later this evening when it gets a little darker," she said with a slight smile, hoping that would satisfy him. "That would be nice," he said quietly.

As she began to rise she noticed that he still looked as if he had another question. "What is it?" she asked quietly. He had his finger on his lip, a habit she had noticed in the videos she had watched. He seemed to do it as a nervous habit or when he was deep in thought. She found it endearing. He asked, "Are the others alive here now, in this time?" After a slight pause, she responded, "A long time has passed since yesterday, Paul. That is something I'd rather not get into. I hope you understand."

Looking down, he closed his eyes briefly before grabbing the pack of cigarettes and lighter from the coffee table. In one smooth movement he rose from the couch and walked outside to the patio. Pondering all that had happened in the last twenty-four hours, he frowned slightly as he thought of yet more questions to ask Emily. He looked up to the sky for a moment before he lit the cigarette.

She thought of going out to talk to him, hoping to convince him that some things are better left unknown. She decided against it as she watched him.

She had always thought that John was the more handsome of the four thinking Paul had a babyface. She chuckled to herself and thought how wrong she was. He was in fact very masculine. Something that wasn't always conveyed by the thousands of pictures that were taken of him. She thought he must have known his appeal as the 'cute one' and played it up in the photo shoots they had to endure.

She watched him as his hair blew in the breeze. His deep brown eyes scanning the horizon as he took another drag off his cigarette. There was something about him that she couldn't put her finger on. His looks combined with his personality were mesmerizing. She began to understand the hysterical reaction that girls had around him and the other three back in the early 60's. He was kind, intelligent, incredibly talented and funny, a perfect man she thought wistfully as she scolded herself.

Exhaling, he put the cigarette out in the ashtray. He thought that Sam had been an agreeable chap, and although the entire situation blew his mind, he wasn't uncomfortable or too fearful. He still felt he had a right to know certain things. It was his life after all, but he didn't want to put any more pressure on Emily. This will certainly make for some intriguing music later, and there is nothing wrong with being trapped with a beautiful woman for a few days.

Looking up, he caught Emily's eyes as she watched him from the kitchen. For a few seconds, they held each other in a long-distance gaze. He shivered from the overwhelming yearning he had for her. Emily blushed slightly as he looked back at her with an intensity that she had never experienced before. She knew that the next eight days were going to be an exercise in self-control.

Closing the door quietly as he returned to the kitchen. "It is quite pleasant out there," he said trying to sound casual. She brushed her hair behind her ear and said, "It will be nice to get some fresh air. Can I get you anything before I get to work?"

Hours later she finished the case she was analyzing and closed her laptop. She went to the kitchen and saw that Paul was sitting outside with the guitar propped against the table. He was leaning back in the chair as he smoked a cigarette. She wanted to go out and see if there was anything she could do for him, but he stood and stretched, grabbing up the guitar before walking to the door. "It's a lovely evening," he commented as he closed the door behind him. She smiled as she turned to look for something to cook for dinner. She heard him humming as he placed the guitar in the living room.

She sensed him behind her, almost letting the knife slip out of her hand. "Can I give you a hand? I'm feeling quite useless?" he inquired. "Yes, thank you," she said handing him the knife as she no longer trusted herself. She busied herself retrieving the plates and silverware. "You know, when I have time, I'm good in the kitchen. I had to learn to cook after me mum died. I'd love to prepare something for you," he said. She grinned at him. "Of course. Anytime I don't have to cook is fine with me," she laughed.

As he finished she asked, "Would you like a drink?" He looked at her with a smile, "Yes indeed that would be enjoyable." "Wine or Scotch?" she asked. "Wine, please," he answered. She poured them each a glass and suggested they sit outside.

"This is quite a nice home you have here Emily," he commented as they sat down. She smiled at him, "Thank you, I like it. It's a quiet neighborhood and I feel safe here." "Is it common for women to live alone now?" he asked as he lit a cigarette. "Yes it is," she replied with a small smile.

"Your home, it's in the city?" she asked. He glanced over at her, "Near. It's close to the studio, so it is very convenient. The others live out of town a bit, but not too far," he replied with a smile. After a moment had passed she asked, "How are you doing?" He paused before answering. "Honestly, I'm still a little unnerved by everything," he said quietly.

She leaned in towards him and covered his hand with hers. "Everything will be alright. I promise," she said reassuringly. "Thank you," he said almost in a whisper. They sat quietly enjoying the cool breeze. "Would you like me to get your jacket for you?" she asked. He looked at her with a smile, "No, I'm fine. Thank you."

He lit another cigarette as he inquired, "May I ask you something?" She looked over at him with a smile, "Of course. What is it?" He looked down before he spoke, "Are you seeing someone?" She was a little taken aback but chuckled softly. "No, I don't seem to find the time. I've been so busy with work," she said with her voice trailing off. He looked over at her with a boyish grin, "Me as well."

He got up to retrieve the wine bottle from the refrigerator. She sighed as she thought how easy it was to be with him. She realized with a slight pang how happy he would make someone someday. He walked back outside with his ever-present smile and poured them each another glass. "Are you hungry?" she asked. "Not quite, can we wait a bit?" he asked.

She nodded, "Of course." He sipped his wine and asked, "Do you need to go into your office tomorrow?" She shook her head, "No, I'm lucky to have the kind of job that I can do remotely." He looked slightly confused, so she explained. "I can work from home, and besides that you are my main concern right now."

He smiled back at her, "I think I like that." She once again caught herself staring at him as he looked away. He really was a good-looking man. She thought of all the pictures she'd seen of him during the time she was researching the jump. He was taller than she imagined, and his eyes were absolutely riveting. He turned and smiled. "You look deep in thought," he said as he lit another cigarette. She stammered slightly, "Oh no, not really. I enjoyed listening to you play earlier," she added. "Thank you," he said with a slight blush on his cheeks.

She smiled at him as he looked back at her. He was a little taken aback by the feelings he felt when he looked at her. He had been with so many women these past few years, but there was something special about her that he couldn't put his finger on. He had never felt this comfortable with a woman before. It was taking all his strength not to reach out to her and pull her into his arms.

"It's getting dark," she said, "Let's go inside." He gathered the glasses and the bottle of wine and followed her to the door. She held it open for him and flipped on the light as they entered the kitchen. He poured more wine for them and asked, "Is there anything I can do to help with dinner?" "No, it's easy, I'll just make some rice and stir fry everything, it won't take long," she answered.

After dinner they went to the living room, he sat down on the couch as they continued to chat. "It's been a long time since I've had nothing to do," he commented with a chuckle. "I'm not sure if I remember how to put my feet up and relax."

She remembered the marijuana Sam had brought to him. "Why don't you smoke," she said as she picked up the bag from the table and handed it to him. She went to the desk and dug out her rolling papers. He rolled one up and lit it, sitting back as he exhaled, then handed it to her.

She sat down in a chair across from him. She didn't trust herself to get too close to him. Paul looked at her over the rim of his glass. "I don't bite Emily, come here," he said as he placed his hand on the couch next to him.

She felt a slight blush come to her cheeks as she gingerly sat down next to him. She smiled back at him as she handed the joint back to him. He grinned at her before inhaling one more time. He got up and reached for her wine glass, "More?" he asked as he turned towards the kitchen. "Just a little, please," she answered. She was already a little heady.

He handed her the glass as he sat down. "When we met Bob Dylan, he introduced us to marijuana," he said, adding, "Oh! he was a folk singer back then." She laughed, "Um, I know," she said with a wink. He grinned, "Still around, eh?" he asked. "Yes, he is," she replied.

Paul continued, "We were in New York, He came up to our suite and as we got to know him he asked if we wanted to get high. We didn't know what he was talking about," he chuckled. "Bob was a bit confused, saying, 'but you sang about getting high!' John and I looked at each other quite baffled as Bob continued."

"I get high, I get high, I get high," he sang a verse from I Want to Hold Your Hand. All of a sudden John realized what he was saying. He thought we were singing, 'I get high,' when we were singing 'I can't hide," he finished laughing.

"Anyway, being new to it, we ended up just sitting about giggling. I thought I was coming up with some profound thoughts. I asked our road manager, Mal, to follow me about and write down everything I said," he guffawed.

She laughed with him, asking, "Well? Were they profound the next day?" He looked at her seriously, "No, they were rubbish!" She was captivated by his eyes and the way he smiled down at her. She admonished herself for being so enchanted with him, for letting her emotions take over.

"I did something similar in college," she began, "I got high at a party and went home and wrote a poem, thinking it was wonderful at the time!" Laughing she finished, "It wasn't!"

Paul put the joint down in the ashtray and sipped his wine. Taking her chin in his hand he gently kissed her on her cheek. "Thank you, Emily, for making this entire situation bearable," he said quietly. She was a little flustered as she replied, "Oh, Paul, it's nothing, I just hope that you're comfortable here until we can get you safely home."

He continued searching her face, hoping she felt drawn to him as he was to her. Without hesitation he kissed her lips softly pulling back as he searched her eyes. She was taken aback and blushed slightly as she averted her eyes from his intense gaze. She had never been kissed so sweetly before. Her heart was pounding in her chest as she turned away. She was confused as to how easily she was getting swept up in his charm. Pulling back from him she looked up into his beautiful brown eyes. She believed later it was at that moment she was lost to him.

She untangled herself from his embrace and nervously began straightening up the pillows on the couch and gathering the glasses from the coffee table. "What are you doing?" Paul asked as he came closer to her. He stood in front of her to prevent her from continuing. "Paul," was all she could say before he gently kissed her again.

Pulling back from him, she looked into his eyes. "We can't," she whispered. He swept her hair away from her face with the back of his hand. "I have wanted to kiss you since last night," he continued, "I know it may sound daft, but I have never felt so drawn to a woman before. Tis almost like I was meant to be here with you." Hesitating, she smiled as she reached up and gently ran her finger along his jaw. "We have to be practical. We can't let our emotions carry us away," she said.

He dropped his hand away from her and turned towards the kitchen, saying, "I need a ciggie." What he really needed was to get a hold of his emotions. His hand trembled as he lit the cigarette. He wanted her so badly, but it wasn't like other times when all he had to do was snap a finger and get what he wanted. He knew she was different. He didn't want to scare her away. He realized that maybe this time he would have to prove himself to her before she let him into her heart.

She sat down on the couch as she reached up and touched her lips where his were moments ago. She wanted him terribly but realized that letting herself fall for him would be a mistake. She heard the door open as he came back inside. She watched him as he stood in the doorway from the kitchen to the living room looking at her. "I'm sorry, Emily, I was too forward," he said quietly. "Oh, you weren't. I'm just a little rattled by everything that's happened," she replied with the touch of a smile.

"Getting emotionally involved would be a mistake. You understand, don't you?" She looked questioningly at him as she watched his face, his eyes. He knew she was right. "Of course, I understand Emily," he responded. Turning away from her he ran his fingers through his hair. "I'm a bit tired. I think I'll go to bed," he said. "Sleep well," she said quietly.

Chapter 3

Emily looked at the clock, it was 4:00 a.m. and she hadn't slept at all. Her mind raced as she tossed and turned all night. Her desire for Paul was something she hadn't expected, and it scared her. Throwing back the covers she eased herself out of bed and put on her robe. She stood for a moment quietly trying to gain strength to face the day. She knew that she could fall in love with him, but it all seemed so hopeless. His life was in 1966 and hers was here in 2019. She had always dreamed of finding someone like him and now that he's here he is out of reach.

Laying still with his arms crossed behind his head. He hadn't been able to sleep. He had thought about her all night wishing she were there with him. He tumbled out of bed and threw on his jeans and a t-shirt. He wondered for a moment if his attraction to her was because of the situation they were in. But she made it quite clear to him that she did not want to get involved. He realized that this was something he had never experienced before. He admonished himself. He was learning a hard lesson in humility.

Opening his door quietly being careful not to wake her, he walked down the hall to the living room only to find her sitting on the couch sipping a cup of coffee. Taking a deep breath, he nodded slightly and said "Morning," as he passed by to the kitchen to fix his own cup. She replied, "Good morning." Emily watched him move about in the kitchen fixing his coffee then grabbing his cigarettes he went outside.

She sat sipping her coffee waiting for him to come back inside. She didn't want things between them to be uncomfortable. She heard the door open and watched him as he poured more coffee saying, "Would you like a bit more?" "Yes, thank you," she said as she rose from the couch and walked to join him in the kitchen. He held the coffee pot as she approached him.

"How did you sleep?" she asked as they walked back to the living room. "I don't think I got a wink," he replied with a yawn. "You?" he asked as they sat down. "Same," she said sheepishly.

"We should have made love that always helps me sleep," he said with a serious look on his face that soon faded into a smile and a wink. "I'm teasing you,

Emily," he said when she looked over at him with a blush in her cheeks.

As they settled on the couch, she absentmindedly picked up the remote. She was tired and forgot for a moment how crucial it was to keep the news away from Paul. Looking for a distraction she flipped on the TV to the Today Show. The day began with the morning news show which began by mentioning the upcoming birthday of John Lennon noting his murder 38 years ago. Paul let out a gasp and began moaning, "No, no, no." She quickly turned off the TV and reached out to him taking his hand in hers. "I am so sorry, Paul, Oh I'm so sorry," she said.

He pulled his hand away looking at her with tears in his widened, shocked eyes. She reached for him again as he pulled away from her standing then stumbling to the guest room. He thought he might get sick to his stomach as he leaned against the door trying to catch his breath.

Emily knocked on the door lightly as she called for him. He didn't respond. As she began walking away she heard him say through his tears, "I need to be alone." He lowered himself to the floor next to the bed and began sobbing. The last time he cried like this

45

was with John after a long night of playing at the Cavern back in 1961. They walked across the street to the park and sat on the stone wall and began talking about the deaths of their mums. They hung onto each other as they wailed in pain and loss.

He wept as he rocked back and forth. He felt as if he was falling into a deep hole with no bottom there to stop him. Nothing was real anymore. He was stuck in the future and was helpless to save John or himself.

Turning away from his door she couldn't bear to hear him cry. His heart was breaking and there was nothing she could do to help him. She quickly walked back to the living room cursing herself as she snatched her phone off the table and called Sam. "Sam, I screwed up. I turned the TV on this morning. The first story was about John's upcoming birthday." After explaining what had happened and getting a rare lecture from him. She hung up and sat down to another cup of coffee as she cursed herself.

She remembered something she had seen while researching for the jump to save Paul. A home recording from Paul's house in 1960. It was Paul and John singing a song called 'I Don't Know.' She had skipped by it, having never heard of it, but read some of the commentary written. Some were saying it was a love song about the two of them. She hadn't thought much about it when she read it but now she wondered if there had been something more between the two of them.

When his tears finally stopped Paul moaned and rocked back and forth. How could it be that John was murdered? He was lost in a world that was not his, he longed to go home as much as he longed to make Emily his.

What seemed like hours later he got up and splashed his face with cold water. He thought about showering and shaving, but he didn't have the strength to do much of anything. He sat down at the end of the bed and took a deep breath. He needed a smoke but was embarrassed to face Emily. He opened the door and made his way to the kitchen.

She was preparing lunch when he appeared behind her. Turning around as she heard him enter the kitchen, she was taken aback by his appearance. He had a five o'clock shadow with dark circles under his eyes from lack of sleep and they were swollen and red from his tears. He just stood there looking at her as if somehow she would be able to make all the pain go away.

Her heart shattered as she looked at him. "This is all my fault. I am so sorry," she gasped. She walked across the room to where he stood. Wrapping her arms around his waist, she held him tightly. He responded by leaning into her embrace. They held each other for a moment before he pulled back from her looking deeply into her eyes saying quieting, "You didn't do anything wrong, you see. Please don't kick yourself."

She took him by the hand and led him to the table. They sat down as she watched him for a moment. There was such sadness and fear in his eyes that she didn't know if anything she said could ease his grief. She began to explain, "Please listen to me. The future is different now that we have stopped your own death. Do you understand?"

"I don't," he mumbled as he hung his head. She took his chin in her hand and made him look at her. "Listen to me," she implored. He reached up and took her hand away but continued to hold it. "Emily, I don't understand a bloody thing any longer," he said with a raspy voice.

"The thing about time travel is that the smallest change can bring about a whole different future or past," she began, speaking quietly. "We have already changed your life and I believe we have also saved John's because of it." She took a deep breath, not sure how much she should reveal. She began, "John was never the same after your accident. He gave up on everything, his family, himself. The choices he made after your death were *because* of your death. He was profoundly lost, he chose a different life than you all were leading, I believe it was to escape the anguish of losing you. You weren't there to hold him up and protect him from himself any longer."

Paul lifted his head with a smirk on his face. He asked angrily, "And you're not going to tell me what path he took, are you?" She lowered her eyes to escape his insistent gaze. "I can't," was all she said. "Emily, please," he begged, afraid he was going to start crying again. She remained silent and shook her head. Angered and frustrated he cursed, "Bloody hell," as he turned away from her. Scraping his chair as he got up he walked outside allowing the door to slam behind him.

He had always managed to keep a stiff upper lip and be the one holding everyone else up, but he was at a loss now not knowing where to turn or who to turn to. He lit a cigarette pacing as he smoked, trying to calm himself. He knew none of this was her fault, but he was furious that she kept holding things back from him, things he thought he had a right to know. He also realized in a glimmer of self-awareness that he had gotten used to getting anything he wanted when he wanted it. He was ashamed of himself for reacting so childishly towards her. Looking up at the sky he asked for patience and calm as he turned to go back inside.

He closed the kitchen door quietly and stood looking at her as she sat at the table. She raised her eyes to meet his. "Please try to eat something," she said softly. Although he wasn't hungry he sat down and began eating. "Forgive me for losing me temper," he said as he touched her arm.

"Don't apologize. I don't blame you at all," she said trying to reassure him. "'Tis not you that I'm angry with," he said before he haltingly asked, "Can we rest together? I don't want to be alone." She met his gaze as she answered, "Yes."

He followed her with a slow shuffle to his bedroom. As they lay down on the bed Paul turned to her looking into her eyes. He reached up and brushed the hair from her face and kissed her gently on her forehead. She smiled at him for a moment wondering how she could continue to resist him. He looked at her with such tenderness and vulnerability. It took her breath away.

She closed her eyes resting her head in the crook of his arm. She could hear his heart pounding so fast that she propped her head in her hand and asked, "Are you alright?" He opened his eyes and replied, "Yes, why do you ask?" "Your heart is pounding," she said. He murmured, "'Tis you." She looked away from him as she lay back down and smiled. He caught her smile as he closed his eyes to sleep.

She felt him relax and his heart slow as he fell asleep. She wished she could stay like this forever holding and comforting him. She drifted into a restless sleep. Keeping close to him she prayed he would feel better after getting some rest.

Hours later, stretching as he woke up, he carefully rolled out of bed so he wouldn't wake her. He made his way to the bath and ran a shower. Emily heard him and lay there for a moment or two enjoying the stillness.

Getting up from the bed she accidentally knocked his notebook off the nightstand. She picked it up and she saw that he had written what she assumed were lyrics. It began, 'You found my heart in time to save...' she heard him turn off the shower and quickly set it back on the stand.

She went off to her own room to shower and changed into a pair of black leggings and a soft deep red sweater. Walking into the kitchen she saw Paul outside, a cigarette, or 'ciggie' as he called them, hanging off his lips as he strummed on the guitar. They hadn't talked much since this morning, but she hoped he understood that nothing is written in the stones of time, anything can change.

She joined him outside. It was a beautiful evening, a little chilly but pleasant. As she sat down across from him, he put the guitar down, leaning it against the bench next to him. They sat in silence. After a moment had passed he slowly raised his head and caught her eyes with his. "I know you're right," he remarked calmly with a wave of his hand, "About John, about all of this." She was relieved that he was seeing the bigger picture. She understood how hard it must be for him. "Oh, Paul, if I could take away your pain, I would. I never meant for you to be hurt like that," she admitted.

He looked back at her again, "None of this is easy Emily. None of it." He emphasized, "I know it is not your fault. You've done nothing wrong." She breathed a sigh of relief as she reached over and took his chin in her hand. Raising his head their eyes met, she leaned over and kissed him on the cheek. He looked into her deep green eyes filled with warmth and caring that made him feel safe.

She asked, "Would you like to take a walk?" He responded with a nod, "Yes, that would be enjoyable." They left the backyard taking a path through a wooded area behind her house. They strolled as they enjoyed the cool breeze rustling through the trees.

They were quiet for a moment as they walked. Then he spoke, "When I would go over to Mendips to practice with John, his Aunt Mimi would call us chalk and cheese." She looked up at him with a perplexed look. He continued with a chuckle, "Chalk and cheese is another way to say opposites, different, night and day. I suppose it was because I was polite to her and

John was, well John. She would call for John when I would knock on the door, 'John, your little friend is here," he laughed. She smiled and said, "Tell me more."

He looked up at the sky and with a sly smile said, "John used to always say, 'I'm the leader of the group' We would all respond back to him, 'That's because you fucking shout louder than any of us!" That made her burst out in a fit of laughter.

In the distance, they heard children playing at the neighborhood playground. "Emily, would you like to have children someday?" he asked, "Yes, I would," she answered. "I really haven't thought much about it, being so busy with work and my last relationship put me off of thinking domestically," she said as she wrinkled her nose. "You?" she asked. Paul, quiet for a moment, "Yes, I would love to have children, but like you I've been a bit busy you see," he said with a little laugh.

As they reached the edge of the playground, a soccer ball came rolling towards them. Paul looked up to see who it belonged to. "Hey, over here," a boy about the age of seven yelled. Paul picked up the ball and threw it to the boy. "Here ya go, mate!" He said with a smile.

The little boy with messy blond hair ran closer to them to pick up the ball. "You talk funny," he said.

Paul let out a hearty laugh that Emily hadn't heard before. "I guess I do," Paul answered with a wink. The little boy said, "My name is Johnny, what's yours?" Paul crouched down and said, "My best friend's name is Johnny. I'm Paul. How old are you, Johnny?" "I will be seven years old next month. I can't wait for my birthday! I want a PlayStation!" Paul laughed, "Well, Johnny, have you been a good boy?" "Yep," Johnny replied. "Then I'd imagine you'll get one of those, whatever it is!" Paul said laughing.

The child's mother called for him and gave Paul a wave of thanks as they continued to walk around the park on the path. Emily smiled at him as they continued on. "You'll be a good father someday, Paul," she said. Instinctively, he gently took her hand in his as they made their way back home. Emily's heart fluttered as he held her hand so casually, it felt so right.

Continuing their conversation, he said, "I've always loved kids. Me Da remarried recently, and his new wife has a little girl. Her name is Ruth and she just turned 5. I try to get home as much as possible to see her. She is a doll," he responded. "What I enjoy most about being with Ruth is seeing the world in a whole new way, through her eyes," he finished.

After they got home they enjoyed watching the sun as it began to set behind the trees. Emily got up saying, "I suppose I should think about dinner. Do you like pizza?" "Who doesn't?" he replied. As she stood in the kitchen she watched him as he picked up the guitar to bring it back inside. He opened the door and slid in quietly when he saw her on the phone.

She finished the order and disconnected the call. "I ordered one. It should be here in about an hour. Would you like a drink?" she asked. "Yes, let me get them. You really don't have to wait on me Emily," he responded as he walked to the refrigerator and drew out a bottle of wine.

"How is your leg feeling after that walk?" she asked. "'Tis a bit better," he answered. "We were lucky Emily," he said. "Yes, we were. I was thinking about that earlier. The accident I saved you from wasn't as a result of being hit by a car, rather you were driving," she answered with a questioning tone. "We want to do a little more research on what that was all about. Sam is looking into it."

"Speaking of Sam," Paul began, "You two seem very close. How long have you been working for him?" She looked at him as they walked to the living room. "I suppose we are close. He had studied under my father, so I've known him for a long time. I've been working there for five years now. He and his wife Chris have been very supportive of me since my parents were killed," she responded in a low voice.

"Oh Emily, I'm sorry," Paul touched her arm in concern. "Thank you," she whispered, "They and my younger brother were killed in a plane crash on the way home from a conference. I was in college at the time. My father was one of the original developers of the time travel paradigm we use today. Sam was in awe of him so when I graduated he recruited me to join the time jump team," she added.

Sitting down next to her he looked at her face. Her eyes were lowered, but he saw her pain etched there. "I understand. Losing a parent is the hardest thing. When me mum died I didn't know I could cry, so I played it tough instead," he admitted. "I don't remember ever really crying about it until one night when John was massively drunk, and I took him out of the Cavern to a park across the way. We both sat there and cried and hugged remembering our mothers for hours," he explained. "We've not spoken of it since, but it's always there." He looked down as he remembered. Emily touched his knee with a gentle pat as he reached for her hand and held it briefly as they sat for a moment lost in their own memories.

The doorbell rang making both of them jump. Emily walked to the door and retrieved the pizza. Carrying it to the couch she placed it on the table before heading to the kitchen for paper plates and napkins. "This smells marvelous," he said as she returned. "It does, doesn't it?" She replied, "Well, dig in," she said as she handed him a plate. After they finished Emily cleared everything away as Paul rolled a joint.

Emily was finishing up in the kitchen as he walked through to head outside. He quietly closed the door and stood still for a moment. The news he had heard about John was beyond comprehension, but he believed Emily that maybe somehow they had stopped it from happening in the future. He watched her through the window as she glanced up and gave him a wave.

When she had finished she joined him outside to enjoy the fresh air. They sat quietly lost in their own thoughts. He lit a cigarette and exhaled slowly as he looked at her. She felt his eyes upon her as she turned and smiled at him. "You're staring at me," she said. "Oh, am I? Sorry," he laughed. She looked back at him with a grin, "Don't be sorry. I was just teasing you." Her phone rang. It was Sam. She stood and walked to the end of the patio as she responded to his questions. Hanging up she sat back down. "That was Sam. He wanted to know how you are doing," she volunteered. His eyes met hers as he replied, "I'm doing quite well," he said with a shy smile as he continued to look at her.

"What is it?" she said when she noticed his gaze. Hesitating, he answered, "I was just remembering how nice it was to wake up next to you." She looked into his deep brown eyes. She could not stop herself from getting lost in them. She held his eyes as she said, "It was nice, wasn't it?" She broke away from the intensity of the moment saying, "Let's go inside."

He stood and walked ahead of her holding the door. "You should try to get some sleep Paul. You've had quite an emotional day and the effects of the jump may still be affecting you," she explained trying to convince him as well as herself that it was best to be sensible in a situation that made no sense.

He looked at her with a smile, "I think you may be right. I am a bit tired," he admitted. "I'll see you in the morning," she said as she touched his arm gently, "Sleep well."

She sat down in the kitchen for a moment calming her pounding heart. She chastised herself for feeling as she did. She locked the doors and turned off the lights. Walking past his door she heard him humming as he got ready for bed. She smiled to herself as she closed her door and undressed. She was glad that he was feeling better after hearing the news this morning. As she climbed into bed she hoped she'd be able to sleep.

He laid down and wished she were next to him. The evening had been so pleasant that he almost had forgotten all that was happening to him. He smiled a little remembering her beautiful face and the way she laughed.

Sleep came easy to him and he woke to the sun streaming in the window feeling like his old self. He showered and could smell coffee and bacon as he opened his door to join her in the kitchen.

He stood watching her as she poured herself a cup of coffee. She had on a black
t-shirt and a pair of jeans that hugged her slim figure. He walked up behind her and said, "Morning!" She jumped in shock which made him laugh. Gasping, she said, "Oh goodness you frightened me!"

"I'm sorry Emily!" he said with a laugh. "I'm just not used to someone else being here," she said as she reached for a mug. "Did you sleep well?" she asked. "I did," he replied.

"Would you like breakfast outside?" she asked. "Yes indeed," he answered. "Great, I'll be there in a minute," she said as she handed him his mug. He stepped outside and lit a cigarette as he sipped the coffee listening to the birds greet the morning sun.

As he saw her coming outside he went and held the door for her as she carried the tray. "Thank you!" she said with a grin. "This looks marvelous," he said as she put the tray down on the table. She had made scrambled eggs, bacon and there were croissants with jam. "I might get used to all of this if you're not careful!" he said with a laugh. She was glad that he seemed better this morning. "Well I want to make sure you're happy," she responded. "I need to go to

61

the store for some things. Do you need or want anything?" she asked. He thought for a moment, "Coke and milk." She nodded, "OK, anything else?" He shook his head.

When they had finished he took the tray and carried it back into the house. "I'll clean up here. I want to be useful," he smiled. She grabbed her purse and keys from the counter and said, "Will you be alright here alone for a while?" He turned to her, "I believe I am able to look after meself Emily," he said with a silly frown. She couldn't resist and reached up and touched his face before giving him a kiss on his cheek. "I won't be long," she said as she headed out the door.

Upon returning home she was gathering the bags from the back of her car when he appeared beside her. "Let me get those," he said as he took them from her. Mimicking his comment earlier, "I might get used to this if you're not careful," she said with a grin. She saw that he must have been working on a song as the guitar was laying on the couch. She thought to herself how strange it would be to hear the song he wrote here in her home.

Looking over at him as he set the bags down on the counter she smiled to herself. She really could get used to having him here. He looked back at her asking, "Do you mind if I have one of these now?" He said pointing to the coke. "Of course not, you don't need to ask me. I want you to feel comfortable here. Help yourself to anything you want," she said.

He winked with a twinkle in his eye and an irresistible grin. "Does that include you?" he said teasingly. She smiled up at him and swatted his arm. Her heart skipped a beat as she turned away to finish putting up the groceries. He got a glass down from the cabinet and asked, "Would you like one as well?" She shook her head. "No, thank you," she replied.

He went into the living room and sat down on the couch grabbing the guitar and began strumming as she walked in. "Will this be bothering you?" he asked as she sat down at her desk. "Of course not. I love hearing you play," she answered.

Deep in thought as she did the analysis of the material she was working on she didn't notice that he had stopped playing. She turned around to see him seemingly deep in thought. "Are you alright?" she asked quietly. "Yes," he replied. "Just trying to bash out some lyrics. I need a ciggie," he said as he got up and turned towards the kitchen. She watched him as he went outside. She stood and stretched before she gathered the glasses from the table.

As he turned to walk back into the house she noticed his face seemed clouded over with tension or worry. She didn't know which one. He closed the door as she stood there looking at him. Neither spoke as their eyes met. He felt as if an unseen force was flowing between them. She turned away afraid of what would come next. He walked towards her slowly and said quietly, "You are like a light shining through all of this madness." He gently kissed her forehead as she touched his arms. She waited speechless unsure of what to do or say. She could not breathe from the overwhelming emotion running through her.

Instinctively, Paul took her hand and kissed it softly. She cautiously moved her hand to his face stroking his cheek while she looked into his eyes one last time before kissing him deeply. She exhaled slowly as she drew back from him. He wrapped his arms around her small waist and pulled her closer. He breathed in the scent of her hair before pulling back to catch her eyes with his.

Cupping her face in his hands, kissing her softly, in awe of the raw emotion he felt. God knew he had had so many women, but this was different. He slowly exhaled as she reached up and traced her finger along his cheek. Her eyes locked on him.

Surprisingly, somehow finding the strength she backed away from him. "Paul, I can't. I'm sorry," she whispered fearing that he would hear her heart pounding in her chest.

Stunned at the magnitude of the desire he felt as he had kissed her and then her unexpectedly breaking away from him, he was almost dizzy with bewilderment. "My God Emily, you have nothing to be sorry about," he said in a voice husky with passion. "I'm the one who should apologize. I promised you I wouldn't do that again."

Feeling as if she was able to breathe again she looked up at him and said, "Let's agree that no one is to blame. It seems we are both fighting a battle neither is meant to win," she whispered.

She squeezed his hand as she gave him a small smile. "We have to be logical," she said trying to convince him as well as herself. He looked at her with his eyes half-closed. "Emily, nothing about this situation is logical," he replied.

She nodded her head with a sly smile, "Well, that is true Paul. After all, you could be my grandfather." His eyes opened wide as he began laughing, "Emily, that's daft!"

Just then her phone began ringing. It was Sam asking if he could stop by on his way home. He told her he had some news.

After lunch Paul went to rest while she finished up the project she was working on. When she was done she went outside to wait for Sam just as he pulled into the driveway. "Where's Paul?" Sam asked as they walked to the porch and sat down. "He's sleeping. I think he's still recovering from the jump and all that's happened," she answered. "Do you want anything to drink?" she asked. "No thanks, can't stay long. We have a babysitter tonight. Chris and I are going to the Fox to see a show," he answered.

"What's the news?" she asked. He hesitated for a moment. "Emily, it looks like the car that tried to run you two down was a deliberate act," he said. She sat upright saying, "Ramsgate?"

"The director still feels that they must be involved in this whole thing. We are checking. I wanted to keep you abreast of everything as we look into it," he finished.

Just then they heard the door open as Paul came out to join them. "Hello, Paul. How are you doing?" Sam asked as he stood and extended his hand. "I'm doing well Sam. Thank you for asking," he answered as he sat down.

"I just wanted to stop by and check on you before I headed home," Sam explained. "Well that is thoughtful of you," Paul said with a smile as he lit a cigarette.

"Is there anything I can do for you or is Emily taking good enough care of you?" Sam asked with a grin. "Emily is treating me quite well," Paul answered. She smiled at Paul before turning to Sam. "I want to give Paul a little diversion, but having trouble trying to figure out what to do."

Sam thought for a moment, "Those concerts at Newtown Park are still going on. They usually have food trucks there too," he answered. She nodded, "Oh yeah, I forgot about that." She was thankful that he didn't bring up the real reason for his visit. Paul didn't need any more stress than he was already under. Sam got up as he needed to get home. "Well, I better get going before Chris wonders where I am!" he said cheerfully.

After Sam left Emily asked, "Did you have a good nap?" He yawned and replied, "I think so." She began checking her phone to see if there was a concert at Newtown Park that evening. There was. She looked over at Paul with a smile. "There is a concert tonight at the park near here. It's a tribute band playing Beach Boys music. Would you like to go? They'll have food trucks and it's so pretty out tonight," she said hopefully. He nodded his head, "I'd love to. I am particularly fond of the Beach Boys. But what is a food truck?" He asked with a smile.

"Oh, they're great. They are trucks that are really kitchens on wheels. They cook all sorts of wonderful food like tacos, burgers and other things. You'll like it," she responded. "Sounds like fun. What time does it start?" he asked. "In a couple of hours, but we should go earlier to get a place to park," she said.

He sat back and said, "We have quite a friendly competition with the Beach Boys, I think that Rubber

Soul inspired their Pet Sounds record. We would try to outdo each other all the time," he smiled. She reached over and patted his hand, "And that gave us all the music we love," she said with a twinkle in her eye.

After going inside Emily searched for a hat that Paul could wear. She was still a little nervous that he may be recognized if they went out in public. She found an old Braves cap and went to find him to see if it fit. He was sitting on the couch strumming the guitar. "Here, try this on," she said as she handed it to him. He took it from her and plopped it on his head sideways as he made a funny face. Laughing, she sat down next to him. She took the hat and adjusted it pulling it down a little. "Why do I need a hat?" he asked.

"I don't want to take the chance that you'll be recognized," she answered. He screwed up his face a little and asked, "Emily, who in the world would notice me?" he asked sincerely. She finished adjusting the hat and sat back trying to find the right words without giving him too much information. "Well, you know, some people are still fans of The Beatles and ..."

"Ah-ha!" he said as he took off the hat and put it on the table. "Please carry on," he said as he sat back crossing his arms. "Oh, Paul," she said as she swatted his arm, "You're trying to trick me!" He countered laughing, "You started it!"

"I'm afraid to tell you too much. It would change the way your life will play out. Do you understand?" she answered. He nodded, "I do. But haven't we already done that bit of damage?" he asked as she lowered her head while she nodded saying quietly, "I suppose so."

"Emily, I was just teasing you," he said softly. "No need to be sad." She smiled up at him while contemplating. "I'm not sad. I'm just trying to figure out how much I can tell you," she said honestly. He sat back and let her mull things over. "I don't want you to tell me if you'd be in trouble with Sam," he added. "Oh, it's not that I would be in trouble. I just don't want to disrupt or change your life any more than we already have," she replied.

"Let me put it this way, umm," she began. He put his finger to her lips saying, "Not to worry Emily, I'll wear the hat without asking any more questions. I don't want to pressure you." She grinned at him and said, "Oh, and you can't shave either," she said. He crossed his arms trying to put up a feign protest. "And why is that?" he asked.

Picking up her phone she said, "Because, these are also cameras and I don't want anyone taking your picture and splashing it all over the place." "I still don't understand, but I'll take your word," He said as he put the hat back on and grinned at her.

When they arrived at the park and found a spot to lay their blanket down. They opened the picnic basket she had packed holding wine and glasses, cheese and crackers. Soon the band began playing and they listened as they sipped their wine. She glanced over at him as he listened with a smile on his face lost in the music. She leaned towards him as the song ended, "Having fun?" she asked.

"Yes," he replied with a wink. "I'd fancy being up there right now but since I can't, I'd like to try some of that truck food." She laughed and looked around at the choices that were parked there. "Let's see. There are burgers, Greek food, tacos, and desserts. What would you like?" she asked.

"Can we try all of them?" he asked jokingly. He wandered to the taco truck while she stopped at the

Greek one. She stopped and picked up two funnel cakes for dessert. They met back at the blanket and nibbled on the food while they finished watching the concert.

The last song performed was, 'God Only Knows.' It had always held a special place in Emily's heart. She leaned on Paul's arm as they were both lost in the song. He smiled down at her and placed his arm around her as it ended. They sat quietly for a moment as others around them gathered their things to leave.

Walking back to the car, Paul took Emily's hand. She glanced up at him as he did with a smile. He loaded the basket and blanket into the car as she got in. She thought to herself how wonderful it was to get out and watch him enjoy the sights, the food and, of course, the music.

She drove while he chatted away about The Beach Boys and how they would always try to outdo each other. "Their latest record, 'Pet Sounds,' is marvelous," he said with glee. "I believe that Brian is a genius," he finished.

When they arrived back at the house Paul rolled a joint while she cleaned out the basket and put it away.

Walking into the living room, she said, "That was fun. Did you enjoy yourself?"

"It was marvelous!" he replied. As he rubbed his cheek he said, "This beard has to come off. I'll be right back."

He walked back to the guest room. She sat for a moment before deciding to pour them some wine. She went to join him and bring him his glass. Peeking her head around the corner she held the glass out to him. "Thank you love," he said with a smile beaming through the shaving cream on his face. He had taken his sweater off and just had on a black t-shirt. She thought to herself how adorable he looked. She smiled at him as she sipped her wine leaning against the sink.

He saw her staring and gave her a wink. A little embarrassed she started to leave. "Wait love, I'll be done in a moment," he said as he touched her arm. She settled back again against the sink. "I absolutely hate shaving, but I hate having a beard as well," he shrugged.

"I think you look great either way," she said with a grin. "A lot of men now just wear a two- or three-day beard. I think it's kinda sexy," she finished. He looked at her with that beautiful smile and said, "Well, Emily, it would have been nice to know that before I shaved." She just continued to smile at him as she sipped her wine.

After a little while having had more wine with a little smoke she began to feel slightly tipsy and could feel her guard starting to drop. Trying very hard to fight the urge to reach over and stroke his cheek and kiss his beautiful lips. Seeing her staring at him, he looked at her with a crooked smile as he cocked his head. "I'm sorry, I was daydreaming," she said with a smile as she began to get up.

"I suppose I should head off to bed," she said with a yawn. He reached out and took her hand. "Sleep well sweet Emily," he said as he pressed her fingers to his lips looking at her with hooded eyes.

She had just enough wine and pot to respond by saying, "Okay, that's enough! You're doing that on purpose!" Pulling back with a mock horror on his face, "Why, Emily, I don't know what you mean!"

"You are deliberately trying to seduce me with your, your…" she stuttered, "your English ways!"

"English ways?" he said unable to control his laughter. Seeing him laugh like that made her burst out into peals of laughter herself. Barely able to catch her breath she said, "Yes, you do it all the time!"

"Do what?" he said trying to stifle his own laughter. "And what exactly are 'English ways?" he teased. She looked over at him still laughing. Finally catching her breath enough to talk, "Kissing my fingers. Calling me sweet Emily and Love. Those English ways!" she said with a grin. "Ah, I see," he said with a wink. "And that! That wink! You do it on purpose! Just to get me to fall for your charms!" she said as she grabbed the pillow next to her and hit him with it. "Stop it!" she said with lighthearted indignation.

As she turned to get up, he picked up the pillow and threw it at her. She turned around and snatched it up and threw it back at him. Before long, they were in a full-fledged pillow fight. Laughing and trying to dodge the other's pillows. Paul threw one at her that she tried to side-step and ended up falling back onto the couch. He picked up the pillow and stood above her as she held up her hands in surrender. "I give up! Stop!" she said still laughing. He dropped the pillow and put his hand out to her, she took it as he gently helped her stand.

Both out of breath they stood for a moment looking into each other's eyes. She began to turn away, afraid of the yearning for him she had inside. He stopped her as he touched her arm, "Emily," he whispered before kissing her lightly on her lips. She responded by reaching up and cupping his face in her hands and then kissing him deeply before drawing back and gazing into his deep brown eyes.

"Oh Paul, we shouldn't," she whispered, knowing it was too late. She needed him and he needed her. He hushed her with a gentle kiss. Without a word spoken he took her hand and led her to her bedroom. Taking her into his arms he slowly began kissing her again as he unbuttoned her blouse showering her with kisses he caressed her moving his hands down her body. He took her beauty in as her naked body was glowing in the moonlight coming through the window.

His longing made him fumble while trying to remove his own shirt. Emily pulled his hands away and started unbuttoning it for him as she looked at him seductively. She touched his chest gently as she let his shirt drop to the floor. She showered his body with kisses as she slowly moved her hand down his stomach looking up into his eyes he leaned down to kiss her again.

As his lips met hers she shivered slightly with anticipation. They stood still for a moment watching each other's faces. The intensity in his eyes was almost too much for her. Making her want him but at the same time making her feel somewhat shy. He began an urgent onslaught of kisses from her lips to her throat and then back up to gently cup her face in his hands as he murmured his need for her. He lowered her to the bed as he hovered over her watching her eyes as he touched her gently moving his hands slowly over her breasts.

He had made love to so many women, but now, here with Emily, he felt almost as if it were his first time. He wanted to show her how he felt about her. How he needed her. He wanted to make her feel as if she was the only woman in the world. As he felt her warm skin under his fingertips, he could barely breath from the passion he felt.

He ran his fingers down her body while his other hand was entangled in her long soft hair. She murmured his name as he covered her mouth with his again. She ran her hands down his back trying not to dig her fingernails into his skin. She had never wanted anyone as much as she wanted him.

A moan escaped from her lips as he continued to touch her. Looking into his eyes she saw such raw emotion that made her head spin. Her body began to shutter as he continued to watch her face. She blinked her eyes open as her body began to relax. She wrapped a leg around his as he gently took her hands and held them above her head.

Leaning over her kissing he continued to devour her lips as her eyes were locked on his and filled with desire. He wanted this moment to last forever. Then at last the urgency took over as they moved in unison together as their desire for each other heighted. Finally letting the cascade of unstoppable emotion wash over them as they became one in that moment and forever.

They collapsed together, both gasping for air. After a few minutes Paul leaned on his hand as he watched her face and smoothed her hair on the pillow. "That was beautiful. You're beautiful," he said sweetly as he kissed her again.

She looked up at him and smiled. "You are too," she said as she brushed the hair away from his eyes. He lay back down and gathered her into his arms entangling their legs so that he could feel all of her. "I want to stay like this forever," he whispered in her ear.

She smiled and ran her fingers along his jaw before kissing him deeply as she moved to rise above him. "We don't have forever, but we have today," she whispered huskily as she trailed kisses down his throat to his chest.

All reason had faded as they made love again and held each other all through the night. Not ever really sleeping but living in that dreamlike state between reality and fantasy. They lived a lifetime of love that night and into the morning. They must have dozed off as the sun began peeking through the curtains. Moaning slightly, Paul instinctively reached for her, wrapping his arms around her as she curled her sleeping body next to his. As he held her he realized she had saved his life and then gave him a new life.

Hours later after sleep had finally won them over they each woke up to a different reality, a new life. Paul woke first, opening his eyes to see her curled up next to him, her hand gently laying on his chest. Not wanting to wake her he marveled at her beauty. He realized with wonder that all he wanted at this moment was to protect and cherish her forever. Watching her face as she slept, he lightly traced his finger along her jaw and over her lips. She stirred slightly, moving her hand to his waist.

Emily, feeling his gentle touch didn't open her eyes wanting to keep each second, each minute, each hour from slipping away. She held her breath for a moment and opened her eyes still not believing she was wrapped in his arms. She had never understood true joy before he came into her life.

His eyes shone back at her. He kissed her as he brushed her hair away from her face. "Morning," she murmured. There was no awkwardness. No doubt. Neither spoke as they were lost in each other's eyes. Paul broke the silence as he whispered conspiratorially, "Do you mind if we stay in bed all day. I don't want to let you go."

She grinned up at him as she responded, "Mmm, but let me get us some coffee first." Moving to get up he said, winking, "I want to have a go at that coffee machine." He got out of bed and she marveled at him as he headed out the door.

He appeared in the doorway holding two cups of steaming hot coffee looking quite proud of himself. With a huge grin on his face and his hair messy from sleep, she thought she had never seen a more perfect man. She walked towards him and took the mug he held out to her. She began snickering as she climbed back into the bed.

"Are you laughing at me Emily?" he asked with a silly smile. "No, of course not, I just remembered an interview of yours I watched." He rolled his eyes, "God, they can be so daft," he confessed. She continued, "The interviewer, a man no less, said to you, 'Paul, you're so beautiful." Groaning as he put down his cup, "Oh, please don't remind me of that. I've never heard the end of it from, well, anyone," he laughed. "He was right," she said as she leaned over and kissed him.

He said, "That reminds me of the premiere of 'A Hard Day's Night,' in London. We got to the theatre and there was quite a crowd gathered there. John muttered under his breath, "Push Paul out first, he's the prettiest." She laughed so hard she almost spilled her coffee on the sheets.

Paul told her another story, "George's humor is so dry, but people may miss it since his delivery is straight-faced. When we had our audition with George Martin at EMI down in London, it was our last shot. Walking into the studio we were dead nervous, but excited. After about an hour of recording they called us up to the booth to listen to what we had done so far. George Martin said, 'If there's anything you don't like, tell me.' In his usual deadpan voice George said, 'Well, I don't like your tie to begin with.' I was horrified as were John and Ringo. We were thinking, 'Well, he's blown it now'. After a brief silence, instead of getting angry, he let out an uproarious laugh."

They sat quietly for a moment and then wondering she asked, "How do you and John write together? Does one come up with the words and the other the melody?" "Not really," he replied, "I don't know, ummm…it varies actually. Sometimes I come up with a finished song and sometimes John does. We work with it together adding to it or taking away from it until we bash it out, but we always say we both wrote it. John will come to me with a half-written song and we finish it together. If I come to him with one he will say, 'Well, that's no good. And that's good,' until we get it right. Tis what we agreed upon early on."

He thought for a moment, "When we started writing together, we'd finish a song and I would write across the top of the page 'another Lennon-McCartney original'," he said with a laugh. She smiled, "How many have you written?" He leaned back against the pillows as he thought, "I don't know. Maybe a hundred or so, we don't keep track. Early on we would write songs for other people. It was fun seeing our written songs hit the charts for our friends. We gave many songs away. The Rolling Stones, Peter and Gordon, Cilla Black and Billy J Kramer were a few but now we really don't have the time any longer."

She studied him as he got up and walked to the window and pulled back the curtains. As the sun streamed over his face, her thoughts wandered to the impossible as she watched him carefully. In her eyes he was the most beautiful man she had ever seen. In all aspects from his chameleon ways of appearing so young to his unshaven street-smart look. She never tired of watching him. But it was his kindness and humility that made him so attractive. She got up and went to him. Reaching up she brushed his hair away from his eyes. "What is it love?" he asked her as he held her hand and kissed her fingers. "It's nothing. Just daydreaming a little," she quietly answered. "Me, as well," he whispered.

Sam called and drew them out of the moment. Paul began kissing her neck from behind as she muffled a giggle and swatted him away. Sam heard her laugh and wondered what was happening between the two of them. He imagined Paul was intrigued by Emily, who wouldn't be, she was lovely, kind and very smart. He had the charming personality that the girls seemed to swoon over. He hung up intending to get a better idea of their relationship this afternoon. He didn't want either one to get hurt and cursed under his breath that it may be too late.

Chapter 4

Sam brought news from the director who had intended not to get involved with this project in the beginning. Now as he had become aware of the glitch and the apparent involvement of Ramsgate, he was anxious to have it resolved. Unfortunately, there is no expeditious way of a resolution because of the matrix jump needed to get Paul back hours earlier than he left was causing some problems and they needed some extra time to be sure it was done correctly. And of course, the most important aspect is that they needed to make sure that once he was home, he would be safe from Ramsgate's reach.

Paul nodded to them, still mystified, not understanding much of what they said, but he did understand that he would have more time with Emily. That suited him fine. He was in his own thoughts of trying to find a way to be with her forever. He had to make sure she wanted the same.

Paul stood up to get himself more coffee. Sam glanced up as he left the room. "Is he okay?" he whispered to her. "Um, yes, he's fine considering we have whisked him across the universe so to speak," she replied, "No pun intended." "How is he handling the news of John?" he asked. "It was rough, very rough on him, but I convinced him that we may have saved John by saving him," she responded. Sam asked her how they were getting along. Emily sighed as she looked at him. "Sam, he is such an interesting man. There is so much more to him than I ever imagined. I always believed he was just a pretty face," she said with a laugh.

He could tell by the tone of her voice that she was conflicted. "Emily be careful. I don't want to see you hurt in all of this." Paul hummed that sweet melody again as he poured himself another cup of coffee. "Anyone else need a bit more?" he said while peeking his head around the doorway. "No thank you," they both said in unison.
Emily walked Sam outside. Giving her a quick hug, he said, "I was wondering if you'd both like to come for dinner one night soon. Chris is dying to meet him," he laughed. "Sounds good," she said as she kissed his cheek adding, "I'll call Chris to see what works for her."

After Sam left, Emily unpacked the bag he had brought. More cigarettes, coffee, tea, wine, food and a few folders from the office for Emily to review. She took them and put them on her desk, realizing she didn't have any interest or motivation to look at them. It seemed all she cared about was Paul, making him happy for the short time they had left together. She had lost interest in her work and in her life here alone.

He sat at the kitchen table as she emptied the bag. He was lost in thought wondering to himself about all the love songs he had written without ever understanding love, until now. Since he has been here he was brimming with ideas and melodies. Drawing him out of his thoughts Emily said, "Sam wants us to go to dinner at their place sometime soon. His wife would like to meet you. Would you like that?" "Yes, that would be enjoyable," he replied.

Glancing up at her he noticed her looking rather down. "Emily, are you alright? Did Sam say something to upset you?" he asked protectively. She stated, "No, of course not. I'm fine. This has been such a whirlwind. I guess I'm a little confused." He laughed. "I know how you feel," he said while getting up and crossing the room to her. He was usually so optimistic and happy. Being here, knowing he may lose her, made him feel lost and afraid. He had tried but couldn't imagine living life without her.

Paul slid his arms around her waist and nuzzled the back of her neck. She turned to face him and smiled wondering how she would go on without him when he was gone. "I'll tell you what Emily," he whispered in her ear, "Sam is a nice enough bloke, but if he upset you, I'd have to set him straight." She smiled at his bravado. "I'm fine, really," she said afraid he might guess the real reason. She was falling in love with him and she was frightened.

As the day's past they had gotten used to their routine of waking together. Emily would work on her cases while Paul would work on his music. Occasionally, Emily would forget that it would all end soon. He would be home and safe from the terrible accident. Making music with the band and changing the world. While she would be left here with her memories and the love she had for him.

It would be a week before he would go back to his home in the past. She planned on making his time here happy. She decided they needed to get out and see a little life outside of the house. She thought she would take him out to dinner and hoped he would enjoy it.

She wanted to take him out shopping to buy some things he needed. She dug out her tape measure to take his measurements. Laughing, he said, "I feel like I did when we were measured by Madame Tussauds for our wax figures." She looked up at him while she placed the tape measure around his waist, "I'll bet that was strange seeing yourselves in wax." He replied, "It was fun, but you're right, it was a bit daft."

Walking into the large department store he was astounded at the choices and the size of the store. Finally, finding the men's department, she stood back and watched him. She realized he was looking very confused as he picked out several shirts looking for the size. "T-shirts you are a large and trousers you are a 32/36. Do you want to try these on?" She asked as she held up a pair of dark jeans.

"So, are you happy with what we got?" She asked as they walked to the car. "Yes indeed. Thank you. It will be nice to get into something new," he replied, "Just a little embarrassed about you paying for everything." "It's fine Paul. Please don't worry about it," she countered with a smile. Sighing as he slid into the car, "But I do worry Emily. It's not right," he said. "And, why is everything so bloody expensive?" he laughed.

Later while they were getting ready to go out, she poured herself a glass of wine. Paul was taking a shower and she could hear him singing as she passed the guest room. Smiling to herself she thought I could listen to him all day. She took extra care with her makeup and her hair, piling it on top of her head into a soft bun. She put on a dress she hadn't worn since last Christmas. A deep blue silk empire waisted dress that accented her figure perfectly.

She walked into the living room where he was waiting. Looking quite handsome in a white dress shirt, a green tie and the dark jeans they had brought. Paul turned around and slowly exhaled and whistled as he looked at her. "We can't go out with you looking like that," he joked, "All the men and maybe some of the women will want to snatch you away from me." She laughed and said, "I could say the same thing, you look quite handsome."

Emily had decided they would try a new little Italian restaurant that had recently opened. She wanted the evening to be special for him. Backing out of the driveway she noticed Paul clutching his armrest. His knuckles were almost white. She stopped and asked, "Is something wrong?" Sheepishly he said, "I must admit Emily I'm terrified in a car unless I'm the one driving." She leaned over and gave him a kiss saying, "I'll be careful. I promise."

The restaurant wasn't too crowded being a Thursday evening. They were seated in a quiet booth near the back of the room. As they settled in their waiter approached their table. "Good evening, my name is Cooper. I'll be taking care of you tonight. May I get you a drink? He asked. Emily smiled up at him, "Yes, thank you. I'll have a chardonnay please." Turning to Paul he asked, "And for you sir?" Paul grinned at the young man. "I'd fancy a scotch," he responded with a wink.

Paul was happy to be out in public without having to hide his face or dodge excited fans. It had been quite a while since he could enjoy himself at a lovely restaurant like this. Emily watched the people around them taking note that no one seemed to notice that Paul McCartney of The Beatles was in the room with them. She began to relax a little thinking maybe her fears were irrational.

As the waiter approached their table with their drinks he caught Emily's eyes and smiled shyly with a slight blush. He placed her wine down and very carefully, almost reverently, placed Paul's drink down with a slight bow with his head. She wondered if he understood who was sitting in front of him. Paul smiled up at him. "Thank ya mate," he said. "You're welcome. The chef is preparing an antipasto for you. Compliments of the house." Before either one could ask why he had gone to retrieve it.

Paul lifted his glass to her with a wink and said, "To you, dear Emily." She raised her glass lightly touching his with a nod, "And to you Paul." Before long the piano began playing. They hadn't noticed it in the corner of the room when they came in. The melody sounded familiar to her when she realized the pianist was playing 'Yesterday' the most famous song that the Beatles had recorded. One that Paul had written.

She turned and looked at him. He sat still, listening. His eyes slightly widened. Not knowing what his reaction would be, she didn't realize she was holding her breath. He looked from the piano and mouthed, 'What?' with a credulous look on his face. She had to laugh leaning over to him, "I guess it's safe to tell you your song is one of the most loved songs even now." She explained that it had been recorded by various artists over the last 50 years. She continued, "I've read somewhere that it has been recorded over 3,000 times, making it the most recorded song ever."

Blushing at the news, he was humbled she realized with admiration. When the song ended he turned to her again. "Emily, I'm gobsmacked," he said. She saw the waiter approaching and he placed the antipasto between them and asked, "Would you like another drink?" Paul looked up at him nodding, "Yes, that would be great." As he walked away, Paul said, "He seems quite familiar to me." "I thought the same thing earlier," she responded.

As they enjoyed the antipasto, he amused her with the story of how he came to write 'Yesterday'. "I awoke with the tune in me head one morning. When I got to the studio I played it for the fellows asking if they had heard it before. The tune was so different from anything I had written before that it took a while, a few weeks until I sat down to finish it. The words didn't come to me for a few more days. So, in the meantime, I just put nonsense words together with the tune." He continued laughing, "I think it was something like, scrambled eggs, oh my baby how I love your legs."

Laughing she noticed their food arriving. The waiter first set her plate of chicken marsala in front of her with a smile. He then turned to Paul, placing his order of veal piccata in front of him carefully. "Did you enjoy the antipasto?" he asked. "Yes, it was quite good. Thank you," Paul answered with a grin.

After they had finished eating, she sat back and watched him watch the other patrons enjoying themselves. He was amused by the fact that about half the men in the restaurant were bald. A complete 180 in style from 1966 and the long hair he wore. He wondered out loud how he might look bald. Emily giggled at the thought. The waiter came by with the dessert menu and after they ordered something to share Emily asked him if he would take their picture. She wanted something to hold on to after he left.

The pianist finished his set and was sitting at the bar taking a break slowly stirring his drink as he looked around the place. His eyes fell on them and Emily felt butterflies in her stomach realizing that if anyone there would recognize Paul it would be him. As if on cue, he leaned to the bartender and said something that made them both turn to look at their table.

She quickly signaled to the waiter to bring the check. They had to get out of there. Paul, feeling her urgency asked, "What tis it?" She whispered, "You may have been noticed." At that moment two couples entered the restaurant and headed to the bar, greeting the pianist. She hoped that would give them enough time to make their way to the exit.

Once outside, as they were getting into the car, she said laughing, "Well, that was a close call. Let's get home before a mob of teenagers comes running down the street." "It's not a bad thing being chased by hundreds of girls," he replied with a wink.

Arriving back at Emily's place they settled themselves on the couch. Feeling the moment was right Paul began, "Emily, tell me why you think I need to go back." Surprised, Emily just stared at him for a moment. "Paul, it's where you belong. You still have a lot of work to do." She ran her fingers up his arm as she said, "The reason I was sent there was to save you and to change the course of your life and The Beatles."

Stopping her, he waved his hand, "That right there, Emily, you or Sam or anyone for that matter don't know what I need or want, you see." Continuing, "I am more than grateful to you for saving me life, but I believe it is my turn to have a say in what happens here on out." Standing he began pacing a bit trying to gather his thoughts. Emily stood to go to him, but he motioned for her to sit as he began. "I can't imagine living my life without you Emily." She felt her heart flip in her chest, "Paul, we have to be logical…" "No Emily, that's rubbish," he said, "The moment you went back to stop me from getting in my car, all logic was lost, you see? Emily, I've fallen in love with you."

Sitting next to her he took her hands in his and said again, "I've fallen in love with you." Her head was spinning, not sure what to say, what to do. "Paul, I love you too, but…" he cut her off. "There are no 'buts' Emily. It is just us right now. What do we do about it?" He asked, cocking his head and looking at her questioningly. She didn't, couldn't, respond immediately. She was too stunned, "I don't know Paul. I don't know what we should do," she whispered.

Getting up, he went to the liquor cabinet and made himself a drink and poured her some wine. Handing the glass to her he leaned over and kissed the tip of her nose and gave her a wink. "What?" she giggled. "Oh, nothing. I feel like drinking a little too much and then making mad love to you," he said with a gleam in his eyes.

She sipped her wine, looking at him over the rim, frowning as she asked, "You need to be drunk?" "Ha, hardly. I'm enjoying this evening. It was a perfect meal and I'm with the perfect woman," he continued, "Whom I plan to devour later." "Oh? And what if I'm not in the mood," she teased with a little pout.

"We may regret this in the morning," she said. He stood at the liquor cabinet stirring his drink with his finger. "No regrets Emily. Never, if we're together, even if we are hungover," he finished with a laugh as he tipped his glass to her and handed her the joint. She sipped her wine and smoked a little more before handing it back to him.

He began telling her the story of when he was the best man at George and Pattie's wedding. "I got a little bevvied. I found a bow and arrow and was fiddling about with it. I put an arrow right through the bonnet of George's car," he said while screwing up his face. "George wasn't all too happy with me," he finished. She laughed, "I suppose not!"

They made love slowly, cherishing each touch and kiss. They held each other all night, neither moving away. They were one now, neither believing one could live without the other. Waking in the middle of the night to make love again and then falling back into their shared dream.

Waking to the sun they laid there both wishing they could make time stand still. He took her hand lacing his fingers with hers, raising them to his mouth. Kissing each of her fingers with such sweetness, she felt she was being kissed by an angel. "English ways," she murmured with a smile.

Finally, they both got up and began their day. She made breakfast while he straightened up the living room. He was finishing as she called him to the kitchen, "Paul! It's ready." He grinned at the domesticity of it all as he walked into the kitchen carrying the glasses from last night. "Thanks," he said as he sat down to join her, "This looks marvelous."

Her phone rang, "Sam," she mouthed as she answered it. "OK," she said as she listened. Just then the doorbell rang. "It must be here. Someone is ringing the bell," she said as she hung up. "Sam sent some paperwork over," she said to Paul as she headed to answer the door.

Laying the envelope on the table she turned to get more coffee for them. "Um, Emily?" He said as he looked at the envelope. "What?" she replied as she poured the coffee. "This is addressed to Dr. Emily Hilson," he said with a questioning look. "Oh, yes, well," she said as her voice faded. "You didn't tell me," he remarked slowly, "You're a doctor?"

She sat down, "Well, it never came up," she grinned. "I have a PhD in Quantum Physics," she stated. He sat back in his chair. "Alright," he continued, "I don't even know what that is." She smiled, "It's the study of the smallest scales of energy levels of atoms and subatomic particles." He looked at her blankly, "And again?" he asked. Getting up from the table she kissed the top of his head saying, "We can't all be musical geniuses." He snorted, "Who's a musical genius? I'm certainly not." She turned to face him aghast that he would say that, "Paul," she began, "I'm going to say something I probably shouldn't."

She walked over to him and gently sat down on his lap brushing his hair away from his eyes. "You and John are considered one of the greatest songwriting teams ever," she insisted. "Now, don't let that go to your head, but it's true. And don't tell Sam I told you," she emphasized. He pulled back a little with a look on his face that she couldn't read. "What is it?" she asked. "Nothing. I'm just curious as to why people would say that, but I'll take your word," he said. She was again amazed at his humility which was part of what made him so attractive to her.

She gave him a kiss as she got up. "I've got to work," she said as she walked into the living room with the envelope. He filled his cup and picked up the guitar on the way to the sunroom.

She read through the file as she listened to him play when he began singing quietly. Whatever he was working on was beautiful, she got up and went to stand in the doorway that separated them. "It's lovely," she said as she watched him. He looked up and smiled at her. "I'm an inspired man," he said with a wink. He stood and walked to her picking her up and spinning her around. She giggled, "Paul, put me down. You'll hurt yourself," she teased. "I won't!" he declared as he continued to hold her in his arms.

He put her down and slowly kissed her. She sighed as he drew back to look at her. "I'm having a hard time with the words," he said. "Love doesn't describe how I feel about you." Blushing, she turned away. "It's true Emily, it's a real problem," he said as he explained walking backwards towards the kitchen, "A real problem."

She stood there for a moment lost in the warmth and love she felt for him and from him. Shaking her head to clear her mind, she sat back down and continued reading the material she was analyzing.

He came back inside saying, "I think a storm is coming this way." She looked out the front window. "You're right," she said as the sky began darkening. Just then a crack of thunder made her jump. "Oh!" she cried from the shock. He laughed from the other room. "Don't laugh at me!" she said teasingly. "Yes, Doctor," he replied with a guffaw. Smiling, she shook her head. "Stop it or I'll come in there and take your guitar away!" she countered. "Ooo," he said as he continued to laugh quietly. "You don't scare me," he said under his breath in a comical voice. "I heard that!" she added.

She worked for a while longer and after finishing put the material in an envelope. Sam said she could bring it with her when they came for dinner, so she placed it on the desk and shut down her computer. Paul was still working so she decided to pour a glass of wine and read the book she had started a while ago. She was so engrossed that she didn't notice him as he walked back into the living room.

He stood for a moment watching her, a glass of wine in one hand and a book in her lap, as she unconsciously played with her hair. He smiled as she looked up at him. "You are beautiful," he said softly. "You're only saying that so I won't take away the guitar," she said with a grin. He leaned over and kissed her on the forehead. "No, I mean it, you are the most beautiful woman I have ever known," he said seriously. She blushed slightly at the intensity of his gaze and his words. She shook herself out of the moment.

Chapter 5

"What do you want for dinner," she asked him as she began to get up. "Whatever is easy, or better yet, let me cook something up for us later," he said. She busied herself with straightening up the kitchen.

Paul grabbed the guitar strumming it as he inhaled the joint he had just lit. Emily joined him, sitting next to him she watched as he concentrated on the chords he was playing, making notes on a pad of paper in front of him. She was mesmerized by his talent, but even more so by his devotion and love of music. She giggled to herself as she remembered an interview he had done with the BBC.

He looked at her and smiled as he leaned the guitar against the side table, he asked, "What is it?" She grinned, "I was remembering yet another interview I listened to, just you, not the others. You were talking about your love of music." He laughed, "That interview was just a few months ago. And I was very stoned," he continued chuckling, "He had asked about my hobbies or something. I'm too busy for hobbies so

I just said, 'I like music.' I don't think that was the answer he wanted."

Getting up as he stretched his arms above his head, "I'm going for a ciggie then I'll get to work in the kitchen," he said. "I'll join you," she offered. He lit a cigarette and turned to her. Looking up at him, finding his deep brown eyes holding her gaze, she took his hand then moving it to her lips and kissed each of his fingers. "Emily, I won't be able to cook dinner if you keep that up," he said with a moan and a smile. "I'll stop," pausing she said, "For now." Hand in hand they walked back into the house as the rain began again.

She smiled watching him as he rummaged through the refrigerator and cabinets searching for something to cook. It was all so domestic. She couldn't help but laugh a little. "What's so funny?" he said peeking his head around the corner. "Us," she replied. "We are like a little old married couple." "That would suit me just fine," he said.

She said, "We're too young for marriage." He turned to her with a quizzical look. "Do ya really think so?" he asked. Realizing that was something that had changed a bit since 1966. She began, "People tended to marry younger in the 1960's. Nowadays it seems people wait until their late 20's or 30's. Getting their careers going before making big life decisions." She waited for him to sit down and handed him the joint. "I'm done," she said, sipping her wine. "They want to have all their ducks in a row so to speak," she continued. "Doesn't sound very romantic," he countered.

She laughed, "No you're right, it doesn't." He sat back and sipped his drink before asking, "How is it some man hasn't snatched you up." She chuckled again, "I guess I've been too busy working to worry about marriage," she replied. "I've never asked you, how old are you?" he asked. She looked at him from under her lashes and replied, "I'm twenty-nine." "Ah, I've always wanted to be with an older woman," he joked as she swatted his arm as he pretended to protect himself.

He stood as he said, "I think some chicken and mashed potatoes are on the menu." "Sounds good. Can I help?" she asked. "No, just keep me company," he answered. He was rummaging in the spice rack while she picked out potatoes for him to boil. "Paul," she began, "Do you want me to peel these?" "No, I want you to sit down and relax," he answered.

"I always find it relaxing to cook," he started, "I don't have much time to do it really, but I enjoy it." She watched him as he flipped the chicken and started to boil the water. He stopped and turned to her, "I always imagined myself married with little ones under foot in the kitchen while my wife and I prepared their dinner," he said. She smiled up at him, "Such a domestic scene," she said, "I can picture that."

She was impressed with the meal he had made for them. "This is delicious," she said as she took another bite. "Thank you. You see I can be useful," he laughed. "I'll clean up in a while. Please join me outside for some fresh air," he said, offering his hand to her. The sun was setting and there was a stillness in the air as they sat down. Paul lit a cigarette and exhaled before turning to her. "I've never been happier Emily," he stated.

Looking at him smiling slightly she said softly, "Really? Of all the wonderful things that have happened to you in the past few years, this is what has made you happy?" He looked down for a moment and raised his eyes to her, "Yes, after everything is said and done, we are all lucky enough to enjoy the lives we've worked so hard for. We've busted our arses for years for the simple pleasures of life. Evenings like this for example. But mostly, my happiness is because of you," he finished.

She sat back and watched him. His hair blew in the breeze and his eyes were shining as he looked back at her. "You look beautiful tonight, Emily," he said softly. She blushed under his intense gaze. "Paul, stop," she said shyly. "You do!" he said, "And I won't stop." He reached for her chin and lifted it as he leaned over to kiss her. "I've never been one to hold back my love, you'll have to get used to it." She ran her finger along his jaw as she held his gaze. She had an overwhelming feeling of utter calm and peace come over her.

Drawing herself away from his gaze as she said, "Write a song for me." "Ah," he began, "But I already have sweet Emily. I want to finish it before I sing it for you," he explained. She sighed and ran her fingers through his hair. "Come, let's go in. It's getting a little chilly," she said as she took his hand. He opened the door for her and locked it behind them. He watched her as she began cleaning the dishes. "Let me do that," he said. "No, you cooked, I'll clean. Go relax in the living room and I'll be right there," she said as she shooed him away.

Paul wandered to the bookshelf, he wanted something to read before going to sleep. As he continued browsing Emily joined him. "I'm dying to read something," he said. "What do you want? Fiction? Non-fiction?" she asked. "Anything really," he replied. "I'm used to devouring newspapers, magazines, and books. I feel as if my brain is being deprived," he laughed. "Here," she said as she pulled a book off the shelf, you may like this," she said. "It's by a very popular author, he writes crime stories and mysteries."

"Come sit," she said as she patted the spot next to her. He sat down and turned the cover of the book open, reading the introduction, "This looks interesting. Thank you," he said absently. She reached over and brushed his hair away from his eyes as she looked at him. He turned to her, "You look deep in thought," he said. "No, not really, just thinking about how being here must be hard for you. We haven't really talked about how all of this is affecting you lately," she replied.

Sitting back, he thought as he sipped his drink. "At first, I was scared. Mostly because I didn't understand what had happened," he said. She said, "They were going to send someone else, but I insisted I do the jump. I thought because we are close in age, you would believe me easier than someone older and more hardened to jumping. Some of my colleagues can be quite by the book."

He thought for a moment. "You mean I could be stuck with some old bloke?" he said with a laugh. She giggled as she moved closer to him and snuggled into his arms. "I suppose so," she answered. "Well, I'm happy it was you. Very happy," he finished.

They sat quietly for a moment his fingers intertwined with hers. "This is lovely," he said. She rubbed her thumb along his finger. "It is, isn't it?" she agreed. "Do you want to start that book?" "Yes," he replied, "I'm going to have a ciggie. I'll lock up and join you in a minute." She straightened up the living room before heading to the bedroom.

She heard Paul come back inside and saw the house go dark as he turned the lights off. She thought how nice it was to have him here, she felt safe. He walked into the bedroom just as her nightgown slid down over her legs. "Now how am I supposed to concentrate on that book after seeing that?" He laughed. She blushed. "You can do it, I believe in you," she said with a laugh. He sat down on the edge of the bed contemplating. "I'll give it a go," he deadpanned.

She climbed into bed and pulled the covers back for him to join her. "Will the light bother you?" he asked. "Not at all," she responded. Paul slid under the covers with the book in hand. Emily snuggled up next to him as he began reading. She drifted off to sleep as she stroked his arm. He read for an hour or so before he realized he was quite tired. Putting the book down and switching off the light, he gently laid down so he wouldn't wake her. He gathered her in his arms before closing his eyes.

As they both woke he caught her gaze and smiled at her as he leaned over to kiss her. She snuggled closer to him. "I don't understand these feelings I have for you," he said running his finger over her cheek. "I imagine this is what true love feels like, but I've never felt it before," he finished. They made love most of the morning. Out of sheer exhaustion they fell into a light sleep.

Waking at noon she untangled herself from his arms and went to shower. Returning to the bedroom she found he was gone. He was in the living room and had settled himself in a chair by the window and was strumming the guitar. "Emily, do you have a pen and some paper?" he asked. Going over to her desk she drew out a pad of paper and a couple of pens. She walked up to him and put them down on the table next to him. He grinned up at her, "Thank you love."

After making sandwiches she joined him in the living room. She decided she'd try to get some work done while he was working on his song. Sitting down at her desk, she opened her laptop and flipped on the two monitors. As they powered up, she leaned back in her chair reading the first file that Sam had sent for her to look over. It was a jump proposal from a governmental agency. Moaning to herself as this always meant twice the paperwork.

She was so engrossed in the file that she hadn't noticed Paul had gotten up and was standing behind her mesmerized by the computer screens. "It's a pretty fancy set up you have there," he said. She laughed, "I suppose so."

As she recalled in 1966 computers took up an entire room. "Just like telephones, computers are smaller and more portable now," she explained. "For instance," she said pointing to her laptop, "This one can go anywhere, and most people now have at least one for work and one for their personal use." He shook his head in amazement. She explained the internet as best she could, realizing computers had not been for the public in his time. "So, you are saying, people can use these things to find out anything?" he asked. "Yes, let me show you," she said thinking of something she could google that wouldn't affect him. Typing in 'Georgia Tech' the university website came up. "This is where I went to college. It's here in Atlanta," she said moving the screen so he could see better.

He was totally flabbergasted as he asked, "Can we look up The Beatles?" Before she could respond, he backtracked, "Oh, sorry, I know the answer," he said with a wry smile. She stood up and gave him a hug. "More coffee?" she asked. "Yes, please, that would be lovely," he answered. They spent the afternoon working, she on the project, him on a lovely tune he was creating. Standing and stretching his arms above his head, he yawned and walked outside for fresh air and a ciggie. She finished up what she had done and sent it on to Sam, shutting down the monitors and her laptop.

Emily went outside to join him. He seemed deep in thought as he sat at the table, a cigarette in one hand, his chin in his other. "Penny for your thoughts," she said as she sat down across from him. "I was thinking about how pleasant it was today, nowhere I had to be, nothing I had to do. It was nice," he said as he put the cigarette out. "But most of all, looking up every now and again to see you there, was the best part of the day," he finished. She looked at him closely. He had a five o'clock shadow and his hair was a little messy. She thought to herself how attractive he is. "It is nice, having you here with me, I loved listening to you play," she said smiling and held her hand out for him.

Chapter 6

Waking up the next morning Emily stood at the kitchen window watching the sun peek above the horizon. Paul had gotten up and joined her sliding his arms around her waist. Without a word, they stood like that watching the daybreak, he sweetly kissed the back of her neck and murmured, "Good morning beautiful." She turned around as she placed her cup on the counter. "Good morning handsome," she said with a kiss.

For a moment she forgot that he would be leaving soon, then it hit her that she wasn't sure if she could live here without him. Seeing her face cloud over, Paul reached out and laced his fingers through hers. "Emily, what are you thinking?" he asked. Not wanting to spoil the day, she said, "Nothing important." She began to clear away the table. "I'm going to take a shower. Do you want anything before I go?" she asked. "No thanks," he answered. "What time are we leaving to go to Sam's place?" he asked. "Six," she replied as she leaned over and kissed the top of his head.

Stepping into the shower Emily let the hot water stream down on her before she began washing her hair. Before long, her tears mixed in with the water from the shower. She cried like that for a while before getting out and splashing cold water on her face. She scolded herself for being so silly and tried to remember that she was lucky to have fallen in love even if he would leave her soon.

Walking into the bedroom, he stopped. He heard her crying. He wasn't sure if he should go to her as he stood for a moment listening and decided to give her privacy. He hoped he hadn't done anything to upset her. Shaking his head, he reminded himself to be gentle with her.

He was in the living room when she came out. Paul reached for her and pulled her into his arms and held her without speaking. They laced their fingers together. He searched her face as they held each other. He took her chin in his hand as he kissed her gently. "Are you alright love?" he asked quietly. "Of course, why wouldn't I be?" she replied looking at him questioningly. "Emily, why do you hide away what you are feeling from me? I heard you crying in the shower." He waited, as she turned away from him slightly.

"I, I..." she began, he interrupted, continuing to hold her chin so that she would have to look into his eyes, "I love you, that means I'm here to hold you when you are sad as well as happy." She lowered her eyes, "Stop Paul, you'll make me cry again," she said with a small laugh. "I was not crying out of sadness. I was crying because all of these emotions overwhelmed me for a moment. You understand, don't you?" she explained. "Yes, of course, I do," he answered, "I am quite overwhelmed meself, but Emily, we have each other now. If you need to have a good cry, do it on my shoulder. Everything will be fine, just watch, you'll see." She began, "but..." He interrupted her again with a kiss, "No buts Emily."

They spent the morning working quietly except for the melody flowing from Paul's fingers. She was deep in thought as she finished up the second project that Sam had sent over to her. She glanced over at Paul as he sat quietly, she sipped her coffee. He must have felt her eyes on him as he turned to her crossing his eyes and sticking out his tongue. It was so unexpected that she almost spat the coffee out all over her laptop. Swallowing as she laughed, "What was that?" He got up as he said, "You looked so serious." He walked over to her and kissed the top of her head. "I'm going to get dressed for dinner," he said as he walked down the hallway.

As they got ready to leave for Sam and Chris' house she asked him if he was comfortable meeting someone new. "Of course, I don't mind," he responded. As they got into her car Emily explained, "Chris is like a sister to me. You'll like her I'm sure." "I'm sure I will," he responded. She was quiet during the ride and wondered if he really was comfortable.

When they got there, he turned to her saying, "Emily, I don't want to create any problems but there may be signs that you and I are..." She stopped him, "It's alright, Paul. I think Sam's already figured it out. If they notice that we look at each other and smile or touch each other they are not going to be angry or shocked, we are all grownups here."

He was relieved. He didn't want to have to hide how he felt about her in front of others. He was in love and he wanted to show it. "So, you're saying Sam won't give me a fist full of fives," he laughed. She responded by kissing him on his lips and giving him a seductive look. "You're torturing me Emily," he said huskily. She smiled and said, "Yes, I know."

They got out of the car and walked up to the door. Sam answered, "Welcome!" He said with a grin, "Come on inside. The boys are spending the night at a friend's house, so it's just us grownups tonight. Paul, I'd like you to meet my wife, Chris," Sam said as he brought Chris closer. "A pleasure to meet you, Chris," Paul said as he leaned into her and gave her a small hug and kiss on her cheek. Chris blushed and stammered a bit. "Really nice to meet you too Paul," she said. Emily gave her a big hug and kiss as well as they all walked into the living room.

"What would you like to drink?" Sam asked Paul. "I'd fancy a scotch if you've got it," he answered. "Coming right up," Sam said on his way to the kitchen. Paul followed him asking if he could help. "No, but please join me. Let's let the girls chat, they haven't seen each other for a while," Sam said. Paul leaned against the counter as Sam mixed their drinks and poured Emily and Chris some wine. "I hope you like steak," Sam inquired, "I'm grilling them out back." "Love it," Paul answered with a smile.

Chris and Emily both looked up guiltily as Sam, with Paul following behind entered the living room. "Now, what are you two talking about?" Sam questioned. Slightly flustered Chris swatted at Sam, saying with a chuckle, "Nothing at all dear." Emily looked absolutely radiant when Paul sat next to her and took her hand in his. Sam knew it was too late to intervene. Emily and Paul were obviously in love and neither could hide it. After a slightly awkward silence, Sam asked Paul how he was handling all of the changes he'd seen.

Paul explained that the most interesting thing was the way people listened to music now. "No records! Amazing," he said, shaking his head. He continued, "Emily is being quite careful about what I can listen to," he said with a wink. "Well, I don't want you to go back home and steal someone else's melody," she said as she gently pushed his arm.

Paul continued, "I am interested in Emily's computer too, but she won't let me near it," he said with a laugh. Chris snickered, "Oh, you don't want to, believe me, it's a rabbit hole. The other day I went to look up a recipe and ended up hours later having learned everything there is to know about how they make chocolate out of cocoa beans!"

Paul had been wondering and asked them about President Kennedy's assassination. "I had offered my meager services at no cost to Mark Lane when he was putting together a film based on his book 'Rush to Judgement'. He asked me why I wanted to score his film. I told him, 'when I have kids and they ask me what I did with my life, I didn't want to say that I was just a Beatle." He paused, "He turned me down. He said it was too controversial and didn't want my involvement to hurt the Beatles or me personally." He continued, "Did they ever prove the Warren Commission wrong?"

A little shocked Emily said, "I didn't know you had offered to do that." He turned to her and replied, "Yes, I was very interested in the whole case, it just didn't seem plausible that Oswald worked alone." Sam commented, "It's widely believed that your viewpoint is right, but nothing was ever proved."

Emily looked at Sam, he nodded. "Paul, one of my jumps was observational. I was there when it happened. I was standing across the street from the grassy knoll and did see someone firing from behind the fence, actually there were four shots from different directions," Emily said. Sam interjected, "We do observational jumps for different organizations and governmental departments. Emily's jump was sent on to the party who contracted us. We don't know what was done with the information."

Paul shook his head, he remarked, "The other fellows and I felt that some of our success here in America had been in part because America needed a bit of cheering up after the assassination. I suppose we brought some fun after the horror." Chris said, "You did. We needed you." Paul continued, "We were playing a concert in Scotland when we heard what had happened. I don't think the audience knew. We had heard he had been shot before we went on. We didn't learn until afterwards that he had died. We all watched the news back at our hotel, so tragic."

"Yes, it changed who we were as a country," Sam said. Paul looked over at Sam and asked, "What happened to Mrs. Kennedy and those sweet children?" Glancing at Emily and then Chris, Sam replied, "Mrs. Kennedy married a Greek tycoon. Caroline became a lawyer and had a family. She's been an ambassador to Japan. John also became a lawyer but sadly, he and his wife and her sister were killed when their plane crashed a few years ago." Paul looked stunned as he shook his head as he said, "How very sad." Emily added, "He was

121

piloting the small plane they were in. His mother never wanted him to fly, but after she passed away, he received his license."

As they continued to chat Sam stood to start the fire for the steaks. "I'll join you," Paul said, "I need a ciggie." Chris smiled at Emily after they had left the room. "Emily, he is so charming. It is so easy to talk to him. You'd never know he was a star," Chris said. Emily replied, "I know. I am constantly amazed at how unaffected he is. And he is so thoughtful and kind." Chris sat back and looked at Emily, "Be careful sweetie, I don't want to see you hurt," she finished. Emily bowed her head slightly and replied, "I am trying very hard to keep things in focus, but we are drawn to each other by something I can't explain." Chris looked at her slyly, "he is incredibly handsome. Funny, I had always thought John was better looking," Emily laughed, "I had thought the same thing."

"Come on, let's join them outside," Chris said while patting Emily's hand. After grabbing a bottle of wine out of the fridge, Chris followed Emily through the patio door. Sam and Paul sat at the table near the pool, their heads slightly bowed close together. Looking at the two of them, Emily knew she and Chris may have interrupted them as they looked quite serious. "Do you boys need another drink?" Chris called. Both looking up at the same time saying, "Yes!"

Emily walked to the table and sat down next to Paul. "So, what are you two conspiring about?" she asked laughing. Not getting a response, she said more concerned, "What is it?" Paul began, "Emily, I was speaking with Sam about," he hesitated for a moment, "about the possibility of you coming with me when I go home." She didn't say anything at first, she was shocked. "Paul," she began before he cut her off. "Emily, we are in love and I can't imagine living without you." She glanced over at Sam as Chris came out the door with a tray. "Let's talk about this later," she whispered to both of them, giving Paul a scolding look.

"Sam, have you started the fire yet?" Chris asked as she came back out of the house unaware of the tension at the table. "No, I was just about to," Sam replied as he stood. He laid his hand on Paul's shoulder, leaning down he whispered something in his ear that Emily didn't hear. Paul looked up at Sam with a furrowed brow and a nod.

Dismayed, she turned back to Paul. "It would have been nice if you had spoken with me first. After all I have some say in this," she whispered, "This is not how things are done …" He interrupted her, "I can't go back without you Emily, but maybe I was out of place," he said quietly. She reached for his hand saying, "Let's talk when we get home." Paul hung his head slightly looking back at her from under his lush lashes with puppy dog eyes. Emily swatted his arm. "And don't you give me that look," she said teasingly. How could she possibly be angry at him, he loved her and wanted her with him.

"Hey, you two," Chris said, "Would you like to eat outside or inside?" Emily, shaken out of the moment, looked to Paul. "Outside would be nice, it's quite pleasant tonight," he answered. Emily stood and asked Chris, "What can I help you with?" "Nothing, sit back and enjoy yourself," Chris replied. After putting the steaks on the fire, Sam asked, "How does everyone want theirs cooked." Paul got up and walked to the grill to keep Sam company.

During dinner, Paul entertained them with the story of how they met Elvis. He laughed as he began, "We were in L.A. on a short break from touring. Elvis was there renting a house as he was filming a movie. We drove up there, dead nervous," he continued, "He answered the door and we all piled into the place. Honestly, we were so excited none of us had the guts to speak to him. So, after a little while he gets up and says, "Well, I'm gonna go to bed unless one of you starts talking to me." Paul laughed as he imitated Elvis' voice. "We all ended up having a good laugh."

Chris laughed as she said, "Do you have any funny stories of John you wouldn't mind sharing?" He looked at her with a grin, "Many," he said laughing. "Remember, John is blind as a bat and absolutely hates wearing his glasses. I remember one instance when we were younger. John had left my house late at night, it was Christmas time. The next day he said to me, "I saw some mad people sitting on their front porch on Mather Avenue playing cards at one o'clock in the bloody morning. The next time I walked by that house I looked for myself and saw that it was an illuminated nativity scene."

He continued, "When we are in the studio, he will lay his glasses down. I'll snatch them up and wear them. He will start looking for them where he thought he had left them. Finally, he will figure out I have them on, he always yells, 'Macca!'" He added. "I can't figure out how I get away with it every time." "Macca?"

Chris asked. "Ah, in Liverpool we abbreviate everything! McCartney becomes Macca, Lennon is Lenny," he answered.

Sam remembered something he had read. He asked, "Is it true that John tied himself to Chuck Berry when you met him?" That made Paul roar with laughter. "Yes! Yes! We were backstage. He had just finished a set and we weren't due to go on for a bit. John looped a rope around his arm and walked to Chuck and looped it on his! Chuck was laughing. Elvis and Chuck are the reason we play, if it weren't for them, there would be no Beatles."

After they finished eating and had gone back into the house. "I've really enjoyed this evening," Paul declared. "It's been quite a while since I've enjoyed such good company and good food!" "Well, we've loved having you both here," Sam declared. "I wish I'd had the chance to meet your boys," Paul added. "Next time," Sam agreed. Taking Paul's cue, Emily rose to gather her things. "Sam, we didn't get a chance to talk about the two separate accidents that I've been analyzing. I'll come into the office tomorrow so we can go over them," she said. "Yes, that sounds good," he replied.

In the car on the way back to Emily's, it was quiet until Paul spoke. "You're upset with me for speaking with Sam," Paul asked while gazing out the side window. "No," she responded. "I'm not upset," she said as she turned into the driveway. Turning off the car, she turned to him, he looked at her waiting. "Paul, there are things we have to talk about before making such a life-changing decision." He shook his head as he responded, "Emily, do you always have to be so logical? We are in love, love is everything, love will guide our way." Emily smiled, as she said, "I am a scientist, and you sir are a hopeless romantic."

She reached up and brushed her fingers on his cheek, "I love you Paul, but we have to..." she whispered. He interrupted, "Stop trying to make this complicated Emily."

"You're asking me to give up everything, I need time," she said with a slightly raised voice. Knowing she sounded abrupt saying, "I'm sorry." Paul lifted his head and looked at her for a moment. He didn't say anything as he opened the door. "Don't be angry," she said as she got out of the car. "I'm not angry at all Emily. I thought you felt as I do. I thought we meant everything to each other," he said as he began walking into the house. "Don't walk away from me," she said in exasperation.

He stopped, drawing a cigarette out of the pack, lit it, then slowly turned around to face her as she walked toward him. With his hands raised in mock surrender, he continued to look at her without speaking. She brushed past him saying, "Finish your cigarette, we'll talk when you come inside," she said as she closed the door behind her. She realized with a moment of insight that he was hurt and didn't know quite how to handle it.

She was pacing in the kitchen when he cracked the door open. Peeking inside, "You're not going to throw something at me head are ya?" He asked with a smile. Laughing she walked towards him. "Paul, my head is spinning is all. I am sorry I was short with you," she finished. He held her never taking his eyes off of hers. She continued, "I love you and I do want to spend the rest of our lives together. Everything is moving so fast. I suppose I'm a little scared. You understand, don't you?" He touched her cheek, and said, "Of course I do. I am too. I promise you, everything will be fine. You'll see."

Emily stared into his deep brown eyes, she realized besides being a hopeless romantic, he was an eternal optimist. "There's so much to consider," she began. He threw his head back and laughed. She was a little startled, "What's so funny?" She asked, pulling away from him. He tried to stifle his laughter but couldn't quite stop. "My sweet Emily, you are so sensible. Yes, you are right, there are things to consider, but being together is not one of them," he finished. "We will be fine my love, you just watch."

She reached up and ruffled his hair as she whispered, "Stop laughing at me," she said with a kiss. He looked at her with such tenderness. "Emily, we will work everything out. When we go back, I will always be there for you. You don't have to be afraid," he said. "I will guide you and help you when you need it." She was lost in his eyes, his voice, his words. He kissed her forehead and then her cheeks, working his way to her lips.

Chapter 7

Emily woke up slowly the next morning, after a night of making love, she was sleepy but happy. She came out of the bathroom and saw that Paul was quietly snoring as he lay with one arm thrown over his head. She stood and watched him for a moment before she turned to leave. Making her way to the kitchen and poured herself a cup of coffee and sat down hoping it would wake her up a little. She would go into the office at 10 to speak with Sam about the discrepancies between the two accidents.

Lost in thought about how her life was about to change, she didn't hear Paul as he padded into the kitchen. "What time are you going to see Sam," he asked as he sat down. "I told him I would be there around 10," she answered. "Are you going to be alright here alone for a while?" she asked. "I'm a big lad Emily," he said jokingly. She smiled at him, thinking, how on earth she was so lucky to have fallen in love with him. He grinned back at her, "What?" he asked. "I was thinking about how much I love you," she replied. "Ah, but I love you more," he said teasingly.

"Let's sit outside for a while," he said. She poured herself more coffee and made some toast and went outside to join him. Placing the toast on the table, she sat down. Paul looked at her and ran his fingers through his hair, "Emily, I just now realized that we will have a family, children and grandchildren! You have made me dreams come true and I cannot wait to watch each day unfold for us."

She was taken aback by his joy. Laughing, she said, "Well, how many children do you think we should have?" He put his finger to his lips and thought for a moment, "Three, four, five..." She giggled, "I remember watching an interview with George and Pattie after they got married and how many children they wanted to have. Pattie quickly said 3 while George deadpanned and replied 39." Paul laughed, "George is a funny guy." He stopped himself from asking her how many they actually had, he was learning not to push her. "I can't wait to introduce you to all of them," he said.

They sat quietly and enjoyed the fresh air and the sun as it began warming their skin. "Paul, are you sure about all of this?" She asked, breaking the silence. Placing his cup on the table, he reached for her hand,

"The only thing I want is you. I want us to be together forever. I want to wake up every morning next to you. I want to hold you when you're sad, and I want to celebrate with you when you are happy." He continued, "I would give up everything I have to be with you Emily, don't ever question my love for you, it's endless."

She was mesmerized by the intensity in his eyes and the magnitude of his words. A tear slipped down her cheek. He wiped it away with his thumb and kissed her lips tenderly. She was too emotional to respond right away, she held his gaze for what seemed like forever. Braving a smile, she kissed him on the cheek and brushed his hair away from his beautiful eyes, "I don't know how to let you know how much I love you. I don't have a way with words as you do," she said softly.

She didn't know if it was the emotions of the moment, but she suddenly felt a little queasy. She stood to go into the house as he asked, "Are you alright?" "Yes," she answered, "Just a little overwhelmed I suppose. I'm going to lay down for a while before I get ready to go into the office." He stood as she did, giving her a hug and a kiss. "I'll clean up these dishes, you go rest," he said.

She made her way to the bedroom and by that time she was feeling sick to her stomach. Sitting on the bed, she took deep breaths and began to feel a little better. After a short time, she felt well enough to get ready to go to the office.

Walking down the hall to the living room she saw that Paul was sitting in the chair gazing out the window. Deep in thought, he didn't hear her come up behind him. She gently placed her hand on his shoulder. "Hi there," she whispered. He moved to put the guitar down and stood up, taking her in his arms, "How do you feel?" he asked. "Better. I'm leaving now, you can come with me if you'd like," she offered. He stepped back, "No I'll be fine. I'm almost done with the song and I want to read," he replied. She looked at him closely, he seemed a little down. "Are you alright," she said. He responded with a nod, "Of course I am. I was just thinking about, well, everything."

She kissed his cheek, "I won't be long. I'll bring us something for lunch," she said as she turned to leave. "Be careful," he said as she walked out the door. Getting into the car, yet another wave of nausea hit her, shaking her head as she sat for a moment before backing out of the driveway and heading down the street.

Sam was waiting for her in his office. He greeted her with a hug, "How are you?" he said. "I'm fine. What have you found out?" she asked hesitantly. "It's definitely Ramsgate," he said as he handed her a folder. Her heart sank as she whispered, "No." She began flipping nervously through the folder. "How long have they been in control?" she asked. "From what I can see from '64 just before they toured the U.S. for the first time," Sam answered.

"What do they want?" she asked. Sam sat back and looked at her. "They want to control the masses, and they are working to do that through The Beatles," he finished. "How?" she asked. "LSD. Once they had John they thought they had all of them, but Paul wouldn't go with the program." Confused, she said, "I don't understand." Sam looked at her sympathetically, "They needed all of them to get with the program. Paul wouldn't go along and take the LSD even after months of John and the rest goading him."

Sitting back in the chair she began feeling sick again. "Why do they need him if they have the others? What difference does it make?" she questioned. Sam walked to the window thinking before turning back to her, each one of them has a certain following. John the intellectuals, George the spiritual, Ringo the younger kids and older people, Paul has the teenagers especially the girls. Their biggest demographic," he finished. She looked up at him almost on the verge of tears. Fighting off the urge to scream and cry she said, "We have to stop them," she whispered.

She stood and began pacing as she thought, "They are targeting him because he doesn't want to influence their fans." She was visibly shaking as Sam said to her, "Emily, we will figure something out. Let me work on it and I will keep you updated." He hugged her to try to calm her down. "You know you can't go home with that furrowed brow, he'll know something is up," he said.

Continuing, Sam said, "I looked into Paul's interest in the Kennedy assassination. I think that may have played a part. A high-profile figure like Paul working to uncover the truth would have been problematic. His involvement would have caused intense public scrutiny. I believe MI-6, MI-5, Ramsgate and the CIA all agreed he had to go." She looked up at him agreeing, "I suppose you're right. Can you find out more about that?" "Of course. I will need some time.

We may have to postpone his jump back at least for a little while," he said.

She said, "What can I do? Dad had a contact at Ramsgate as I remember he..." Interrupting her, Sam shook his head, "I've been in touch with him already. I'm still waiting to hear back," he said. She sat back down feeling overwhelmed. "Do they know he's here?" she asked. "Yes," Sam answered, "But don't worry about that right now. They guaranteed that they would not come after him here." She looked at him and rolled her eyes, "Really, Sam, and you believe them?" she said.

She remembered hearing stories about Ramsgate when her father would discuss them with his colleagues at dinner. They were ruthless in their efforts to use mass mind control to sway public opinion. She shivered as she remembered the plane crash that took her parents and brother. She always felt Ramsgate was involved. Her father was close to revealing the time travel paradigm that they use today, and she believes Ramsgate was threatened by that. She looked at Sam as she said, "We are dancing with the devil Sam." He sat on the end of his desk and nodded in agreement, "Unfortunately, we don't have a choice, Emily. Not if we want to save Paul's life."

She abruptly stood up and said, "What if he doesn't go back? What if he stays here? The Beatles will have the future they always had, but Paul will be alive." He looked at her and saw that she was quite serious. He was silent for a moment, considering the possibility. "Emily, I'll work on that and let you know what I come up with. But we must tread lightly with any plan we develop. It has to satisfy everyone involved." She nodded in agreement.

Sam thought for a moment and then continued, "We will have to talk to him. He will have to be the one to decide if he wants to stay here or go back." She looked at him and nodded in agreement, "Do you want me to talk to him or should we do it together?" she asked.

"I think we should speak with him together," he answered. "All right," she sighed. As she turned to leave she handed the folder back to Sam as she gave him a hug. "Keep me updated," she said as she walked out the door.

Sitting in her car she tried to calm herself. She was still shaking from the news. She didn't want to alarm Paul, but it was going to take all her strength not to show her fear. Ramsgate was relentless and she knew as well as Sam that beating them would take a miracle. She sat there for a moment trying to digest all that she had learned from Sam. Her stomach feeling queasy again. Before stopping to pick up lunch she swung by the store to pick up a few things.

Pulling into the driveway she saw Paul sitting on the patio reading. She watched him for a moment until he looked up and waved as he rose and walked towards her. "I missed you," he said. "I missed you too!" she replied, trying to keep her voice light. He took the bags from her and set them on the table. "Let's eat lunch out here. It's beautiful out today," he said. She wasn't hungry but tried to eat as they chatted.

"Did you finish your song?" she asked. "Nearly," he said. "Just have to fine tune it." "How was your meeting with Sam?" he asked. "It was fine. He is still working on the discrepancies that were found. He'll let me know what he finds," she replied sounding as casual as she could.

She wanted to busy herself and appear as calm as possible. The news she had heard was hard to digest. He must have noticed that she was tense and asked,

"Emily, are you alright? Did something happen at your office that you're not sharing with me?"

She slowly sat back down with a sigh. How can she explain this all to him? "We've run into some complications, but Sam is working on it. Please don't worry," she finished. He reached for her hands, standing and drawing her close to him. "I trust you both. I don't want you to be upset," he said as he ran his finger along her cheek. "I'm fine," she said with a small smile.

They finished clearing the table and went back inside. Paul grabbed his book and settled himself in a chair by the window. She made some tea and put some cookies on a plate for him. Setting her mug down on the table she walked to him and handed him his tea placing the cookies on the side table.

She sent Sam a text conveying that the sooner they explained things to Paul the better. She asked him to come by for dinner tomorrow at 7. He responded almost immediately with a 'yes' and told her to keep her chin up. She smiled at his kindness. She finished her coffee and got up to go to the kitchen. Paul looked up at her as she stood, putting his book down next to him and picking up his own cup.

Breaking the silence, she said, "I've invited Sam for dinner tomorrow so we can explain everything to you." He leaned against the counter and watched her as she cleaned the mugs. He nodded his head and said, "I'm worried about you Emily. You're not acting yourself." She turned to him and smiled, "I'm just a little tired is all," reaching up she touched his face and gave him a kiss.

He went back to his book, and she went to her desk to see what more she could find out about Ramsgate's involvement with The Beatles. She was deep in thought when she looked over at Paul. He had his finger on his lip and his head leaned back. He was fast asleep. She smiled as she leaned back in her chair to watch him nap. She loved him so deeply that she was overwhelmed for a moment. She vowed at that moment that whatever happens, she will stay by his side, here or there.

Turning back to her computer she saw that Sam had sent an email. Opening it, she leaned forward to read it. He again confirmed the dinner and let her know that he had spoken to his contact at Ramsgate. He had news he would share with the two of them tomorrow. She sent a quick reply and shut down the computer.

Paul stirred from his sleep and the book on his chest fell to the floor with a thud. Reaching down to retrieve it he looked around for Emily. He then heard her in the kitchen. She peeked her head around the corner to see if he was awake yet. "Hey, sleepyhead," she said quietly. She walked to him, putting her arms around his waist. "Feel better now?" she asked as she softly kissed his lips.

"Yes, indeed. I'm getting spoiled with all this rest and relaxation," he chuckled. She reached up and ran her finger along his jaw to his lips tracing the shape of his mouth before kissing him gently.

He instinctively pulled her tighter to him. He kissed her deeply as they held each other. Drawing back from her for a moment as he took in her beauty. Her deep green eyes smiled back at him. "What are you thinking about?" she asked. "Us," he said sweetly. She loved his Liverpudlian accent making 'us' sound like 'ooos'. She laid her head on his chest not wanting him to see the worry in her eyes. The thought of him being in danger was too much for her to carry, but she knew she had to be strong for him, for them.

Chapter 8

Waking up early the next day Emily was restless from all that she and Sam discussed. When Paul finally dragged himself out of bed and into the kitchen she poured him coffee asking, "Would you like to go on a road trip for a day or two? We can drive up to the mountains. I think we need a change of scenery."

"I'd be dead chuffed," he answered. She planned to take him to Helen, a small tourist town in the north Georgia mountains modeled after a German valley village. "Great, we can leave in the morning," she said.

Later, Paul was outside when Sam pulled into the driveway. She could hear them laughing as they came into the kitchen. "Hi, Sam!" she said as she leaned in and gave him a kiss on the cheek. "We're eating healthy tonight you two so no complaints!" she said as she took the salad out of the refrigerator. "Can I get you a drink Sam," Paul asked.

"Yes, thanks, whatever you're having is fine," Sam replied. Emily poured a glass of wine and waited for

Paul to finish mixing the drinks before stepping outside to enjoy the beautiful weather.

They all sat around the table as Sam leaned back in his chair and took a sip of his scotch and nibbled at his salad. Looking at Paul and then back at Emily, he smiled. "How are you holding up?" he asked Paul once they were done eating. "I'm doing fine," Paul responded as he lit a cigarette.

Sam began, "Paul, have you ever heard of Ramsgate?" Paul looked up as he exhaled, thinking, "No. What is it?" Sam shifted forward in his seat. "It's an organization based in England. It bills itself as the 'Ramsgate Institute of Human Relations,' basically a nice sounding cover for what they really do," he said. "And what do they do?" Paul asked. Emily spoke up, "They work to control the masses." "Alright," Paul said, "And again, what does that have to do with me?"

Glancing over at Emily, Sam took a deep breath and continued. "Early in your career, right after you appeared at the Royal Variety Performance in '63, they took notice of The Beatles as a way to control and manipulate the younger generation, your fans." He paused and sipped his drink watching Paul for his reaction. Paul looked confused as he leaned in and said, "I don't understand." Sam resumed, "They tried to infiltrate your managing company, the inner circle of The Beatles, to have a closer inside look at the phenomenon that you were."

He continued, "Once you received your MBE's they felt they had the control they wanted. You were then part of their orbit so to speak. The Beatles were the biggest source of money for England at the time. But, they wanted more."

Paul shook his head, "We just have Brian and his assistants. There's really no company," he said warily. Sam said, "That's what they found out. They tried a few ways to get in and then," he paused again, "They figured out a way, through John." Paul sat back, stunned, "How?" He asked quietly. Emily reached for his hand as she said, "Through LSD. They wanted to use The Beatles to spread the word about LSD."

Paul stood up and lit a cigarette. He began pacing as he thought. "George's dentist slipped it into their coffee one evening when George, Pattie, John and Cyn were at his place for dinner," he remembered. Sam nodded, "He was part of the plan." Sitting back down he looked from Emily to Sam and asked, "And again, what does this have to do with me?"

Sam finished his drink and set it down on the table. "They know that you are not keen on it and they want you out of the picture," he said quietly. "The incident Emily saved you from wasn't an accident," he took a deep breath as he continued, "They tried to murder you." No one spoke as they waited for Paul to digest the news. He looked up at Sam asking quietly, "And the car that tried to run us down that night that was them as well?" Sam nodded.

Emily watched his face as she reached over and touched his hand. He looked at her and then back at Sam. He cleared his throat before saying, "On Boxing Day last year we put out a story that I had a moped accident in Liverpool while I was visiting me Da." Pausing for a moment, "It wasn't a moped accident. I had gotten roughed up by a few fellows." Emily looked at him in surprise while Sam nodded as if he already knew.

"They repeatedly told me I had better fall in line, but at the time I didn't know what they were talking about. I thought they were going to kill me." He finished quietly. Emily stood and gathered their glasses. "I'll get us another," she said in a whisper as she turned to go into the house.

145

Letting the door close behind her she let out a small sob. She didn't know if it was fear or the thought of someone hurting him or that they may continue to try again. She pulled herself together and fixed their drinks hesitating for a moment before joining them. She looked out the window to see Sam give Paul a pat on the back as Paul hung his head.

"Sam, I'm afraid I haven't been up front with you and Emily," Paul said as he saw her approach. "I thought I could control it, but..."

"Control what?" she asked. He stopped her with a wave of his hand as he stood and began pacing.

She sat back and waited for him. "It began while we were filming Help! There were mysterious men who would appear on the set. They would just watch me, not really speaking to anyone, but seemed to be allowed to be there."

He said as he sat back down. "Then it all started. While we were filming in the Alps. John and I were in the bar of the hotel one night after filming. We played a set. We were all having a good laugh, it was just like the old days."

Her mind flashed to the pictures she remembered seeing the two of them smiling and laughing as they played. Her heart dropped as she waited for him to continue.

Sam shifted in his chair as he sipped his drink watching Paul. "We left to go back to our rooms. I had just said goodbye to John when…" He stopped for a moment as if he was unable to continue. "Three men jumped me. They covered me mouth and dragged me out to a car," he said quietly.

Emily involuntarily gasped as she reached out and touched his hand. He laced his fingers through hers as he continued. "They took me to a place not far from the hotel. I don't know where it was as they had my eyes covered with something." She sipped her wine trying to calm herself as she realized her hands were shaking. Paul picked up his glass and downed what was left.

He looked at Sam and then back at Emily giving her a small smile. "They held me there for what seemed like an eternity. Turns out it was only that night and the next day. They took turns beating me as they laughed. I didn't understand why this was happening to me.

What had I done? There was no reasoning behind the beatings but just a constant pounding. It was a joke to them but to me it was just plain terrifying," he finished in a whisper.

Sam leaned forward, laying his hand on Paul's shoulder. "Paul, that was Ramsgate. They wanted you out of the way. They knew that out of the four, you wouldn't be able to be controlled."

"Well, they are bloody right," he said as he stood to refill his drink. "Another?" He asked Sam as he walked towards the house. "Yes, please," Sam replied.

Emily sat back as she shook her head. "This is all too much," she whispered to herself. Sam nodded his head in agreement as Paul walked back outside with a bottle of scotch.

"So," he began again. "It was a rough time for me. I was being pressured by the other fellows to drop LSD. They would not understand that I was not going to go down that road with them. I could feel a bit of a separation from the rest of them at that point. But we carried on. It's what we did. What we had to do."

"Excuse me, I'll be right back," Emily said as she got up and walked to the house. Her heart was breaking, and she didn't want what she was feeling to show in front of Sam and Paul. She poured more wine and tried to catch her breath. Watching them for a moment through the window she could see Sam was talking to Paul as he nodded his head listening to what Sam was saying.

She joined them as Paul reached over and touched her arm. "When it happened again, the 'moped accident,' they broke my front tooth and busted up my lip pretty good. I refused to get it fixed for two reasons. I wanted to show them I wasn't afraid of them. What I was afraid of was the dentist dosing me as he did to John and George."

He let out a short laugh. "Brian was furious with me. I even filmed a couple promos looking like that, but at that point I didn't care anymore." He sat back and finished. "I finally went home to me Da's and got it fixed before we came here for our tour." He sat back with a sigh, "That's all I know. I never found out who they were or why they were doing that to me and not the others.

Sam thought for a minute before asking, "Is there anything else? Other times you felt threatened?" Paul looked over at him then at Emily. "I've spent a lot of time alone lately. My house was finally done being refurbished. I wrote a lot. Went out very rarely. I did notice a black car with dark windows outside my gate. Mostly at night, there were too many birds hanging about during the day." He looked over at Emily with a smile, "Sorry, I mean girls." She smiled back at him as she took his hand.

"I'm sorry that happened to you Paul, really I am," Sam said. "I've been looking into a resolution of this for you Paul, we're not at 100% on this yet, but there are two options in the works." Emily looked at Sam perplexed at this revelation. "You haven't mentioned anything to me," she said softly. "I wanted to have a better grip on the possibilities before I said anything to either of you," he responded.

Taking a deep breath Sam continued, "My contact at Ramsgate has agreed to two scenarios. The first one, we jump you back and you fall in line. Meaning, promote to your fans the use of LSD and other drugs." Immediately, Paul stated firmly, "No, no, I won't do that."

Sam sat back and looked at Paul, "I didn't think you'd go for that either, but I have to give you all the information I have," he said calmly. He continued, "Once they had your replacement ready he began promoting the use of LSD, I believe it was around June of 1967 he did an interview stating he takes LSD. He actively participated in the plan to distribute LSD to audiences at music festivals in the United States such as the Monterey Festival in '67."

Paul was visibly shaken as he listened, shaking his head, asking rhetorically, "Who gave him the right to use my name for such nonsense?"

Emily asked, "What's the other scenario Sam?" He smiled slightly as he continued, "My contact at Ramsgate has agreed that if you choose to stay here, they will finance it. Meaning, they will match your earnings from September 1966."

Paul didn't speak for a moment, then said softly, "Thank you Sam. I need a bit of time to think about all of this." Sam stood up and held his hand out to Paul, "I'm going to leave you two alone. There are still a lot of details to work out, but I'll keep you posted." Paul took his hand and said, "Sam, thank you for everything."

Sam gave him a pat on the back. Emily gave Sam a quick hug before saying, "Oh, I forgot to tell you, we're going up to the mountains for a few days." He nodded, "Good idea. When you get back, I should have more information for you Paul." Paul nodded, "Thanks again Sam."

Paul turned back to Emily, gathered her up in his arms and held her tightly. She pulled away slightly as she gently kissed his lips. She closed her eyes and sighed. "Are you alright?" she asked. "Yes," he responded. "I just need a moment to try to understand everything," he said. He took her hand as they went inside.

She sat down on the couch as he stood staring out the window. She waited for him to digest what Sam had told him. He spoke without turning around, "I had hoped to take you home with me. I wanted to show you my world, but I can't go back just to get caught up in all of that nonsense again," he said quietly. "I want to stay here."

She stood and walked to him, touching his face, looking into his eyes. "You have to be sure that it's what you want, what's best for you. Maybe you should take more time to…" he stopped her, "I know what I want, and I know what I don't want. I don't want to spend the rest of me life looking over me shoulder, afraid I'll be beaten and murdered if I step out of line," he said. "I love you Emily and I want to build a new life here with you," he finished.

She looked into his eyes as she held his face in her hands. "I love you too Paul, but you have to be absolutely positive about this," she whispered. He took her hands away from his face holding them as he said, "I've never been one to hold back when I decide I want something. I've not done it before, and I won't start now. I suppose that has gotten me into more trouble than not." He paused before kissing her and looking deep into her eyes, "I want you Emily. I've waited my whole life for you. I just didn't realize it until we met."

She looked at him with tears in her eyes. She was speechless for a moment. He leaned down and gently kissed her lips. "If you'll have me that is," he teased. Smiling back at him, "I love you Paul. I always will. I just want you to be sure." He pulled her into him and kissed her with the kind of passion she has never known. She needed him too and would do whatever it took to keep him safe.

They were emotionally exhausted and went to bed early. She watched his face as he began to fall asleep. He was so beautiful she thought to herself. She knew she shouldn't think of him in that way, but he was angelic looking with his pale skin and huge dark eyes. She shuddered as she thought about what he had been through and the beatings he endured. She stroked his chest lightly as she snuggled into the crook of his arm. Listening to his heartbeat as she closed her eyes to dream.

In the morning as they got ready to leave Emily was excited that he would now be able to enjoy the music that came after The Beatles. She had put together a playlist for the car ride on the way up north. Appreciative of his fear of being a passenger in the car, she suggested he smoke a joint before they left. She grabbed her bag off the bed and went to the living room.

He was waiting for her in the living room staring out the front window deep in thought when she joined him. He gave her a quick kiss before taking her bag from her as she locked up the house. As they settled into the car she pulled out her phone to allow it to sync up with the car speakers. Before starting it, she said, "I've put together some songs for us to listen to on our drive. What you are about to hear is because of the four of you." He looked at her curiously, "What do you mean?" he said.

"Remember the night when we jumped back, you asked me if The Beatles had made a mark? Well, they did, you did, everything that happened after you was because of you," she finished as she watched his face.

He still looked perplexed as he said, "Do you mean others are playing our tunes?" "Well, yes, but mostly because people heard you and realized they could make music too," she answered. "Everyone you are about to hear said they wouldn't be where they are if it weren't for The Beatles." He blushed slightly at her revelation. "So, tell me, do people know who we are even now?" He asked carefully. She leaned over, taking his hand, saying softly, "Yes sweetheart, yes they do."

He sat back in his seat and smiled as he squeezed her hand before letting it go. Letting out a slow breath, he shook his head in amazement. She laughed as she started the car, "I don't want to tell you too much more. After all, I don't want you getting a fat head."

She backed out of the driveway and headed toward the highway. She pulled into the coffee shop and ordered two coffees. Flipping her phone on she smiled at him as she punched in the playlist and let the music begin. "This is a British band called Queen. This song is called 'Bohemian Rhapsody,' she said. "I read that the lead singer would draw pictures of you when he was younger." He laughed as he said, "I can't begin to tell you how many drawings we were sent. Some of them were quite good."

On the very first note Paul was taken away. She smiled as she watched his whole demeanor change. She was constantly amazed at the effect music had on him. She turned the volume up when they hit the highway letting him enjoy the full impact of the song. He kept turning to her with a look of pure joy on his face. His eyes would widen every now and then when the song would change from one second to the next.

When the song finished he motioned her to stop the music saying, "That was bloody marvelous! They managed to put so many levels into just one song." She smiled at his joy. Next she played 'Stairway to Heaven' and then 'Suite Judy Blue Eyes'. She knew that The Beatles had befriended David when he was with the Byrds and she wanted him to hear what came after that. "I am beyond myself," he said, "This is all so good! But they all are so long, it's amazing they are played on the radio," he commented.

She smiled to see him so happy. They were almost to Helen when she turned the music off for a moment. "We're almost there. Let's check in a while and you can hear more later," she said. "Thank you. You don't know what this means to me," he said.

After getting the key and chatting with the real estate agent she got back in the car and headed down the road to the cabin. As they settled in they saw there was a balcony overlooking the river. It was a cozy place with a big overstuffed couch and a fireplace. Paul placed their bags on the floor in the bedroom and turned to look at her. She swept her hair away from her face as she caught him looking at her intensely. "You look beautiful," he said. For some reason she felt shy and vulnerable under his penetrating gaze. She lowered her eyes as he came towards her. He lifted her chin gently and kissed her before enveloping her in his arms.

The stress of the last day had taken its toll and they not only desired each other, but they needed each other. They had a yearning for the other that they never felt for another before. His gentle kissing became more intense with a hunger for her. This beautiful and intelligent female who had become his life line and his love. She wanted him to be safe and to love her always. They took each other in completely with an unstoppable veracity until they were spent.

Hours later they realized they were famished and began getting ready to go out to dinner. "What are you in the mood for?" she asked. "Anything really," he replied. "Hmmm ...let me think there is a good German restaurant, a steakhouse, Mexican…" she listed until he said, "Steakhouse sounds good to me." "Great, it's just down through town," she said.

They were seated at a little table by the window with a lovely view of the river and the main street. The waitress took their drink orders and reeled off the specials for the evening. She left them to peruse the menu. Emily put hers down and watched Paul. He felt her eyes on him and peeked over the top of his menu with a wink. "Do you know what you want?" he asked. "Yes, you?" she asked. He nodded as he put his menu with hers.

The waitress was at their table and stood nervously as she looked at Paul. "What can I get for you tonight?"

she asked. "I will have the filet, medium, baked potato and Caesar salad," Emily said. Paul laughed, "I will have the same, except medium rare please. Also, can we have a bottle of champagne?" he added. Emily looked at him with a grin. "Champagne?" she said. He leaned back casually glancing at the scene outside. "Yes, I thought it would be nice for a change," he said smiling back at her.

Emily sat back and watched him as he marveled at the normalcy of being out again without the hassle of being recognized. He looked at her with a light in his eyes she had rarely seen. Happy that he was comfortable and relaxed. "We can take a walk after dinner," she began, "There are some cute shops to explore if you'd like." He didn't respond right away, "Love to, are there any clubs here, places where they play music?" he asked.

Sitting back smiling. "I think so, just around the corner," she answered. "Would you like to go there?" she asked. Smiling, he responded, "I'd love to." When the champagne came and the waitress had left them alone, Paul raised his glass to hers. They touched glasses and sipped the champagne.

After they had eaten they took the stairs down to the street. Strolling arm in arm window shopping, stopping for a moment, they sat on a bench and watched the tourists wander by. They watched as families enjoyed the cool fall evening and the children were being treated to huge ice cream cones. Stopping in a wine shop, they picked up a few bottles and headed back to the car where they stashed them in the trunk.

They pulled into the parking lot of the club and already could hear the music pulsating as a crowd of people waited to get in. They took their place in line and were soon let in and headed to the bar. Paul ordered their drinks while she scanned the room for a table. Spotting one about to be free, she motioned to him and headed to it. It was near the stage and she knew he would enjoy being close. He finally reached the table and set the drinks down just as the band finished their set.

Before they left the stage, they announced that it was talent night and the next set would be dedicated to anyone who would like to join them on stage for a song. She turned and looked at Paul and saw a glimmer in his eyes. "I think I'll have a go at that," he said as he leaned towards her. She laughed as she patted his hand, "I think you should!" They chatted while enjoying the atmosphere of the place.

When the band gradually got back up on stage the lead singer was on the mic. "Okay, do we have any brave souls out there tonight?" The applause went up as a young man rose from his seat encouraged by the table of his friends who cheered him on. Paul glanced at Emily with a smile. Matt climbed up the steps to the stage, squinting as the lights hit him. He spoke with the band for a moment before standing at the mic. The band started the song he had requested and after a bit of a false start he crooned out a beautiful ballad. When he had finished, he was greeted by wild applause from his friends as well as the rest of the bar. No one clapped harder than Paul. The band again offered the mic and Paul rose from his seat with a grin and a wink at Emily.

Emily was a little nervous but sat back sipping her drink as she watched him chat with the band. She couldn't hear what they were saying but then Paul turned around with a bass guitar strapped around his neck. He began by playing a few chords and then stopped and turned and said something to the rest of the band who all broke out into fits of laughter.

She realized it was because he was wearing the bass upside down so he could play it. Then, at his lead, they started again, and she knew the song right away, 'Kansas City.' When he began singing everyone clapped along as they recognized it. The band was following his lead and at some point the entire place became riveted to Paul on the stage.

When they finished the crowd applauded wildly. He took the bass from around his neck and began handing it back but was stopped by a band member who waved his hand to the cheering crowd. "One more song. One more song," the crowd chanted. Paul looked down at her with a grin and gave the crowd a shy wave as he turned to the band to tell them what to play next. The crowd erupted when he sang the first note of, 'Long Tall Sally.' She was in awe as she watched him. His presence on stage was spellbinding. Never missing a beat or a note, he finished with a screaming flourish. Once again the crowd, along with the band, gave him a loud round of appreciation.

He shook hands with the band and hopped down from the stage. "Whew," he said as he gave her a quick kiss on the cheek as he sat down practically downing his entire beer. "Need another?" she asked with a chuckle. "Yes," he said gasping. She got up and headed to the bar, "Hi, can I…" she didn't get to finish as the bartender poured her wine and Paul a beer saying, "It's on the house." She grinned at him and headed back to the table. She put the drinks down and whispered in his ear, "These are on the house. You made an impression." He grinned, saying in an exaggerated Texan drawl, "Oh shucks Ma'am, that's mighty fine of them."

They decided to call it an evening a little while later. As they got up to leave the crowd once again gave him wild applause. He waved and gave them a shy smile as they walked out into the fresh air. Laughing, Emily dug in her purse for the keys asking, "Have you ever thought of doing that for a living?" He put his finger to his head thinking. "Hmm," he responded, "Maybe." She leaned over and gave him a kiss, "You were fantastic. Just imagine, I had a front row seat to see Paul McCartney," she said laughing.

Back at the cabin Paul took a quick shower while Emily unpacked their things. She sat cross-legged on the bed waiting for him to finish. She thought about how he may miss performing and wondered if he had yet realized that part of his life would more than likely be over. Shaking her head, she decided not to bring it up tonight. Best to let him enjoy the fun he had had at the bar. She watched him as he walked out of the bathroom with just a towel while running his fingers through his damp hair.

She smiled up at him as he leaned over and kissed her forehead. "How did it feel?" she asked. "Marvelous, I needed that," he said as he sat down next to her. "But what I need more is you," he said kissing her, "Right now." He laid down bringing her along with him as he engulfed her with kisses as he murmured, "I'd rather be here with you than playing in front of a crowd." She looked up at him locking her eyes on him, "I love you Paul and I will do everything I can to make sure you are happy." He looked into her eyes saying, "Just being with you is all I need or want." She reached up and touched his cheek, then kissed him slowly. They tenderly caressed the other in a way that made their love making heighten with inclination that peaked rhythmically together. They fell asleep in each other's arms satisfied and complete.

Paul was the first to wake up. He quietly slid out of bed and went out to the balcony with a cup of coffee. Listening to the river below he enjoyed the sound of the birds and the wind rustling the trees. He felt Emily's hand on his shoulder and reached up to touch her. She leaned down, kissing the top of his head before sitting next to him. She was enjoying the fresh breeze as it swept across her face. He reached over and took her hand in his. "Emily, thank you for this," he said, "It has been good to get out and enjoy ourselves." She nodded, "Yes, it has been nice." She wished this moment could last forever. She had never been happier.

Getting up he asked, "Coffee?" "No, thanks. There's a great breakfast place here. Let's go there and then we can go exploring for the day," she replied. Just then her phone rang. It was Sam, "Hi Sam," she said as she answered. Listening for a moment she then handed the phone to Paul, "He wants you." "Hello," he said as he got up and walked to the bedroom.

She sat back and listened to the water flowing below. He walked back to the deck and handed her the phone. "He wants to have me come to the office when we get back," he explained. "Did he give you any more information?" she asked. "I told him what I've decided. He did say things were looking good, but I'd have to go through something called acclimation," he said with a questioning lilt to his voice. "Did he explain that to you?" she asked. "No, he said you would have the honors," he replied with a smile.

"Okay, let's get ready and I'll explain over breakfast," she answered as she walked to the bedroom.

They sat in a small booth at the back of the restaurant and Emily began, "Acclimation is basically what it sounds like. It is a process of getting you adjusted to your new environment. A lot has happened in the world since 1966." He nodded in understanding. "Can you fill me in on a few of the high points now?" he asked.

She sipped her coffee as she thought before saying, "In 1968 Martin Luther King was assassinated in Memphis." He looked shocked while remembering The Beatles time in Memphis not long ago. He said, "Somehow, that doesn't surprise me at all. We were afraid for our lives there after John's 'Jesus' comment. The KKK was threatening his life. When we were doing our second show in Memphis, someone set off a firecracker. We all looked at each other, thinking the other had been shot. It was terrifying." She reached for his hand across the table. "I'm sorry. I hadn't heard about that," she said. He shook his head, "What is wrong with people?" he said softly. She looked at him and replied, "There is a lot of sickness in the world."

After a moment she continued, "A few months later Bobby Kennedy who was running for President at the time was also assassinated." He sat back stunned. "No," was all he could say. "Yes, 1968 was the year of upheaval," she finished. As they ate, he was thoughtful, asking rhetorically, "How did that family survive all the tragedy they've endured?" She shook her head, "They have persevered. One of Bobby's grandsons is now in Congress."

Wanting to lighten the mood, she changed the subject. "I thought we could take a drive after breakfast. It's very pretty up here," she offered. "Yes, that would be very pleasant," he answered. "Are you alright?" she asked. "Yes, just a bit shocked is all," he responded. As they walked to the car she took his hand squeezing it as she smiled up at him. They spent the day exploring the waterfalls and hiking trails that were in the area. They stopped and bought apples and honey from a roadside stand and brought them back to the cabin in the late afternoon. They were exhausted, so they grabbed a quick dinner and went to bed early.

Paul woke first, sliding out of bed, he settled on the balcony and enjoyed the peace and quiet. He heard Emily's phone ring and got up and saw it was Sam calling again. He picked it up and answered with a bright, "Hello Sam! It's me."

"Hi Paul, sorry to keep pestering you two, but I have some news," Sam paused, "We've gotten final approval for you to stay. Your money has been transferred to an account here at the company. When you get back I'll get it set up into your own account," he finished.

"That's marvelous!" Paul responded, "May I ask, how much it tis?" Sam smiled to himself before saying, "The amount has been adjusted to today's market rate." He continued, "In 1966 your net worth was $3,334,000. The amount waiting for you in the account is $24,843,000." There was silence, "Paul? Are you there?" "Yes Sam," letting out a deep breath Paul grinned, "I'm a bit speechless, but dead chuffed."

"When are you coming back?" Sam asked. "This morning," Paul answered. "Why don't you and Emily come by the office around 10 tomorrow." Sam said. Just then Emily wandered out of the bedroom and gave him a smile as she fixed a cup of coffee. He said to Sam, "Emily just got up. I'll let her know and we will see you then."

"Morning love," he said as he took her in his arms. "Sam?" she asked. "Yes, he wants us to go to the office at 10 tomorrow," he answered. "Did he have any news?" she asked sitting down at the table. "Yes," he replied as he fixed himself another cup. "Well?" She said with a smile anxiously awaiting his response.

He sat down across from her and looked into her eyes and he took her hands and held them. "It's done. Ramsgate has agreed and has already transferred me money into an account here. Sam wants me there tomorrow to get it signed over to me own account." She stroked his fingers as she listened. "That was fast," she said. "Yes indeed. The nice part is that they have adjusted it to today's value." Her eyes widened, "Wow, that's a nice surprise," she said.

She continued to sip her coffee as he looked over at her. "Aren't you going to ask me how much it tis?" He said with a grin. "It's your money, Paul, but if you'd like to tell me," she answered. He looked at her cocking his head, "Why wouldn't I tell you. I don't want to have any secrets between us Emily," he finished sounding a little disappointed. She got up and sat on his lap brushing his hair away from his eyes as she gave him a kiss. "I'm just teasing you," she whispered. "How much is it?" she asked. "Well, apparently I was worth $3,334,000 but that is now valued at $24,843,000," he explained.

He moved to get up placing her in front of him. "I want to buy us a house big enough for a dozen kids and a couple of dogs," he said as he spun her around laughing. "How about a couple of kids and a dozen dogs," she countered. He kissed her and agreed, "Maybe you're right," he said as he put her down. "I'm thrilled for you Paul, I really am," she said as she turned to head to the bedroom. "Emily?" he said, "Wait." She turned back towards him noticing an unfamiliar look in his eyes, "What is it?" She asked as she reached up and touched his face.

He drew her closer to him, his arms wrapped around her waist. "I can't wait to give you everything," he said softly. "You already have. You've given me your heart and that is all I need," she whispered in his ear. He shivered slightly aware that their love was the most powerful emotion he had ever felt. Words, for once, failed him as he held her tight never wanting to let her go.

Chapter 9

Before Sam could transfer his money to his bank account, Paul would need a new identity. Paul and Emily had talked about it on the way home from their trip. They had let Sam know what he had decided so the paperwork could go forward. They pulled into the parking lot of her office. She turned off the car and faced Paul. "Ready?" she asked. "As I'll ever be," he answered.

Sam was waiting for them when they arrived. "Morning," he said as Paul and Emily entered his office. "Good morning, Sam," Paul said as he shook his hand. He had all the paperwork laid out on his desk. Glancing down at it and then back at Paul. Emily gave him a quick kiss before saying, "I'll leave you two to all of this." "Wait, Emily I need you here," Paul said as he stood. Sam sat down and waited, watching them. "Paul, this is your business, not mine, I thought you'd want privacy," she stressed. Sam rose from his chair, "You two talk and I will be back in a few minutes," he said as he walked out the door closing it behind him.

Paul looked at her, confused, "This is our life now Emily, not mine alone," he said. "I don't want to step on your toes," she asserted. He became a little exasperated as he said, "I don't understand. Explain to me how it would be stepping on my toes," he said. "Paul let's not do this now…," she began as he interrupted her. "Maybe we should wait then. Come back tomorrow after we've gotten all this straight." He was hurt and a little angry as he began walking to the door. "Paul wait, stop," she pled.

He countered as he spun around, "I'm not the one making this difficult. I'm not the one trying to keep our lives separate. I'm not the one…," he stopped as she walked to him and put her fingers to his lips. "I'm not trying to make this difficult. I was trying to be considerate. I'm sorry I upset you," she said quietly as Sam opened the door. She turned to him with a smile and said, "Okay Sam, we're ready." Sitting down across from Sam, she took Paul's hand and squeezed it as he looked back at her with a solemn glare.

"Alrighty then let the fun begin," Sam said trying to lighten the mood a little. He handed Paul the first file which held his new identity: James Michael Mohin. He had decided on his real first name, his brother's name and his mother's maiden name. All the documents he would need were there: a social security card, birth certificate, passport and a driver's license. The next folder held a check for $24,843,000. He slowly picked up the check and said, "I never would have believed that my little ditties would earn this much money." Sam laughed, "Don't forget, as soon as we have your accounts set up, money will be deposited quarterly from your residuals for the music that you had written up until September 1966."

Emily smiled as Paul looked over at her with a grin. Sam began, "Right now, let's get that money into a bank account," looking at Emily he finished, "I thought it would be a good idea to use the bank the company uses for now, until he decides how to invest." She nodded, "As good as any," she answered. Paul sat back and folded his hands in his lap as Sam finished, "Done," Sam said. "You'll receive your debit card and checkbook in the mail in a few days. Paul, looking confused, "Debit card?" Emily smiled. "I'll explain later," she said as she reached over and squeezed his hand.

"Now," Sam continued, "We have to get you acclimated. There will be some sessions here that will be pretty intense, but I'll be right there with you and, if you'd like, Emily can be there too. "Paul looked at her and smiled as she replied to Sam, "Of course I'll be there." Then after those sessions here you can study on your own with Emily's help. When would you like to start?" he asked. Paul replied, "Can we start tomorrow? I'd like to rest up a bit." "Let's make it the day after. There is really no rush," Sam answered.

They all stood up and Emily gave Sam a hug and invited him and his family for dinner soon. "Let me check with Chris. I'll let you know when we are all free, between the boy's baseball and soccer practice, I never know what's going on," he said with a chuckle. Paul gave Sam his hand, "Thank you Sam. I'll see ya soon."

They got in the car and Paul looked at Emily saying, "I need to speak with you when we get home." She was taken aback slightly at his stiff tone, answering quietly, "Certainly." She turned the radio on for the short ride to her place. "Do you want lunch?" She asked as they unlocked the door. "No, not right now," he answered. "Come sit with me," he said, taking her hand. She sat on the couch next to him. "First off, I want to apologize for getting heated earlier," he continued, "Second, nothing of mine is only mine any longer. Nothing. I want you to understand that."

She looked at him and saw only sincerity in his eyes. She was overcome for a moment. "We have to take everything slowly," she said as she stroked his hand. "I should have talked to you before we got there. I don't want you to feel that you have no privacy anym…" He hushed her with a kiss, "We have a lifetime to spend together and when one or the other of us needs solitude, I believe the other will understand. But, right now, Emily, I need you with me to guide me and love me and tell me what a debit card is." He smiled down at her as he kissed her on the cheek. She responded with a gentle kiss on his mouth. "I'm here," she whispered in his ear.

Chapter 10

Paul woke first, leaving Emily to sleep peacefully as he took a shower and went to fix the coffee. He was nervous about the day ahead. Emily finished filling him in on the events of 1968, but he knew he had a long way to go.

Emily stood wrapped in a towel looking in the mirror when Paul appeared behind her. He reached around her and put her cup on the sink counter in front of her. She smiled at him in the mirror as he pressed himself to her from behind. "Nervous?" she asked. "A bit," he said as he pulled her hair away from her neck and gently kissed it.

"Don't be too anxious. The first day will just be a review of some of the major events that have taken place since '66. We've already covered some, so it will be more of the same. Sam will be leading today, and I will lead tomorrow," she finished. "I've been meaning to ask," he began while sipping his coffee, "Is Prince Charles King now?"

She laughed, "Nope. Queen Elizabeth is still going strong." "You're kidding me," he said with a grin. "No, she's 93, been on the throne for 67 years. Prince Charles was married to a lovely woman, Diana, but they divorced, and she was killed in a car accident in 1997 in Paris. They had two boys, William and Harry. I'm sure Sam will tell you all about it today," she finished. Paul replied, "That is remarkable. I wrote a little ditty about the Queen after we received our MBE's. It wasn't published, it was just for fun. I called it 'Her Majesty'." Emily looked at him saying, "I didn't know you wrote that. We will be going over Beatle songs and how your friends honored and remembered you. They did publish this song. It was the very last song on their last Beatle album."

He hopped up and sat on the counter as she finished putting on her makeup and fixing her hair. "Will there be others there," he asked curiously as he put his hands under his legs. She nodded, "Yes." She had seen so many pictures of him sitting like that. It reminded her of a little boy trying to keep himself still. She stood in front of him leaning over to kiss him. "Let me get dressed then we can go," she said as she turned away.

He gathered up their cups and took them to the kitchen. He was waiting for her outside when she was ready. She locked the door and as she started walking towards him, she threw the car keys at him. "You're driving," she said. He was shocked but excited as he slid in behind the wheel. "Just remember, we're in America, stay on the right side of the road," she laughed.

He pulled into the office parking lot and found a spot and switched off the car. Turning to her, he handed her the keys and gave her a kiss. "I feel like a new man!" he said as he got out. She laughed as they began walking towards the door. Sam was there to greet them as they walked in. "Morning you two," he said shaking Paul's hand and giving Emily a hug. "Ready?" he asked. Paul nodded as they walked down the hallway to a room with a TV screen on the wall and a table full of paperwork. Sam began by explaining what would be taking place. "We've put together a show that will highlight the major events since 1966. You can stop it anytime you wish," he said showing Paul how the remote control worked. "You can also take notes and write down any questions you may have."

Paul looked over at Emily and then back at Sam, nodding his head, "Okay, let's carry on," he said.

When Sam turned on the TV, the first few hours were filled with moon landings, Vietnam, the countercultural revolution and civil rights movement. Paul sat back and stretched as Sam flipped off the TV. "Time for lunch," he announced.

"Any questions so far?" Emily asked. "Not really. There was nothing too surprising," he said as he took her hand. "Do you mind eating in the cafeteria? It will save some time," Sam said as they walked down the hall. "No, of course I don't mind," Paul replied. Walking into the cafeteria Emily was greeted by a table of three, "Hey girl! Long time no see!" one of the women said. "Hi Kim, how are you?" Emily responded.

As Kim got up to give Emily a hug she noticed Paul standing there and stumbled a little feeling as giddy as a schoolgirl seeing her crush pass in the hallway. Paul had always been her favorite Beatle, and she couldn't believe he was standing right in front of her. "Kim, this is Paul," Emily said with a smile. She put out her hand, "Nice to meet you, Paul," she said. He took her hand and leaned over and gave her a kiss on the cheek. "A pleasure to meet you," he gave her a wink. She blushed furiously as she reached up and touched her cheek where he had kissed her. Paul grinned at her as Emily introduced him to the others.

An older man was seated there as well, he stood shaking Sam's hand. "So, this is the one that got away from me," he said, putting his hand out for Paul. I was scheduled to do the jump before Emily here was chosen. I'm Ken, nice to meet you, Paul," he finished. "Pleasure to meet you Ken," Paul replied. A younger man with dark blond hair and glasses was biding his time as he waited to introduce himself, "I'm Alex, nice to meet you, and welcome," he shook Paul's hand heartily. "I'll be helping out tomorrow, see you then," he finished excitedly.

"Everyone's quite friendly here," Paul said as they made their way to an empty table. Sam and Emily both laughed, "They've all been dying to meet you," Sam said as they sat down. Paul looked at Emily with an uneasy glance. "Are you alright?" she asked as she leaned over towards him. "Yes, it just seems strange that they would know who I am," he answered. Sam laughed again, "You've been the talk of the place since you decided to stay, but everyone here is beyond trustworthy, so no worries."

After finishing lunch Paul stood as he said, "I'd fancy a ciggie," Emily led him to another door down the hallway that opened to a courtyard. "Here, you go sweetheart," she said as she opened the door for them to go outside. He lit a cigarette and exhaled before turning to her looking quite serious, saying, "So that's the old bloke I could have been stuck with?" Emily burst out laughing.

"You are so bad!" she whispered. He took her hand and kissed it. "Yes, I am," he responded in a low voice.

At 6:00 Sam stood and switched off the TV. "I think we can call it a day," he said as he gathered the folders together that were spread across the table. "Do you have any questions?" Paul stood and handed Sam the notepad that had been in front of him. "Yes, if you wouldn't mind answering these," Paul said handing it to him. On the first page he had written, 'for Sam's eyes only.' Sam walked Paul down the hall to Emily's office where she had been working while she waited for the session to be over.

He patted Paul on the back as he continued down the hall to his own office. "All set?" she asked. "Yes, I'm a bit tired," he answered. "Would you like to stop and get something to eat on the way home?" she asked as she shut down her computer and packed her laptop in her bag. "Yes, that would be lovely," he responded as he took her bag.

Sam sat back in his chair and began reading the notepad that Paul had handed him. There were a few questions, including a couple about Nixon and Vietnam, but then he read further. He chuckled as he scanned the page:

1) I need you to take me to a jewelry store (shhhh, it's a secret)
2) Do you have the name of an estate agent?
3) I want to buy a car, recommendations?
4) Please keep the above away from Emily! (with a smiling face and a wink)

He slid the notepad in his briefcase and locked it up and headed home. Chris and the boys were waiting for him to arrive before having dinner.

Chapter 11

Paul and Emily slid into the booth of a little pub near the house. The waitress took their drink orders before either said anything. "So? What do you think so far?" Emily questioned. "It's all very interesting, nothing really surprising yet," he answered as the waitress brought their drinks. "I gave Sam a list of questions. He said he'd answer them tomorrow," he finished. She sipped her wine and looked at him. "The whole thing won't take too long," she started, "Then we'll just handle things as they come up."

After dinner they drove home and settled in for the evening. Paul was very tired, "Emily, I'm shot. I may go to bed early tonight," he said with a yawn. She leaned over and stroked his hair, "I'll join you. It's been a while since I was in the office and I'm tired too," she said. "I'll be with you all day tomorrow. We are going to show you what happened with The Beatles and music in general," she told him. He brightened up a bit with that news. "Good, I'm looking forward to it," he said as he stood. "Come, let's go to bed," he said, offering his hand.

By the time Emily had finished in the bathroom, Paul was fast asleep quietly snoring with his arm thrown above his head. She stood and watched him, his chest gently rising with each breath. She was overtaken with relief that he was safe and joy that he was here with her. She carefully climbed into bed so as not to wake him but sensing her nearby, he turned and wrapped his arms around her and pulled her close to him.

Arriving at the office the next day they saw Sam getting out of his car. He greeted them with a wave. "Paul, can I have a word before you start today?" he asked. "Yes," he said as he gave Emily a kiss before she went to get things ready for the day. Walking to Sam's office, he was greeted by Kim whom he had met the day before. She smiled a shy smile and blushed as she passed by him. He chuckled to himself as she seemed to trip while turning around to look at him. "I've got a couple ideas for you regarding your questions," Sam started. First, here is the business card from the realtor who sold us our house," he stated. "He's good and he will really listen to what you want before dragging you all over to look at houses."

Paul took the card and put it in his pocket. "Thank you, I'll ring him up," he said. Sam continued, "What type of car do you want to look at?" Paul grinned and said, "Well, two actually. I want to get Emily a new one as well. I thought a sports car of sorts for me and something more practical for her." Sam replied with a chuckle, "Let me think about that one. There are quite a few new types of cars since you last drove."

"Now as far as jewelry stores go Tiffany's is going to be your best bet. There is one not far from here. If you want to keep it a secret, which I'm sure you do, I can run you over there this weekend. We'll tell the girls we are grabbing a quick lunch," he finished. Standing Paul said, "Thank you, Sam, and remember not a word to Emily. I want it all to be a surprise." Sam nodded with a grin, "No problem. I didn't even tell Chris. I'm afraid she wouldn't be able to contain herself," he said with a laugh. "Well Emily is waiting for me. I better get going," he said as he shook Sam's hand.

When he entered the room, he saw the young man he had met the day before with Emily talking at the front of the room. "Morning," he said as soon as they both looked up. "Good morning Mr. McCartney," the young man said. "Please call me Paul and if I remember correctly, you're Alex?" "Yes," he answered, "Shall we start?"

Alex began by playing a few clips of other musicians talking about The Beatles' influence in their lives and their music. Paul sat back in his chair and watched quietly. After about an hour Paul said, "Can we stop for a moment?" Alex paused the tape and went in search of coffee for all of them while Emily and Paul wandered into the courtyard. "How are you doing?" she asked as she kissed him on the cheek. "I'm a little overwhelmed honestly," he replied.

After returning from their short break, Alex continued sharing quotes from people like Steve Jobs: "My model for business is the Beatles. They were four guys who kept each other's negative tendencies in check. They balanced each other and the total was greater than the sum of the parts. And that's how I see business. Great things in business are never done by one person, they are done by a team of people."

And from the author Kurt Vonnegut: "I say in speeches that a plausible mission of artists is to make people appreciate being alive at least a little bit. I am then asked if I know of any artists who pulled that off. I reply, 'The Beatles did.'

Paul put up his hands, "Wait, wait, I'm a little gobsmacked right now. Can we take a break?" he said with a smile. Walking outside, he said, "Emily, we never set out to be anything other than a little dance hall band. I'm shaken that so many people consider us worthy of all that praise." She reached up and stroked his cheek giving him a kiss, "You should be proud. Those people are talking from the heart because you all had a huge effect on music and the culture," she said as they walked back to the room. He looked at her with a perplexed look, "We were all just having a good laugh."

After breaking for lunch Emily began the afternoon session. She was nervous as it would explain in detail how he was replaced and what occurred after his 'death'. Paul sat down as Emily began, "Paul, this is not going to be easy, so you tell me when you've seen enough, and we'll stop for the day." He just nodded and sat back to listen to her explain the rationale for keeping his supposed death a secret.

She went and sat down next to him. "Brian, George Martin and the rest were told to keep quiet. If any spoke out there would be dire consequences. They had already lost you and they each didn't want to lose another," she stated. He shook his head asking, "God,

Emily, why?" She looked at him and simply said, "It was part of the control they wanted over all of them. They didn't want questions which is why they all began putting clues in the music and on the album covers," she got up to continue.

As she began again he sat back in his chair with his hands behind his head. "The first clues were on their next album. The album was called 'A Collection of Beatles Oldies," she paused looking back at him. "The cover of the album had the first clues they put out," she said as she showed him a picture of the cover, a psychedelic painting. He took the photo and examined it closely asking, "Who is this?" Pointing to the man sitting casually in a chair. "That is the one who replaced you," she said as she watched his face.

She pointed to the car in the background, "That was also a clue. Do you see how it's about to run right through his head and printed next to it 'To the Original.' She handed him another picture. This is the back side of the cover. It showed the four of them when they were in Japan just a few months ago, but with Paul towards the back of the picture wearing a Japanese robe, surrounded by an eerie mist.

"Why 'Oldies,' that makes no sense at all?' he asked as much to himself as to her. She sat down next to him. "Your friends had to be very clever," she said pointing to the drum where the word was written. "OLDIES, if you move one space over on the O and L it turns into PM, PM DIES," she said, as she wrote it out on a pad of paper in front of him. He stared at what she had written for a moment. A look of sadness and vulnerability crossed over his features.

She touched his hand and gently asked, "You Okay?" He didn't look at her or respond right away but kept his eyes on the picture she had handed him. "This picture was taken in Japan, the robe I have on, I've still got it," he said quietly. Just then they both turned as they heard the door open. Sam peeked his head in and said, "Hey, it's getting late. Chris wants you to come over for a bite that is if you're up to it." Emily looked at Paul, he shrugged saying, "Of course, sounds quite pleasant." "Great, the boys are excited to meet you, but beware, they will probably want you to play a song for them," he said laughing. Paul got up slowly and said, "I'd be delighted."

He was quiet on the way to Sam and Chris' house. She was aware that everything he had seen would take a while to sink in. "Hey," she said as she pulled into the driveway, "We don't have to do this if you're not up to it." He sat for a moment before replying, "I'm fine really. Let's carry on." Chris stood at the door as they walked up the path waving at them saying, "Come in! The boys are excited to see their Aunt Emily, and of course to meet you Paul." Right behind her were Zak and Stephen jumping up and down with excitement. "Hi you two!" Emily said as she scooped them both up with a bear hug. She gave them each a great big kiss before putting them down. "Zak, Stephen, come here. I want you to meet Paul. Paul, this is Zak and Stephen," she said.

"Well, hello there!" Paul began, "I've heard a lot about you two!" Zak, who was just two years old shyly walked closer to Paul and handed the piece of paper that was clutched in his small hand. "Well, what do we have here?" Paul asked with a smile as he crouched down. "I draw a picture of you," Zak said in a small voice. Paul took it and looked at it quite seriously. "Well I'll tell you I've had lots of pictures drawn of me, but I think this is the best one yet," he said as he showed it to Emily.

Stephen, who was four, stepped closer and seriously stuck his hand out, "I'm Stephen, Daddy said you can sing us a song," he said. Paul laughed as Sam cut in,

"Now Stephen, I said if he wants to." Paul shook Stephen's hand and said, "I'd be happy to Stephen, maybe in a short while." Chris took Zak's hand as she led them into the kitchen. Sam was already there mixing drinks and pulling the hamburger patties out of the refrigerator. "Boys go wash your hands. God knows what you've been into," Chris said as she began mixing a salad.

Paul leaned against the counter and looked over at Emily with a thin smile. Sam said to Paul in a low voice, "You holding up?" Paul turned slightly to face him saying something that Emily did not catch. Sam patted him on the shoulder as they continued their muted conversation while heading outside to start the grill up.

Chris asked, "How did he handle things today? Sam said you were going over The Beatles history?" Emily hesitated for a moment watching Paul and Sam outside, "I'm not sure, he says he's fine, but he's not his usual self. But really who can blame him, it's a lot to digest," she replied as the boys came running through the kitchen headed outside. "Whoa, slow down there guys!" Chris said as the door slammed behind them.

Emily watched as the boys both ran up to Paul, each taking one of his hands and pulling him away to the other side of the patio. "Oh, goodness," Chris said with a laugh, "I think they are trying to get Paul to catch the frog they saw out there this morning." Emily laughed as she watched the three of them searching with their heads down looking quite serious. It made her heart burst with love. Sam said something that made Paul look up at him with a smile.

"Come on. Let's go outside," Emily said, picking up the salad bowl. Soon the four of them were sitting around the table enjoying the boys still searching for the frog and the smell of the hamburgers sizzling on the grill. Paul sat quietly, hands clasped, and his head slightly bowed. Emily reached over and covered his hands with her own. "Hey, we can skip tomorrow if you'd rather, give you a break," she said softly. He leaned over and kissed her cheek, "I'm well," he replied weakly.

Sam, overhearing their conversation spoke up, "Paul, I've got an idea. I could use a day off. What do you say and I get together, and I can show you around the city?" Paul smiled conspiratorially as he answered, "I'd be dead chuffed, Sam." Emily smiled at him when

Chris asked, "Chuffed?" Paul chuckled a little, "Oh, it means I'd be delighted. I keep forgetting where I am."

After dinner, Paul requested a guitar and sat with the boys in the living room as he sang, 'Yellow Submarine.' Sam, Chris and Emily stood in the doorway watching as the boy's face shone with excitement having heard it 100s of times before. They clapped their hands when he finished and begged him to play it again. "No, no boys, maybe next time," Sam said as he ushered them away.

Paul stood and leaned the guitar next to the chair he had been sitting in. Emily and Chris said their goodbyes as Sam walked Paul out to the car, "I'll pick you up at 10," he said. "Sounds good," Paul replied as he got in the driver's seat and smiled at her as she handed him the keys. Emily slid in and waved at Sam and Chris as they backed out.

Chapter 12

He was quiet as he reached over and put his hand on her leg, she covered his with hers. "That was enjoyable. The boys are quite energetic," he said wistfully. She smiled at him and agreed, "Yes, they are. I love them dearly." As soon as they got in the house Paul went to roll a joint. "I need to relax a bit," he said when she walked into the living room. She sat down and watched him as he lit it and exhaled and leaned his head back. "Are you sure you're alright or should I just stop asking you that?" she questioned as she took the joint from him. "I'm fine really today was a bit intense is all," he answered with a slight smile.

They sat for a while in silence. She slid closer to him touching his chest as she kissed him gently on the mouth. He reached over and held her face in his hands. "I love you," he whispered in her ear as he nibbled on her earlobe. "That tickles," she sighed.

Paul pulled her close as she laid her head on his chest and listened to his heartbeat. "I missed you," she whispered. He gave her a lopsided smile as she continued, "We haven't made love in two days," she laughed. "Has it been that long?" he asked with a chuckle. "Well, we'll have to work to make up for that," he said as he hovered above her gently kissing her face. He took her hand and led her to the bedroom. They both finally drifted off to sleep staying in each other's arms until the sun broke through the window the next morning.

Emily rose quietly while he was still sleeping. She went to the living room where she noticed Chris had been texting her. 'Since the boys are running off on us today, I've made an appointment for us at the spa. I'll pick you up at 10.' Emily smiled as it certainly had been a while since she pampered herself she thought as she sat down with her coffee. She replied and got up for more coffee when he wandered into the kitchen looking sleepy. She poured him a cup and ruffled his already messy hair. "Chris and I are going to do girly things while you and Sam are off doing manly stuff," she said.

"I'm not sure what we'll be doing is 'manly stuff' but it sounds like you and Chris will have a good bit of fun," he laughed. "Are you feeling better this morning?" she asked as she poured him more coffee. "I am happy to be taking a break," he answered. "What are you two going to do today?" she asked. "I'm not sure, I'd like to get to know Sam a little better so whatever we do will be fine," he said.

While Emily was in the shower Paul quietly opened her jewelry box and took out a ring. He thought it would be the best way to gauge her ring size. He slid it into his pocket as he heard her coming out of the bath. He looked up when he heard the doorbell ring and said, "I'll get that," as he walked out of the bedroom. She could hear them all chatting as she walked down the hall. "Ah, there you are my love," Paul said as he went to kiss her goodbye as he checked his pocket to make sure his wallet with his new debit card was there.

He and Sam got into Sam's car as the girls got into Chris'. "Well, what first?" Sam asked. "Let's go to the jewelers first. We can carry on from there," Paul replied as he sat back and enjoyed the ride. Sam took the back roads over to Peachtree Road and pulled into the parking lot of the upscale mall.

Once inside Tiffany's, Paul began browsing the rings in the display case. He shook his head and looked at Sam as he said, "I've got something different in mind." An older gentleman overheard the conversation and made his way over to where Paul

196

and Sam were standing. "May I help you find something?" the man said with a highbrow accent. Paul smiled, "I'm looking for an engagement ring, but I'm not sure I want the typical..." the man stopped him with a wave of his hand. "Can you tell me what price range you'd be comfortable with?"

Paul looked at Sam and smiled. "I would be happy at $150,000-$200,000 give or take," he answered, looking at the man behind the counter. "Surely," the clerk said as he turned to retrieve a tray of rings from the back of the store. They saw him lean in and speak with a young woman who glanced their way.

She approached them and asked them to step into their side room. They walked in to find a comfortable room which held a couch and two beautiful brocade chairs. "Please make yourselves comfortable," she said as she offered them something to drink. "Coffee, wine, water?" she asked. "Nothing for me, thank you," Paul said as he sat down in one of the chairs. Sam waved her off with a shake of his head sitting down on the couch.

While he was waiting Paul began tapping his foot to a beat that was running through his head. With great fanfare the gentleman came in bearing a tray of rings followed by a young lady with another tray.

He sat them gingerly on the table in front of Paul and he said, "These are within your price range with the exception of a few. Please look them over and see if any are to your liking." They were all remarkable with brilliance that dazzled the eye, but Paul was immediately drawn to a cushion cut chocolate diamond surrounded by white diamond baguettes set on a delicate gold band. He picked it up and he looked at it more closely before handing it to Sam. "What do you think?" he asked. Sam looked at it and responded saying, "I think she'd love it." The clerk smiled as he took it from Sam and held it for Paul to inspect again. "You have good taste sir," he commented as he admired the ring himself.

Paul looked up at him and asked, "How much?" The man took a deep breath intending to add a little drama, "This ring is a 6 and 1/2 carat chocolate diamond with 2 carats of white diamond baguettes. It is priced at $185,000." Without flinching, Paul withdrew Emily's ring from his pocket, "I don't know her ring size, but this is hers," he said handing it to the clerk. The clerk took the ring and shuffled off to assess the sizing leaving them alone.

Sam let out a long breath before saying with a laugh, "She will love it Paul. Please, just don't tell Chris what you paid for it. I'd never hear the end of it." Paul laughed as he gave him a wink. The clerk came back in and was thrilled to announce that the rings were both the same size as he handed Emily's back to Paul. "Marvelous, will you box it up?" Paul said while withdrawing his wallet and handing the gentleman his debit card.

"Let's go get some lunch," Sam said while they were leaving the store. He pulled up in front of a popular local restaurant where they went in and got settled in their booth. The waitress took their drink orders while handing them the menus. She took notice of Paul right from the start, flirting with him as she reeled off the lunch specials. Sam sat back watching. Paul seemed to take it in stride and gave her a small smile as she touched his shoulder before taking their order.

After she had collected their menus and walked away Sam leaned over to Paul and said, "I suppose you're used to that?" "What's that?" Paul said looking up at him. "Women, fawning over you," he answered. Paul laughed, "Truthfully, I hadn't noticed. It's a funny thing but all I can think about is what Emily is doing right now."

After lunch Sam drove Paul around the area pointing out neighborhoods that he thought both Emily and Paul would like. Paul was especially drawn to one neighborhood in particular and asked Sam to drive through it again. The houses were large, but not too flamboyant. "Give my guy a call and tell him what you like here. He will work out a time to show you a few," Sam said as he pulled out of the neighborhood.

They drove back to Emily's and saw the girls were still not back. Paul opened the door and they went inside. Paul asked Sam, "Would you like a pint?" "Sure, thanks," Sam answered. They had just sat down at the kitchen table when they saw Chris and Emily laughing as they got out of the car. Paul quickly got up grabbing the Tiffany's bag and went to hide it in the guest room before the girls came inside.

Paul greeted them at the door and picked up Emily swinging her around planting a kiss on her lips. "Missed you," he said as he put her down. "I missed you too," she replied, taking his hand as she gazed up at him. "Did you have fun? What did you do?" she asked as they sat down. Sam spoke up, "We had lunch and I showed him around Buckhead."

Chris looked at Sam, "I've got to pick up the kids will you be coming straight home?" "Yes Ma'am," he said in response with a grin. As he headed out the door he turned around and gave Paul a wink. Emily turned to Paul as they left and asked, "What was that?" "What was what?" he responded with a lilt to his voice. "That wink," she replied. "Oh, I have no idea," he answered with a look of feigned innocence.

He quickly changed the subject and said, "Did you have a nice day?" She went to him hugging him around his waist, "Yes I did I've got pretty nails and toenails," she said as she let go of him and began walking towards the living room. Before she could get very far he grabbed her hand and pulled her back to him. She let him draw her closer to him as she gazed into his deep brown eyes putting her arms around his waist.

"Sam took me to look at a few neighborhoods today. He gave me the name of the estate agent they used when they bought their house." She looked at him in surprise. "Really? What's wrong with this house?" she asked as she touched his cheek. "Nothing at all but I thought we may need something larger. We might as well do it now before things get too hectic. I would like to have a studio where I can work. I think I would enjoy writing songs for others," he said. She looked at him with a smile as she said, "Buckhead is pretty pricey." "I think we can manage," he said as he gave her a kiss. She laughed a little realizing how silly that sounded, "Yes, I suppose you're right."

Hesitating for a moment she said, "I wanted to talk to you about something." He looked at her as she continued. "I've thought about what you said about your money. I need to tell you that I have money too. I want to be as open about it as you were," she stopped and looked at him to gauge his reaction. He was a little shocked but happy that she was being candid with him.

"When my parents died they left me with a good bit of money. I am not sure how much I've got, maybe $800,000. They also left me their house which I sold for $500,000 and bought this one for $300,000. I have it in a money market account, so I really don't think about it too much." She finished adding, "I thought you should know." He leaned over and kissed her. "Thank you," he said softly as he searched her eyes. "It means the world to me that you shared that," he said. Kissing him again she snuggled closer while he stroked her hair. She closed her eyes and felt a wave of love and peace sweep over her.

Chapter 13

The next morning as Emily prepared for the day's session Paul sat down and watched her and Alex as they discussed something quietly before she gave him a smile as she left. Alex turned to Paul, "I am going to continue where Emily left you yesterday. I'll explain the coded messages and hidden clues in the cover of the next album. He flipped on the TV screen and the front cover of Sgt. Pepper's Lonely Hearts Club Band appeared.

Paul leaned forward slightly looking intently at an album cover that he would never have imagined. Alex began, "This was released on May 26, 1967, eight months after you 'died'. Your replacement was the driving force behind this LP, but your friends made this a tribute to you in your memory. For an hour, he went through the clues on the cover, the foldout and the back cover. He began explaining the hidden messages in the songs on the album when Paul with a wave of his hand asked him to stop, "I need a moment."

Paul walked outside and lit a cigarette. He looked across the courtyard and could see Sam's office. Sam was sitting at his desk talking to someone else in the room. When he heard the glass doors open behind him, he turned slightly, it was Emily. She didn't say anything as she came and stood by his side. He finished the cigarette and turned to her, searching her eyes, "Will you join us this afternoon? I need you," he said slowly. "Of course," she said as she took his hand and squeezed it.

The afternoon was spent explaining to him all the clues and hidden messages all the way through to the last album The Beatles recorded, Let It Be. He was exhausted, confused and agitated when they finished. "There are more clues and insights from other bands as well," Alex said as they all stood.

Alex continued, "Your friend Mick had an especially hard time dealing with your 'death' and often gave your replacement the brunt of his anger." Paul stopped him as he looked at him with a cold hard stare. "Am I to feel bloody sorry for him?" he spat out caustically. Alex was taken aback slightly by Paul's anger and stammered, "No, no, I..." Emily stepped in and stood in front of Paul saying something Alex couldn't hear.

Emily turned to Alex, "Thanks, we will see you tomorrow." After Alex had gathered his papers Emily turned back to Paul but before she could say anything he had turned and was walking out the door. She finally caught up with him as he stood waiting for her by her car. Without speaking she pulled out onto the street for the ride home. She glanced over at him as she came to a red light and noticed he was looking out the window with his finger at his lip. She reached over and gently touched his knee. He didn't respond to her gesture as he just stared out in a daze.

When she pulled into the driveway he got out of the car and was unlocking the kitchen door before she even started to move to get out of the car. She stepped inside the kitchen as he was pouring himself a drink. She stood in the kitchen doorway watching him as he grabbed the guitar and went to the sunroom. She turned to get dinner started and poured a glass of wine as she fixed a salad. She heard him get up and fill his glass again.

She walked into the living room calling him, "Paul?" He was already heading back to the sunroom when he stopped but didn't turn around. "Hey, look at me," she said calmly. He turned slowly to face her. His face was ashen, and his eyes were hard. Her heart broke as she began walking towards him when he stopped her with a wave, "I need to be alone for a bit," he said harshly as he turned away.

Dismayed, she went to the kitchen and sat down. It wasn't like him to push her away like this, but she understood the day had been filled with the reality of his former life. He had filled his glass again and walked past her as he went outside. She sent Sam a text, 'having a tough time after today. Taking tomorrow off.' Sam replied quickly with a thumbs up.

Not sure if she should go outside to try to talk to him, she watched him as he stabbed out his cigarette and stood staring off into the distance. She sipped her wine as he turned to head back inside. He let the door close hard behind him as he looked at her with a blank stare. "Please talk to me," she pled quietly as she held his eyes.

He slammed his empty glass along with the bottle of scotch down on the table, grabbed a chair, turned it around and sat down noisily. "What exactly do you want me to talk about?" he asked dismissively while he filled his glass again as she said, "That's your fourth glass. You…" He interrupted her, "Don't tell me how much I can drink Emily. You're not me Mum," he spat vehemently. Startled at his anger she didn't say anything for a moment. Shakily she stood and began walking away saying, "We can discuss this in the morning when you're sober."

"Emily, I thought you were all about talking. Where in the bloody hell are you going?" he said vehemently. He had gotten up and was moving towards her. She put her hand up and said, "I'm not going to talk to you while you're drunk don't come near me," she turned to leave him alone with his bottle.

He reached out and grabbed her arm and spun her around. She was shocked as she tried to pull her arm away from him. He held her still as he glared at her. "Paul stop it," she said as calmly as she could. He continued to hold her saying, "What do you want me to talk about Emily? The weather, the latest news on the telly or what style shirt I wear? Or better yet, shall I talk about someone walking into my life, leaving me totally forgotten? Yes indeed, let's talk about that."

He let her arm drop as he turned away from her with a smirk on his face and walked back to the kitchen where he poured more scotch as he sat down with a clamor. She stood there for a moment unsure what to do or say.

She turned around to face him. "No one forgot you Paul." He stood there staring at her as if she hadn't spoken. "Why do you think I jumped back to save you?" she asked. He shook his head and turned away from her walking outside letting the door slam again behind him. He was shaking from anger and frustration.

She waited for him to come back inside, pacing the living room, trying to find a way to help him. He had come back inside and was pouring himself yet another. "Paul, my God, you're going to be sick as a dog in the morning if you keep drinking like this," she said. He just looked at her with a blank stare as he lifted the glass to his lips. "Please just stop," she said as she sat down next to him laying her hand on his knee. He instead gulped down what was left in the glass and brushed her hand away as he got up for more.

She went to her bedroom resisting the urge to slam the door but made sure it was locked. She was shaking with frustration and appalled at his behavior. Her mind was reeling. She understood today had been hard on him but his belligerence towards her was something she hadn't expected. Deciding she needed to calm herself, she ran a bath. As she turned on the faucet, she heard him knock at the bedroom door. Ignoring him she undressed and slid into the hot bubbly water. He knocked again, this time harder as he said, "Emily, open the bloody door." She responded coldly, "I'm taking a bath."

He went back out to the living room sitting down hard on the couch. He knew he was drunk but he didn't care as he sipped what was left in his glass. He was tired and angry and needed to lose himself in the bottle tonight. He thought to himself how hurt Emily looked when he raised his voice to her and grabbed her arm but in his current state he didn't dwell too long on it. He just wanted to forget the day and everything he had learned. He was trying hard to forget the things he'd heard that he didn't want to believe. He got up to go outside when he thought he heard her door open.

She finished her bath and slipped into a nightgown and robe and sat on the bed. She didn't want to stay in here all evening, so she quietly cracked the door open. Making her way down the hall she stood for a moment to calm herself. He was coming in from having another cigarette, a drink in his hand. He clumsily locked the door. He turned around to see her standing there. "Why don't you come to bed?" she asked gently.

He didn't reply as he put his glass on the counter. Turning slowly to look at her he said bitterly, "I'm gutted. Is that what you wanted to hear?" "Paul, you have every right to be angry but right now you are behaving like a spoiled child," she said. He looked at her with disdain as he shook his head and laughed.

She moved closer to him to comfort him, but he side-stepped her putting his hands up flippantly as he brushed past her. She stood in the doorway watching him as he sat down clumsily on the couch saying, "I'm going to bed now. You can sleep in the guest room tonight." She turned to walk back to the bedroom having mixed emotions of being annoyed and helpless at the same time.

He laughed bitterly as he mumbled under his breath, "Bloody bitch." She was trying to be understanding, but that pushed her over the edge. She walked to him as he stood and drew her hand back and slapped his cheek hard. He reached up and touched his face where she had hit him with a bewildered look on his face.

She backed away from him saying, "I don't know who you are right now. I don't care who you are, and I don't care how much you've had to drink. Don't ever speak to me like that again!" She made her way to her bedroom and slammed the door locking him out.

After hearing her door slam he sat back down and put his head in his hands as he began to weep. He was exhausted from the upheaval he had been through. He was lost and afraid. He thought to himself I've done irreparable damage to Emily with me hateful behavior. He got up and stumbled into the guest room, laying on the bed without undressing. He tossed and turned all night waking with a massive headache and a broken heart.

She woke up with the sunlight streaming through her window listening to the silence. She was dreading the day ahead as she showered and dressed for what may lay ahead. Opening her door, she quietly walked past the guest room. She could see him as he lay there sleeping still wearing his clothes from yesterday. Gathering her things for the day she left the house without saying goodbye. Still very shaken she couldn't bring herself to face him.

When Paul finally made it to the kitchen he was feeling the effects of the scotch from the night before as he carefully made a cup of tea. He thought she may be in her room, but after checking he noticed her car was gone. Slamming the counter in the kitchen with his fist he went to the living room and picked up his phone. He punched in her number only to hear her voice asking him to leave a message. "Damn it to bloody hell," he cursed out loud. He thought of calling Sam but decided that he needed to make things right between Emily and himself without involving others.

Throughout the day he tried to call her several times, but she wouldn't answer her phone. He knew he needed to pull himself together and spent the day napping and playing the guitar although his heart wasn't in it. He thought about all that he learned the day before and tried to calm himself whenever he felt the resentment begin to rise in him. Late in the afternoon he was outside enjoying the sunshine thankful that his head had finally stopped pounding when she pulled into the driveway.

Emily saw him there as she pulled in. She took a slow deep breath as she got out and began walking towards him not knowing what kind of mood he would be in.

She was a little uneasy. She nervously brushed her hair behind her ear. She stopped and looked down at him as she lightly touched his shoulder, "If you won't or can't open up and talk to me," she paused, "Maybe you should stay with Sam and Chris while you're acclimating. I don't want another evening like last night." She waited for him to respond to her, but he sat silently, sighing she turned to go into the house.

He sat frozen in shame and hurt. He needed her and didn't want to leave but didn't want to stay if she wanted him to go. Walking into the house he waited until she came out of her bedroom after having changed her clothes. "If you don't want me here I'll go," he said quietly. "I don't want to be a burden to you. I'll go gather my things," he stated. She shook her head and sighed as she watched him walk away. He either hadn't listened to her or he wanted to leave, she didn't know which it was, but she didn't have the energy to argue.

He stood in the guest room for a moment before he began looking in the closet for a bag to put his things in when Emily appeared in the doorway. "I let Sam know we'll be there soon. They will be expecting you," she said quietly as she watched him. He sat down on the bed too exhausted to respond. She waited for a moment watching him, wanting to go to him, but he gave no indication he wanted her there. She turned and walked down the hallway to the living room sitting down on the couch and waited for him to finish.

He came out with his bag walking past her to the door without looking at her or speaking. She sat paralyzed for a moment before joining him outside. He stood waiting for her by her car. She hit the key to unlock the doors and he lifted his bag into the back seat. She slid behind the wheel and started the car as he got in. Neither spoke, neither knew what to say to the other.

They arrived at Sam and Chris' and sat in the driveway for a brief moment before he moved to get out. "Paul?" She said softly as he began to open the door. "Yes Emily?" He responded as he looked at her with sorrowful eyes. "I hope you will find your way." He didn't respond as he got out of the car, grabbed his bag and walked to the door.

When Emily finally got back home she let herself release all the emotions she was feeling. She cried in helplessness. She loved him dearly but felt what he was facing was far too much for her to handle alone. She hoped Sam would be able to get through to him without all the emotionally charged feelings that were between them. But she missed him already and she was heartbroken that he chose to leave instead of opening up to her. She thought her love could pull him through but began laughing at herself as she thought how silly that sounded. She shook her head and wiped away her tears wishing he was there with her.

The next morning, she arrived at work early and spent the morning deep in a case she was working on. Drawn out of her thoughts as Sam knocked on the door. "Hey, can I come in?" he asked. "Of course," she replied. "How is he?" she asked as he sat down. Sam thought for a moment before answering, "Honestly, he's not doing all that well, but he insisted on continuing today. I just left him with Alex. I was thinking he would benefit from working with Mark." She nodded in agreement.

Mark was the lead psychiatrist there and had worked with others who had decided to stay after a jump. "He may resist that, you know?" she replied. Sam nodded, "I know. I've broached the subject with him already and he didn't seem to eager." She chuckled, saying, "He can be stubborn. I think it has to do with the way he was raised and the time he came from. There was such a stigma back then when it came to mental health."

Sam leaned back in the chair and asked, "How are you doing?" She paused, "I'm alright I suppose. I am devastated that he chose to leave." Sam looked back at her with a smile, "I don't think he was thinking clearly, I think he needs you more than he's ready to admit." She looked at him thoughtfully. "He's pretty direct. I'm not sure you've got that right," she countered.

Sam said, "Chris talked to him and he told her it was what he thought you wanted. He didn't want to be a burden to you." She rolled her eyes as she responded, "It was *not* what I wanted. I wanted to help him, but he wouldn't let me."

Sam could see the doubt and hurt in her eyes. "He loves you Emily, I think he'll come around," he said softly. "Oh, Sam, it was horrible," she hesitated for a moment, "I slapped him." Sam looked at her with surprise. "You slapped Paul McCartney?" he said jokingly. She smiled at him, "He called me a bloody bitch," she whispered as she noticed Mark about to knock on the door. "May I join you?" he said. "Of course, Mark, come in," she said.

The three of them talked about how best to help Paul get through his acclimation. Mark started by asking, "First, I've been told he's seen most of what occurred before he got here in general terms," he said. Sam nodded, "Yes, but he's having a tough time learning about his replacement," he said. "Of course, he is. That is to be expected," Mark said. "Sam let's give him a day or two and then I'll begin working with him if he agrees. I don't want him feeling he's being pressured in any way, that would only add to his discomfort," Mark suggested.

Looking kindly at Emily, "Emily, what you have to understand, what we *all* have to understand, is that he has been extraordinarily famous since he was very young, he's used to getting his own way and he's used to being taken care of. I suspect that his feelings of being out of control are making this all the harder for him to cope with." She was relieved that he understood what was happening to Paul. "Thank you, Mark," she said.

After Sam and Mark left she tried to concentrate on work, but her mind kept wandering to Paul. She so much wanted to walk down the hall and wrap him in her arms. She stood to stretch her legs and looked out the window to see him standing in the courtyard with

Sam and Mark. Paul reached out to shake Mark's hand with a wary smile.

As the three of them turned to walk back into the building she sat back down at her desk feeling an overwhelming sadness. She admonished herself for feeling this way after all she wanted him to be alright and if that meant without her, well then she thought, that was for the best. As long as he can get through his acclimation and begin his new life here she would be happy for him. She packed her laptop into her bag and thought it best if she works from home for the next few days to avoid running into him. She wanted to give him the space he needed.

As she walked outside to get into her car she saw Paul and Kim walking to Kim's car. Paul smiled at something Kim had said as they got in. Emily stood frozen with shock. She was confused and felt pain in her heart that she had never felt before. She got into her car and sat for a moment. She was visibly shaken as she put her car key into the ignition.

When she arrived home, she was still shaking as she poured a glass of wine. She couldn't comprehend that he could move on that quickly and already be looking elsewhere. She sat on the couch and began to cry. At that moment she received a text from Chris. 'Paul's not here. Is he with you?' She replied with a simple, 'No.'

Emily was beginning to calm down as she poured another glass of wine. She still was shocked about seeing him with someone else. Chris responded, 'Sam had to stay late at the office, so he said someone was driving Paul back here, but he hasn't arrived yet.' Emily let out a heavy sigh before responding, 'He left the office with Kim. Maybe they went to grab some dinner. They looked quite chummy.' She hit send instantly wishing she hadn't. It sounded petty and jealous. She had some more wine as she gazed out the window trying to talk herself into feeling happy for him instead of sad for herself.

Hearing her phone buzz, she walked to the couch and sat down as she picked it up. Chris had responded, 'Em, don't you think for a minute he's interested in anyone else. He has been mooning around here like a lost puppy.' Emily was feeling a little tipsy and she was tired of being the one always in control and sensible. She responded back, 'Don't fall for it. He'll be just fine!' She got up and poured more wine knowing she'd regret it in the morning but at this point in time she didn't care.

She picked up the phone and sent one more message to Chris, 'I'm working from home the rest of the week to avoid running into him. Come over for coffee tomorrow. I need to pick your brain about where I should go on vacation.' Earlier in the day she had sent Sam a request for some vacation. He hadn't approved it yet, she made a note to remind him tomorrow.

Chris responded saying she'd be there at 10. Emily settled on the couch sipping her wine and trying to keep her mind off of the man she had loved and lost in such a short period of time. She kicked herself remembering the vow not to get involved with him and now she was paying the price. A few minutes later Chris sent one more text, 'He's home. I thought you'd want to know he's safe.' Emily wrinkled her nose as she tapped in her response, 'not my concern any longer. See you tomorrow.' She sat back and sighed heavily, eventually getting up and heading to bed without dinner.

Paul had come in while she was texting with Emily and sat down at the kitchen table to chat with the boys who were finishing their dinner. Chris walked into the kitchen and offered him a beer as she tried to gauge his mood. "How was your day?" she asked casually.

He glanced over at her with a small smile and a shrug. She patted his hand, "It'll get easier Paul, just give it time."

Stephen looked at Paul and asked, "Why don't you like Aunt Emily anymore?" "Oh, Stephen." Chris said, "That's not a polite question." Paul looked at Chris before turning to Stephen, "I love Emily, but she and I are having a rough patch and she needed some time to be alone." Chris smiled at Paul as he turned back to look at her.

"Boys go get your PJ's on it's almost time for bed. I'll be upstairs in a minute to tuck you in," she said as she began clearing the table. Turning to Paul, "Do you mind waiting to eat until Sam gets home? He shouldn't be long." "I don't mind at all," he answered as he sipped his beer. After she got the boys to bed, she walked back into the kitchen to fix dinner when she noticed Paul outside smoking. Just then Sam pulled in and they were chatting as they walked towards the house. She wanted to reassure Paul but felt it would be better to wait until she saw Emily the next morning.

Chris knocked on the kitchen door before opening it, "Hi Em," she said as they hugged. "How are you doing?" Emily poured them coffee as she answered, "I'm alright," she said with a shrug. Chris smiled at her, "He misses you," she said gently. Emily looked at her with doubt in her eyes, "He seems to be moving on just fine. And besides it's not my concern or business anymore," she said with a smirk.

Chris firmly said, "Emily, he said that Kim needed to make a stop at the store to pick up a few things. Kim insisted they stop for a drink. I don't think you have anything to worry about." Emily looked back at her with tears stinging her eyes and tried to smile. "I'm not worried, he's Paul McCartney after all. He will be fine. He'll find someone here to be happy with," she said with a sigh.

Then changing the subject, "I want to go on a vacation. I need a change of scenery. Any ideas where I should go?" Chris leaned back, "Do you think right now is a good time for that?" she asked. "Chris, it's really out of my hands now. He's working with Sam, Alex and Mark, and I need a break from everything," she said firmly. "Now, seriously, where should I go?"

Chris watched her friends face, she hated seeing her like this, "Well, there's always a cruise." Emily shook her head, "Too many people." They chatted about different places where Emily could go without her really deciding on one. "I guess I'll think about it," she said sounding a little dejected.

Chris looked at her and said, "Maybe you should put it off for a while, until things are more settled for Paul." Emily gathered the coffee cups and placed them on the counter as she turned to Chris shaking her head. "I love him very much Chris. I thought he loved me too, but he obviously doesn't. I feel like a naive little fool." She continued, "I need to get on with my life."

Chris stopped her, "Oh Emily! You are so wrong! He's not going to say anything to me, but I can see the pain in his eyes when he thinks no one is looking. Or the look on his face when someone says your name. He loves you Emily," she finished. Emily smirked and shook her head, "He wouldn't have left me if he did," she said softly. Chris gave her a hug as she left, "Keep your chin up Em, everything will be fine."

After Chris left she settled in at her desk to work. She resent the vacation request to Sam before she logged into the secure mainframe and began working. She was so engrossed in the project she hadn't realized how late it was. She looked at her phone and noticed she had missed two calls from Paul. It made her heart break, but she put the phone down and went to fix herself dinner.

Sam had just gotten in from work when he saw Chris and Paul sitting by the pool talking. Paul's head was hung down as Chris leaned over and patted his hand. He went outside to join them carrying a couple of bottles of beer. "Here ya go," he said to Paul as he handed one to him. "Thanks Sam," Paul said as he leaned back and opened it. "I was telling Paul about my conversation with Emily today," Chris continued, "She wants to go away for a few weeks," she said.

"I know. She sent me a vacation request, but I haven't approved it yet," Sam said with a grimace as he sat down. He glanced at Paul with a wink.

"I feel as if I'm betraying her confidence but," Chris paused, "She honestly believes it's over between the two of you. She saw you leaving the office with Kim the other day and it really threw her through a loop. She feels as if you're moving on without her."

Paul stood abruptly and began pacing, "That is bloody daft!" He continued exasperated as he sat back down, "She won't answer when I ring her. She won't talk to me. I'm sure she's been working from home to avoid seeing me. I don't know what to do."

Sam leaned in as he said, "Would you mind if I tried to talk to her?" Paul looked at him with a half-smile, "I'd appreciate that." Chris patted his hand as he looked over at her with saddened eyes. "I told her not to go anywhere until things were settled between you two. I hope you don't mind," she said. "Of course, I don't mind. Thank you," he responded. Chris continued, "Emily is very headstrong Paul as I'm sure you've noticed. She'll come around." Sam sent a text to Emily and smiled at Paul, "Let's see if some brotherly type persuasion will work."

Emily was sipping a glass of wine and reading when her phone buzzed with a text from Sam, 'Paul would like to speak with you. Can I bring him by?' She put the phone down not sure if she could face him. She thought for a few minutes before replying. She answered as best she could explaining, 'No, he needs to take care of himself. Please tell him I wish him the best.' She paused before sending it as she wanted so much for him to be there with her. But she cared more about his well-being than her own broken heart. She pressed send.

She got up and poured another glass of wine and made a salad for dinner leaving her phone on the coffee table while she ate. When she returned to the living room she noticed Sam had texted her back. She sighed before reading it, 'I think you are one of the smartest women I know, but I think you are wrong here,' he added a smiley face. She chuckled a little knowing how unlike Sam that was.

Then another came through, 'I think he needs you to help him get through this, please reconsider (this is me talking not Paul).' She sat back taking a deep breath and sipped her wine as she considered what he had said, 'Alright, bring him by.' She wasn't absolutely sure she was ready to see him but felt that he should have the opportunity to explain himself. She was nervous to face him but tried to calm herself before they arrived.

Knocking lightly on the kitchen door Sam came in first followed by Paul who stood just inside the door, not sure if he should enter. "Hello Sam, Paul," she said softly as she greeted them. Sam began, "Paul and I have talked and we both agree that there was a miscommunication between the two of you." She looked at Sam and then finally rested her gaze on Paul who met her eyes with his. She replied to Sam while she continued to look at him, "There was no misunderstanding Sam. I told Paul that if he wouldn't talk to me he should leave. He chose to leave. It's as simple as that."

Paul stepped forward as she spoke, "I was trying to do what I thought you wanted Emily. I didn't want to leave you. I need you, and if you agree, I'd like to come back." She shook her head saying, "No, you have enough to deal with without all of this…" Paul stopped her as he stepped closer to her, "I can't do it without you Emily. I need you but more importantly, I love you."

Sam smiled at Emily as she looked from Paul to him. She hesitated for a moment then shook her head, "My main concern is that you get through acclimation. It doesn't help you if…" Paul stopped her repeating, "I need you Emily." Turning to Sam she gave him a weak smile, "I think Paul and I should talk a little more. Thank you for your help Sam." Sam gave Paul a pat on the back and Emily a hug. "See you tomorrow," he said as he opened the door to leave.

She turned to face Paul as he stepped closer to her with pain in his eyes whispering, "God, I'm sorry, I'm sorry, I'm sorry, please forgive me." Her heart melted as she wrapped her arms around his waist and laid her head against his chest. She looked up at him, "Is it you?" she asked quietly. "Yes, and did I say I'm sorry?" he asked with a half-smile.

For a moment she let the tears she had been holding back flow. She had wanted to be strong for him, but her relief overtook her. "Emily don't cry. Oh God, please don't cry," he said as he wiped her tears away and held her closer.

"I'm very sorry I slapped you," she said softly as she reached up and tenderly touched his cheek. "I deserved it, and more. I was a bloody bastard," he said, giving her a contrite smile. "No, I shouldn't have done that," she countered. "Well, I'm sorry I acted in such a way that you did," he replied. He took her face into his hands and made her look him in the eyes, "I can never explain to you how broken I was without you," he said as he kissed her lips tenderly.

"I can't help you if I don't know what's going on in your head," she said as she stroked his hair. He looked at her with sadness in his eyes. "I am terrified and angry," he said softly. "I am angry that me friends and family had to grieve me. I am bloody angry that someone could so easily step into my shoes. I was terrified that I had lost you."

She touched his cheek gently saying with a smile, "That's a lot to be angry about, and I don't blame you at all. No one does. I don't want you worrying about me. I want you to concentrate on *you*." He felt such love and caring from her that he shook his head in wonder.

She smiled at him and kissed him sweetly saying, "I adore you Paul. All I want is to help you, but you have to let me. I can't do it alone. We have to work together." He looked at her and said, "I was selfish. I had forgotten how much you've done for me Emily. I will reach out to you when I'm feeling in over me head, I promise."

Looking up into his eyes, she said, "Are you willing to talk to Mark? I know you've met him." she asked hoping he would agree. He nodded his head, "Yes I did, but I don't..." She put her finger to his lips stopping him from continuing. "He can help you in ways that I can't," she said looking at him pleadingly. He knew it was best to agree even though he was uncomfortable with the whole idea. "Yes, I'll see what he has to say," he replied with a sigh.

She took his hand in hers feeling the tension in him melt away. She looked at him and could see tears in his eyes, "I want to take away all the heartache you're feeling," she whispered to him as she touched his cheek. "You can't love. I need to muck through it so I can carry on," he insisted. She smiled and squeezed his hand as she kissed him, "I love you." He smiled back at her as he said, "I love you more."

She was exhausted emotionally by all that had happened. But she wanted to get the issue about Kim resolved. She hesitated for a moment before saying, "Did you and Kim..." He stopped her as he put his finger to her lips. "Emily, Kim gave me a lift back to Sam's. She had to stop and pick up a few things from the grocer." He continued, "She was quite insistent that we stop for a pint," he said shaking his head. "I really just wanted to get home but didn't want to hurt her feelings." Emily looked at him with a slight frown on her face. "Emily, nothing happened between us. Nothing."

With a small smile she said, "I just couldn't make love to you if you had..." He stopped her with a sweet kiss, "I wouldn't do that to you Emily. I love you far too much." "But you forget Paul that I know about your past behavior with women," she began.

Paul closed his eyes and sighed, "I understand why you are wary about that. But, since I met you I haven't wanted to live like that any longer. I was so tired of all the women passing through me life." He took her face in his hands, "Emily, I admit I took advantage of the opportunities we had with women. But I can't imagine making love to anyone but you." She looked deep into his eyes, "I want to believe you, but it rocked me to the core seeing you with Kim," she said quietly. "I don't want to ever doubt you, but you need to know, I won't be here if you…" He stopped her with a kiss and a smile. "I have waited for you my whole life Emily. I promise you that I will always be here for you and you alone."

Chapter 14

The next morning, she said goodbye to Paul at Sam's office and went to her own office to start her day. As she was getting organized there was a knock on the door. "Hi Emily," Mark said as he entered her office. "Good morning Mark, to what do I owe this honor," she said with a smile. "Looks like I will be helping Paul after all and I wanted to touch base with you before we get started," he answered.

"Oh, so he agreed, good," she said as he sat down across from her desk. "Yes," he answered, adding, "As I work with him I'd like you to keep me posted on any extreme mood swings he may have." She looked at him, "Of course, I will," she answered. "I won't be able to speak with you about what he talks about, but I want you to know I will take care of him," he finished. She thanked him as he left.

Sam took Paul to Mark's office and greeted him with a handshake, "I'm going to leave him with you," Sam said to Mark as he gave Paul a pat on the back. "Thank you, Sam," Paul said. Mark said to Paul as he offered him a seat, "Before we get started, let me say that anything that is said here between us will stay with me. You are free to talk to Sam and Emily as you please about what goes on, but I won't without your permission." He continued, "I may on occasion speak with Emily but only to get her opinion on your progress. Not about anything we discuss between the two of us," he finished. "Thank you, I appreciate that," Paul said with a smile, feeling a little more relaxed.

Mark wanted to make Paul as comfortable as possible, so he suggested they sit outside. He knew Paul smoked and maybe being in a more relaxed setting would help him to open up. They sat down at a table in the shade of a tree. Mark looked around to make sure they were alone and then he looked back at Paul before he began.

"Well, let's get the obvious out of the way," he said with a smile. "I've been a fan of yours since I was a kid. I even saw you perform here in Atlanta in August '65, great show!" Paul laughed, "Atlanta had the best sound system of that tour. Could ya hear us?" he asked. "Yep, even though my sister was screaming in my ear," Mark laughed. Paul blushed slightly, "It would be a bit much when they would scream all the way through the show, but we enjoyed it," he said.

They spent the morning chatting and getting to know each other. Mark would occasionally mention the man who replaced Paul to see what kind of reaction he could illicit regarding Paul's feelings about the man who took over his life. "I saw him play a few years back and he did a rendition of 'Yesterday.' I have to tell you, I didn't think it sounded much like you," he said waiting to see Paul's reaction. Paul sat back anxiously tapping his cigarette on the table before lighting it, exhaling before he responded. "I haven't seen him perform, Emily is being careful about what I can see," he said casually.

Not giving up, Mark pushed a little harder. "He's still touring I hear and even has one lined up for the beginning of next year," he said. Paul jabbed out the cigarette as he looked back at Mark with a blank stare, "Who would keep that up at his age? Surely he's got enough money to satisfy himself," he said in a low voice. "Frankly, I find it embarrassing that people think I would still be performing at that age," he bristled.

Mark smiled, "Perhaps he's still trying to prove himself Paul. He had some big shoes to fill," he said reassuringly. Paul looked back at Mark with a small smile, "Thank you, I appreciate it," he said while rolling his eyes. "No, I mean it," Mark said as he looked up to see Emily walking towards them.

"I hope I'm not interrupting," she said as she stood behind Paul placing her hand on his shoulder as he reached up and laced his fingers through hers. "No, we were just about to finish up for the day," as he looked at Paul he asked, "Tomorrow?" Paul nodded as he offered his hand.

He watched them as they walked away Emily had her arm around his waist as he rested his arm on her shoulder. They stopped a short distance away as Paul said something in her ear. Mark noticed the smile she gave him and the loving way he gently reached up to brush away the hair away from her face.

He had a good feeling about Paul. He knew full well he still had some difficult emotions to deal with, but with his and Emily's guidance he felt Paul would come out of this a stronger man. He still wanted to deal with Paul's feelings about leaving the life he led, his friends, his father and brother, but for now he was glad that Paul had Emily to lean on. Not only was she a brilliant scientist, she was one of the kindest people he knew.

He remembered something he had read about Paul's upbringing, although his mother had passed away when he was just 14, Paul's father along with his sisters, Paul's aunts, had instilled in him respect and manners. It showed when they were all interviewed later. John would be flippant and sometimes rude while Paul would be there to smooth over any hurt feelings.

When a reporter once asked, 'why are you all so horrid snobby?' Paul responded, 'we're not horrid snobby. You expect nice answers to all of your questions. But if the questions aren't nice questions, they don't have to have nice answers. And if we don't give nice answers, it doesn't mean we're snobby. It just means we're natural.' The other reporters gave him a round of applause.

Paul is a good man, he thought to himself as he walked back inside, feeling confident that he could help him adjust to life here. If his upbringing would have been similar to John's, he wasn't sure he would adjust easily or at all.

Mark walked down the hall to Sam's office to fill him in on the progress of the day. "Hey Sam," he said as he settled into a chair across from Sam's desk. Sam asked, "So how is he?" Mark thought for a moment as he ran his hand through his hair, "He's trying very hard to hold in his feelings. It takes time, that's expected." Sam looked at Mark and nodded understanding he couldn't say too much more. Mark thought for a moment, "He seems quite taken with Emily," he said.

Sam smiled, "I believe we are witnessing a case of love at first sight as far as I can tell." He continued, "The day after he arrived here I could sense something between them. It was quite remarkable really." Mark smiled back at Sam, "You may be right, and who better than our Emily to give him a new life? I'm going to be showing him more about his replacement tomorrow, stop by and give him some support, will you?" Sam replied, "Of course, whatever I can do to help."

"One more thing, he is aware of Ramsgate? Correct?" Sam looked at him and replied, "Yes, we told him they were responsible for his 'death' and replacement, why?" Mark said thoughtfully, "I want to be sure he understands the importance of keeping quiet about who he really is." Sam was glad that Mark was concerned about Paul's wellbeing, "Yes, I believe he is mindful that he needs to stay in his lane," Sam replied. "Tomorrow," Mark said with a small wave.

Sam sat back in his chair and looked out the window. He had been having uneasy feelings after speaking with The Director about Paul and his acclimation. He couldn't put his finger on it, but he felt The Director was not all too happy about Paul's decision to stay. Shaking his head, he began straightening up his desk before heading home.

The next morning Mark had set up the TV in his office. He was going to show Paul interviews of the new 'Paul.' He knew it would be tough for him, but this is what Paul had to deal with from here on out. But first, he had to tell Paul about the deaths of Brian, George and their roadie and Paul's good friend Mal. This was something he was not looking forward to doing. The Beatles were like brothers and he knew that he and George had known each other for a very long time. Paul tapped lightly on the door, "Morning," he said. "Good morning, how are you doing?" Mark asked. Paul nodded, "I'm doing well, thank you," he responded.

Mark sat on the corner of his desk as he looked down at Paul in front of him. "Paul, I have some news that you may find hard to deal with," he began. Paul sighed and steeled himself for what Mark would tell him. "A year after you 'died' Brian was found dead. The authorities ruled it a suicide." Paul looked up at Mark with shock and bewilderment in his eyes. "Brian had been hospitalized for depression before, but I can't believe he would kill himself," he said softly as if to himself.

"We are looking into the circumstances of his death, it may not have been a suicide," Mark said. He continued, "There were others who were connected to you who also died under curious circumstances. We are looking into all of them and seeing if there are dots to be connected." Paul looked at him and asked, "Will you tell me if you find anything?" "Of course," he agreed. Mark waited for a moment to let him gather himself before he continued.

"There is more," he paused before saying softly, "Paul, George died in 2001 from cancer." He watched Paul as he broke the news of his friend's death to him. Paul's eyes widened slightly before he looked down at his hands in his lap. "I didn't know," he said softly. Mark said, "I asked Emily not to tell you. I wanted to break the news to you." "We were kids together. He's like me baby brother," Paul said in a whisper. "I know," Mark said as he stood and placed his hand on Paul's shoulder. "If you'd rather take the day off to deal with the news that would be fine with me," Mark said. "No, no, I'd prefer to carry on," Paul said with a wave of his hand.

Mark continued, wanting to get the deaths of his friends out in the open. "In 1976, Mal had moved to Los Angeles, where he was writing his memoirs. One evening he got out of control, probably from alcohol and drugs, and his friend called the police because she was worried he might hurt himself. When the police arrived, he had an air rifle in his hands. They asked him to drop it, but he didn't. They shot him to death."

Paul took in a slow breath and exhaled, "Mal was the gentlest, kindest person I've ever known," he whispered. Mark continued, "He was writing his memoirs, it was in a suitcase, that suitcase disappeared that night and was never found." Mark waited for a reaction from Paul before continuing, "It's said that he was going to expose your replacement." Paul shook his head and looked up at Mark with tears in his eyes. Unable to speak for a moment he cleared his throat and said, "So many people have died because of me. Mark, how do I carry on as if nothing is wrong?" This was the breakthrough Mark had been hoping for.

Mark paused for a moment before responding. "Paul, what happened after you 'died' was not your fault. These people would have died even if Emily had not gone back there that night and saved you. The blame is all on Ramsgate and their need to have total control was/is more important than anyone's life. Being exposed to the world would open up so many questions. They would be destroyed alongside many of the governmental agencies who aided them. So, taking the lives of a few to save themselves was/is, their paramount objective. I want to emphasize the need for you to keep quiet. Granted, they were quite generous with you in allowing you to stay, and giving you the money you had earned, but make no mistake, they will take it all away from you if you step out of line."

Paul drew in a ragged breath and sat back in his chair. Looking up at Mark he said, "I understand, I won't do anything to bring harm to anyone. I can and will keep quiet." Mark sighed as he patted Paul's shoulder, "Good, I know this has all taken its toll on you this morning. Tell me how you're feeling right now."

Paul was silent for a minute before he responded. "Mark, to tell you the truth, I feel like bloody hell. I knew it would be difficult to adjust to my new life here, but this is incredibly painful." Mark nodded, "Of course it is, because you are just as human as anyone else. It would be unnatural if you didn't feel that pain and grief. But, I don't want you to keep it to yourself. That will only lead to nothing but trouble for you and in turn Emily. I want to give you some time before we continue. Go find her and take a break and when you come back you can let me know if you want to stop for the day or continue."

Mark sat down in the chair next to him and placed his hand on Paul's arm. "This is a lot to deal with. We can stop any time you say. You need to just tell me. Please understand, I am here to help you get through all of this," he finished. "Thank you, Mark. I'll be back in a few minutes," he replied. He sat for a moment before getting up to walk to Emily's office.

As he left Mark's office he saw Alex was walking down the hall towards him. He stopped as Alex neared, "Alex, I want to apologize for my behavior towards you the other day. You did nothing wrong." Alex looked at him and replied, "I understand and please don't think twice about it. I'm sure it is very difficult for you right now," he said as he shook Paul's hand.

Paul walked down to Emily's office, but she wasn't there. He was thirsty and decided to walk to the cafeteria. As he stood in line he looked at the few tables that were occupied and noticed Emily was sitting there with a man. She didn't see him as they seemed deep in conversation. She was laughing at something he had said. Paul made his way outside with the awareness that he felt quite jealous, as he had watched her with someone else. Paul had a ciggie and reflected on what he was feeling. He had rarely been in a position to feel that way and he found it very uncomfortable. He stopped for a moment and took a couple of deep breaths before heading inside to Mark's office. As he reached the cafeteria doorway the man that Emily had been sitting with was coming through it. Paul had the urge to stop him and say something, but he kept his head down and made his way down the hallway.

When he got to the office Mark was gone so Paul waited as he finished his coke looking out the window. He watched as the man he had seen Emily with walked across the courtyard in the direction of Sam's office. Feeling slightly lightheaded, Paul didn't hear Mark as he came back in. Mark said, "Hey, are you alright? You're as white as a sheet." Mark said as he walked towards Paul. "Here, sit down," he said with concern in his voice. "I do feel a bit dizzy, I've probably had too much..." Paul said weakly before the room began spinning and everything went black.

Mark quickly got to Paul before he hit the floor. He got his feet above his heart before calling for help. When the medical team came in Emily was not far behind. As the EMT's worked on him he began having a seizure. They had just gotten him on a stretcher as he woke. He tried to sit up but was told not to move.

Then through all the activity he heard Emily's voice, "I'm here. Be still and let them help you." There was an on-site medical facility in the building that Emily had never been more thankful for. As they wheeled him down the hall he began protesting, "I'm fine really," Paul said slightly agitated from the seizure. Mark took the lead on convincing him that he just needed to lay back and let the EMT's do what they could to help him. His pulse was weak as they were working on stabilizing him.

"Emily, I'm fine," Paul continued to protest as he struggled to sit up. She leaned over him ruffling his hair, "No you're not," she whispered with a smile as she kissed his cheek. She took his free hand in hers as they ran an IV and connected leads for an EKG. He gave up his objection with a sigh as the tech began the test. After a few hours and what seemed like dozens of tests, Mark and the other Doctor came into his room with the news. He had what they called an NES or a non-epileptic seizure, more than likely caused by emotional stress since they hadn't found any underlying organic cause.

Paul rolled his eyes, "Well, if I don't feel the fool," he said under his breath. Emily laughed, "You're not superman." Mark explained that the changes he'd been experiencing with acclimation along with the stress he had been under before he got there were more than likely all contributing factors. "Can I get out of this bed now?" Paul laughed. "Yes, but you are to go home and rest. We can pick up in a couple of days," Mark replied.

When Emily and Paul got home, she said, "I need to go pick some things up at the store for dinner and fill your prescription why don't you go take a nap." "Ya know we could have stopped on the way home," he replied as he wrapped his arms around her waist. He began kissing her saying, "Why don't you come lay down with me?" She laughed, "No! I know you!" He began nibbling on her ear lobe. "Stop," she quietly protested, "You need to rest, and we need to eat later. She took his hand and pulled him to the bedroom ordering him to lie down.

She didn't feel comfortable leaving him alone for too long, so she just picked up a few things to get them through the night. When she got home he was sitting outside. She smiled at his disobedience. He walked to the car and grabbed the bags before she had a chance to object. "You are not supposed to be up!" she said. "I feel good. I slept a little and wanted a ciggie," he responded as they got into the kitchen.

She put the groceries away while he made a pot of English tea she had found at the store. She had gotten used to the English habit of having 'tea' around 4 with a small snack and eating dinner a little later. Sitting outside with their coffee and black and white's or biscuits as he called them, she looked at him noticing he still looked very tired. Leaning over to him she put her hand on his, "You scared me baby," she said softly. He looked at her with a small smile, "It was very strange. I had gone to the cafe to get something to drink and I don't remember much after that," he explained.

"You were in the cafeteria? I was there too," she said. "I know, I saw you," he replied. She looked at him questioningly, "why didn't you say something to me?" He was slightly embarrassed as he tried to explain, "You were with a man. You two were laughing and I didn't want to interrupt," he finished. "You wouldn't have been interrupting, that was Sam's brother. I saw him in the hallway, he was on the way to see Sam, so we stopped in for a quick cup of coffee," she said.

When he didn't respond. "Hey, what is it?" she asked. With lowered eyes he confessed, "I was struck with a bit of jealousy I suppose," he said softly. She threw her head back in laughter, "I'm sorry, I shouldn't laugh. But it's nice to think you were jealous," she teased with a wink. When he didn't return her gaze, she said, "Paul, look at me. You will never have to be jealous of another man, ever. And besides, Sam's brother is gay." He was confused as he asked, "Gay? He's a happy bloke?" It made her break out into another fit of laughter. "Why are you laughing at me?" he asked with a frown on his face.

When she got herself under control she reached out for his hand, saying, "I'm sorry, I'm not laughing at you. Nowadays homosexuals are referred to as gay." "Well, that's daft, but a good thing to know I suppose," he chuckled. While they were on the subject she gently said, "There are other words we don't use anymore as well. Such as colored when describing someone of darker skin. They are either black or African-American." She had remembered him using the term colored a few times in interviews and wanted to make sure he didn't innocently offend someone. He nodded, "I have a lot to learn Emily," he said. She patted his hand and gave him a kiss on the cheek, "You will be fine. It's just going to take some time."

Later in the evening, Emily was doing laundry when she heard something out in the kitchen. "Paul?" she shouted. When he didn't answer she went looking for him to find him sitting on the couch with his head in his hands. "Are you alright?" She said as she crouched down touching his knee. "I've been dizzy again and I knocked over a chair in the kitchen," he replied. "Oh, sweetie, here lie down and put your feet up," she said as she helped him. Then, sitting next to him, she reminded him that the doctor said this might happen. "I know, I'm sorry I'm such a drag," he replied with a weak smile. "I'll get you some water and one of the pills they gave you," she said walking to the kitchen.

She texted Sam to let him know just in case she needed his help. He replied that he would get in touch with Mark to let him know. She came back into the living room to find Paul sitting up but he looked pale. "Here, take this and lay back down," she instructed. "No Emily, I feel a bit better," he answered as he sipped the water with the pill. "What is this thing again?" he asked. "It's valium, anti-anxiety/anti-seizure medication. It will probably make you sleepy," she answered. He smiled up at her, "I don't need any help there," he said jokingly. She had gotten him some Gatorade at the store and went to the kitchen to pour him a glass.

By the time she got back to the living room he was asleep. She smiled as she covered him with a throw from the back of the couch. She sat down in the chair across from him and watched his face as he dozed. She was still amazed at how beautiful he was. She loved the way his eyes angled down, his perfect nose and his beautiful lips made him as close to perfect as she could imagine.

Even though things lately had been rough she knew her love for him was never-ending. He could be hard and stubborn at times, but she was beginning to understand his quick wit and inquisitive intelligence. He was *not* as he had been portrayed; a pretty face with no substance. She had read an article once where he had said, 'I vaguely mind people knowing something I don't know.'

He was clever, introspective and incredibly funny. He could be hard at times but yet has a wonderful optimistic attitude that she was sure had got him through his hectic life of the past few years. She knew that he had been on a self-improvement campaign before he decided to stay here. She had no doubt that he would continue once he finished his acclimation.

She stood up and went to the kitchen to straighten up before heading to bed. She heard Paul moan and went to see what she could do for him. He was sitting up and running his fingers through his hair. She bent down and kissed the top of his head. As she did he gently pulled her down into his lap. She smiled as she brushed the hair away from his eyes, neither spoke. It was as if they both knew that words were not enough, never enough to tell each other about the love they felt. He lifted her chin and kissed her seductively. In one smooth movement he stood as he lifted her in his arms and carried her to the bedroom.

Chapter 15

The next day they went back into the office. Paul had insisted. He wanted to get finished with it all and preferred to 'carry on' as he put it. She had already learned that trying to argue with him when he had his mind set was next to impossible. She was beginning to understand his steely determination. It gave her insight into the success that The Beatles had achieved. He was the force behind them pushing them from one level to the next all the while letting them believe it was fate and luck.

Mark checked Paul's vitals and saw that his blood pressure was still a little low. He asked Paul, "do you happen to know what your blood pressure has been?" "I don't know, never remember those things, but I don't think it was out of the ordinary," Paul replied. After Mark had finished examining him they settled in for the day. "I'll give you a copy of the medical records from yesterday and you should talk to Emily about finding a doctor here," he said as he put away the equipment.

Mark then turned on the first video. It was outtakes of The Beatles in the studio and as they were recording. Paul's replacement was quite animated as the video continued. He had sat down awkwardly saying he was stoned. He then began bouncing around imitating the way Paul had shaken his head as he sang. Paul grimaced at his antics. At that point Mark paused the video and looked at Paul. "We get high all the time, but I never behave like an arse," he said. Mark watched him as Paul was visibly repulsed as he viewed more videos and pictures. One picture being a close-up of the man picking his nose for the camera. Paul stood, "I need a ciggie," he said. Mark paused the TV and replied, "Of course, why don't you take a break and see if Emily's free."

Peeking his head into Emily's office Paul said, "Come with me." She stood up and joined him in the fresh air. "How's it going?" she asked. He was noticeably uncomfortable as he answered, "The replacement. I have to say that man is nothing like me."

"No, he's not. There is only one you and he isn't it," she said as she kissed him on the cheek. Speaking softly, he asked, "How could it go unnoticed?" She stood in front of him catching his eye, "People see what they want to see Paul and it's what Ramsgate

253

counted on," she replied. He shook his head, "I feel like he is a caricature of me, not someone trying to pretend he is me," he said thoughtfully.

She looked at him lovingly, "Have you talked to Mark about that? How people can't see what is plainly right in front of them." He shook his head, "Not really, the thought just came to me you see," he stated. She looked up and saw Mark and Sam approaching them. "Emily, Sam is joining us for the afternoon, would you like too as well," Mark asked. "Yes, let me finish up in my office, I'll be back in a few minutes," she said as she walked back into the building.

"Paul, I think you have done a great job getting to the root of your feelings. I want to dig a little deeper this afternoon and I think you'll benefit from having Sam and Emily here with you," Mark said.

Sitting across from Paul, Mark began, "Paul, I'm sorry to have to tell you this, but your father passed away in 1976." He waited for Paul to digest the news. Paul stared at him blankly for a moment in shock before he spoke. "How?"

Mark began, "He passed away from pneumonia. His wife was with him at the time." Patting Paul's hand,

"She said his last words were, 'I'll be with Mary soon.' I'm so sorry," he finished quietly. Paul crumbled at the thought and began weeping. Mark stood and grabbed a tissue and handed it to Paul. At that moment Emily knocked lightly on the door before entering. She was confused for a moment before Mark approached her and whispered that he had just told Paul about his father's death.

She went to him as Mark left the room to give them privacy. She sat down next to him and placed her hand on his knee. He wiped his eyes as he hung his head. She reached up and stroked his hair murmuring softly, "I'm sorry baby. I'm so sorry." His tears finally stopped. He looked at her with hooded eyes, "I'm not sure I can continue on today. I think I'd prefer to go home."

"Of course," she said as she began to stand. He grabbed her hand, "Tell me, did that man go to me Da's funeral?" She took a deep breath as she sat back down. There was really no way to sugar coat her answer. "No, he didn't. He was on tour with his new band."

Paul let her hand go as he stood, "Bloody bastard!" he hissed as he began pacing. "So, you're telling me that the world believes I didn't love me own Da enough to see him off?" She stood and took both his hands in hers, "Paul, please don't worry about that now. I know you're upset but let's take care of you first. Come on, let's go home." She led him to the door as Mark opened it. "Mark, we are taking the rest of the day off," she said as they passed through the door without waiting for his reply.

Paul was quiet on the way home, when she would glance over at him and saw that he was lost in thought as he stared out the window. She pulled into the driveway and shut off the car as they both sat still in silence. Heaving a heavy sigh, Paul swung the door open and slowly got out.

Once inside, she wanted to help him in any way that she could. He was standing at the front window, his brow furrowed, his finger at his lip. She walked up behind him and put her arms around his waist resting her head on his back. He slowly turned and faced her with tears beginning to spring to his eyes again. "I realized when I decided to stay here that people would have died, but this is so hard. I loved me Da and I didn't get the chance to say goodbye." he finished. She reached up and wiped a tear from his cheek with her thumb. "Ah Emily, I couldn't get through this without you my love," he said as he kissed her lips tenderly.

They sat outside as she listened to him tell stories of his childhood. "When Mike and I would stay out too late, Da would lock us out. We would have to climb the drainpipe and shimmy into the loo head first. Hoping we wouldn't land in the bowl," he finished with a chuckle. She giggled at the thought. "Da had it harder than most after me Mum died. He sent us away for months to live with one of our Aunties." She leaned closer to him with a smile. "Why was that?" she asked.

He sat back and lit another cigarette as he thought. "I never knew why really. I never asked him. I suppose he needed time to grieve without us lads under foot," he replied. "I was angry at him for a long time after that. Mike and I didn't get to go to the funeral. I never got to say goodbye to her." Emily instantly realized how hearing about his father today brought up Paul's memories of his Mother's death and the aftermath. She breathed in sharply desperately trying to keep her own tears at bay.

He glanced over at her, "Let's not bother with it anymore," he said with a small smile. He reached out and covered her hand with his. She thought for a moment before speaking up. "Paul, if you'd like I can ask Sam if we can give you a break for a few days. We can get away and relax. Maybe go to the beach," she offered.

He thought for a moment, "It sounds lovely, but I would rather carry on and get finished with it all. But I would love to see the shore. Can we plan on that when this is all wrapped up?" he asked.

They didn't make love that night instead they just held each other silently. When his breathing slowed, and she knew he was asleep, she held him as gently as she could while caressing his arm. He was going through so many painful moments and she knew he would have to endure more. A tear slipped down her cheek as she wished she could shield him from anymore heartache. She turned away from him, not wanting to wake him as she quietly let her tears flow for him. He instinctively turned and gathered her in his arms. Letting their bodies become entangled, she finally drifted off to sleep.

When she woke, he was gone. She slipped into her robe and went to find him. He wasn't in the living room, but the kitchen light was on and the coffee had been made. She looked out the window and saw that he was standing there looking off into the darkness. Quietly opening the door, she walked towards him. He didn't turn or speak when she touched his shoulder, but he continued to gaze through the trees at the half-lit moon. She sat down and waited.

"I woke in the middle of the night," he began, "I've been up ever since." He said as he sat down to face her. "I've condemned John to death. Haven't I? By deciding to stay here, I've let him die." Before she could respond, he said softly, "It should have been me."

She took in a ragged breath, "It *was* you, and yet that didn't change what came after. Paul, you can't do this to yourself…" He interrupted, "I am responsible though Emily, you said so yourself when I first got here." She looked up at him, "Yes, but you have to understand something. You had no control over what would or could have happened. He may have gone off to live in New York regardless. We just don't know."

He stood and stated, "I'm needing more coffee, come, it's chilly out here," as he reached for her hand. She poured them each a cup and placed them on the coffee table while she grabbed a throw from the back of the couch.

Sitting next to him she covered them both. "It's been 53 years Paul. People have died. You can't blame yourself. It will be good for you to talk to Mark. He's helped others in your position. It's what he does."

The sun began peeking through the window when they got up and began getting ready for the day. He was quiet on the way to the office. She tried to engage him but gave up when he reached over and turned the radio up. Switching off the engine he turned to her. She leaned over and kissed him. Smiling, trying to draw him out of his mood. He reached up and stroked her cheek with the back of his hand. "It's hard Emily. I thought I was handling it all, but it's hard," he said softly. She smiled at him, saying, "Have I told you lately that I love you?" He leaned over and kissed her, "Yes, but don't ever stop."

They walked together to the front door. "I've got a few things to do in my office. I'll be there in about 15 minutes," Emily said, giving him a quick kiss on the cheek. Paul walked down the hall to Mark's office knocking lightly on the door. "Morning Paul!" Mark said cheerfully. "Good morning," Paul replied. "I hope you're feeling better today," Mark inquired. "A bit," Paul said with a nod, "I'm anxious to carry on and get everything out in the open." Mark took a deep breath, "I'm glad you feel that way, but nonetheless, if things get too overwhelming we'll stop, alright?" He said giving Paul a pat on the back.

"In 1999," Mark began as Emily slipped into the room and took a seat next to Paul. Mark continued, "A man broke into George's home in the middle of the night. George went to see what was going on and saw an intruder with a knife. George charged him to try and disarm him but instead was repeatedly stabbed. His wife, Olivia, took a lamp and hit the intruder over the head stopping George's attack but then he tried to strangle her. The intruder took off and was later caught. They both sustained injuries and George almost died." He let that digest a minute before continuing, "And, as you already know, John was murdered in New York in 1980." Paul listened as Emily reached over and covered his hand with hers.

"Yes, I learned about John from Emily," Paul responded flatly as Mark continued, "We now believe that both incidents were related. We believe that the same entity that murdered John also tried to murder

George. We also believe that Brian was killed, and it was made to look like a suicide.

Looking at Emily and then Sam, Paul simply said, "Why?" Mark nodded to Sam who continued, "We are convinced they were going to reveal the secret about your replacement. George had always fought the hardest to have it all out in the open. He had discussed it with the others, and they decided that John would be the one to break the story to the press. He was killed days before he was going to go public. That sent George over the edge. He became somewhat reclusive and obsessed with security." "And Mal?" Paul asked. Mark nodded, "He was also murdered therefore keeping his memoirs from the public."

Paul leaned back in his chair with his eyes closed, unexpectedly, he stood and walked towards the door saying, "I need some air." Emily looked at Mark who nodded. "I'll keep you company," she said. They sat on a bench as he fumbled for the pack of cigarettes in his pocket. "Bloody hell," he muttered when he dropped the lighter. She quickly picked it up and flicked it and lit his cigarette.

He stared straight ahead into the distance as he inhaled slowly. She sensed he was putting up walls again, but she was thankful that Mark and Sam were here to help him if he felt out of control. She said, "Don't hold it in, talk to Mark, if you'd like Sam and I to leave you two alone…" he stopped her, "No, I'm alright really," he said quietly. She smiled but thought to herself how hard he was trying not to show vulnerability. She assumed it was because men in his day were not able to show emotions. It was unacceptable and a sign of weakness. She took his hand and squeezed it, getting a half smile from him.

As they got back to the office Mark was looking through a folder. He looked up at them and said, "Let's talk about how you're feeling Paul. I know I threw a lot at you." Paul began pacing back and forth. "I am not sure if I can put into words how I feel. I suppose I am feeling a lot of guilt. Because of my decision my friends suffered." he said.

"Paul, all of this is/was out of your hands. It was Ramsgate's actions and what they were willing to do to keep their deception from getting out to the public is not your fault," Mark replied.

Sam finally spoke up, "The point we are making is this. Although you may want to do something to justify yourself in all of this, you can't. Ramsgate will stop you and they would have no problem hurting the people that surround you now." Sitting back down Paul tried to understand what they were saying.

He looked at Emily and back at Sam. "Are you saying if I came out now and declared him an imposter that they may harm me or Emily?" he asked credulously. Sam replied, "Not 'may harm,' Paul. I don't know at this point if they would even find it a viable option, but we want both of you safe and the best way to guarantee that is for you to keep a low profile now that you are here in this time."

Paul wanted to ask and felt that now was a good time. "I want to see me brother and Richie, I mean Ringo," he stated. Emily looked down, Mark looked at Sam. "Paul, that would be tough to do," Sam continued, "They believe you died. The shock of seeing you, especially as you were back then, may be too much for them. Not to mention that would be stepping on Ramsgate's toes." Paul looked up at him, "Please, there are so few of them here," he finished in a whisper.

No one spoke until Mark said, "Paul, it would put you, Emily and them all in danger, not to mention I am concerned about what it would do to you emotionally, I have to say no." Sam began, "Our first priority is keeping you safe. Ramsgate is quite prepared to shut this whole thing down if you step out of line."

Sighing as he looked at Emily, "What do you say?" he asked. "I have to agree with Sam and Mark. I don't see what you would gain by meeting with them. Nothing would change and I think it would do more harm than good." she finished.

"What about me brother? I know he's alive now, he's me brother," Paul said quietly. Emily looked at him with caring eyes, he seemed so lost and sad. As Sam and Mark again argued the dangers, he hung his head.

Emily watched him closely, as he looked at Sam before asking, "Can we stop for the day?" Emily leaned towards him and kissed his cheek as he reached for her hand. Paul stood and said to Mark, "I'd like to take tomorrow off." Emily glanced at Sam as she busied herself gathering her things together. "Tomorrow's Friday so let's just all regroup on Monday," Sam offered.

Getting in the car she asked Paul if he'd like to stop anywhere on the way home, "No," he answered as he looked out the window. Looking over at her before she started the car, he said, "I'm fine, Emily, can we go now?" Sighing, she backed the car up and began the ride home. He was quiet as they turned into the driveway. When he got out of the car, he stopped and lit a cigarette and didn't look at her as she passed by. She turned to face him with the other night still so fresh in her mind. She wanted to avoid another night like that. "If you're not ok, you need to let me know," she said.

He jabbed out the cigarette and walked into the house. She stood for a moment dreading the evening ahead if he was going to let himself go back to the dark place he had been in. She saw him through the window pouring a drink, she shook her head as she went inside. He sat down on the couch and rolled a joint as he sipped the scotch. He took a hit and sat back staring at the ceiling as he continued to smoke. A small moan escaped his lips as he thought about John, George, Mal and Brian.

He glanced at Emily busying herself in the kitchen. He took another hit as he watched her. His emotions were boiling to the surface as he thought about all he had learned since beginning acclimation. His guilt about not being there for George as he was dying began to overwhelm him. He put his glass down and stood to go to the kitchen, he needed Emily to pull him back into the light.

She sipped her glass of wine as she stood looking out the window. When she turned around he was standing in the doorway staring at her with helplessness in his eyes. "Help me," he said softly as he held out his arms to her. She walked towards him as he began to cry. "I should have been there for all of them," he sobbed. Finally, as his tears subsided he said softly, "I feel so stupid and selfish," wiping his face with the back of his hand. "Please don't do that to yourself," she exclaimed as she led him to the table. Sitting down she took both his hands in hers, "I'd rather see you cry than get drunk again," she said with a smile.

"Ah, Emily, seriously, what would I do without you?" he sighed. "Apparently you'd drink a lot of scotch," she said jokingly. "Let's eat then maybe later I can figure out how to distract you?" She said with a wink. "Come on," she said softly as she held his hand. "Sometimes I think I could go without food forever just as long as I have you here," he said as they walked to the dining room.

He spent some time after dinner playing the guitar in the sunroom. It had always been there for him when he needed to escape, but tonight all he wanted was to be with Emily. He stood and went in search of her and found her on the patio talking on the phone. He watched her from the kitchen as she laughed at whatever was being said. He felt a twinge of jealousy as she looked up at him and waved him outside as she hung up the phone. "Come here. It's beautiful tonight, isn't it?" She said as he leaned in to kiss the top of her head. "Yes, it is," he agreed.

She didn't mention whom she had been speaking with and for some reason that made him uncomfortable. He was quiet as they sat enjoying the evening. She touched his knee as she said, "you're awfully quiet." "Just thinking," he replied looking deep into her eyes. She smiled at him, "I was talking to a friend of mine. I think it's time to introduce you to them, my friends that is," she finished. "I'd quite like that," he responded feeling a wave of relief.

Hesitantly, he spoke again about trying to contact Ringo. She looked at him sympathetically understanding his yearning. "You heard Mark, it would not be good for you or him. Can you imagine the shock at seeing you as you were 53 years ago after believing all these years that you had died?" She tried to appeal to his common sense as she smiled and took his hand in hers. He looked back at her as she continued, "There is Ramsgate to think about too. I am grateful for what they have done for you, but I have no doubts about their cruelty and callousness, and you shouldn't either."

"I suppose you are right," he said as he leaned back and looked at her. "I'd like to meet that fellow who pretends to be me though and give him a punch in the bloody mouth." She was so surprised that she burst into a fit of laughter. Catching Paul's eye, she saw a spark of light there that had been missing since all of this began.

She got up and stretched as she turned to him, "Hmm, let's see if I can take your mind off things," she said with a seductive smile. She led him to the bedroom, "Stay here. I'll be right back," she said. She went into the bathroom to change into the sexy nightgown she had bought when she and Chris had gone to the spa. She opened the door to see him sitting on the bed. He lifted his head to look at her letting out a long breath, "Emily," he said. She walked slowly towards him as he stood.

She slowly took his shirt off as she traced kisses down his chest. As he moved to touch her, she gently took his hands and shook her head no. She felt his desire as she continued to undress him watching his face. He looked back at her with smoldering eyes as his lips slightly parted. Kissing him deeply, she moved her body against his. She pulled back, moving her hands to his chest and gently pushed him back onto the bed. She teased him beyond his limits as he was transported to a place of ecstasy he had never experienced before.

They both lay there unable to move for a moment. He rose up leaning on his hand as he looked down on her. Gently stroking her face as he murmured his undying love. "Emily, I can't begin to tell you how much I love you." She ran her fingers over his chest smiling up at him, "Try," she said seductively. "I have never been in love like this before, you have taken my heart and have given me my life. I will never be able to give you everything you deserve."

She looked up at him, "I don't deserve anything I only want you safe and happy and here with me," she finished with a smile. He watched her face for a moment before leaning down and kissing her lips saying, "There is nowhere I'd rather be than right here with you. Honestly, I can't even imagine a time when I won't miss you when we're apart, won't want to make love to you endlessly, when I won't need you with all my heart. Just wait, you'll see," he finished with a smile. She looked at him as she brushed his hair away from his eyes, "I promise you I will never be far from you when you need me," she said. "Me as well," he replied to her with a kiss.

Sighing, she started to get up. "Wait, you're leaving me already," he laughed. "I'm going to take this off," she said, pointing to the nightgown." "Mmm, no," he said as he gently pulled her back down next to him, "Leave it on," he whispered as he began kissing her shoulder. Making love again, they both fell asleep entangled with each other, waking as the sun shone through the window over their bodies.

They spent the day huddled on the couch looking at houses online. He was flabbergasted that with a touch of a finger you could literally walk through someone's house. She decided to make a list of all the things they each wanted, making the search a little easier. The list grew as he kept adding more and more features he wanted. Giggling, she said, "Okay, stop, stop, what are the three most important things you want."

Sitting back with a sly grin he mused, "Hmmm, number one a studio, number two a swimming pool and number three a library." She smiled and nodded, "Good choices," as she began a new list. Getting up he stretched and walked outside while she typed in all their wishes.

Three different homes popped up. She was scanning through them when he came back inside. "Come here and see what you think of these," she said as she placed the laptop in front of him. They were all beautiful and one was in the neighborhood that Sam had shown him. "I'd like to see these. Should I call the estate agent that Sam told me about?" he asked. "Yes, if you'd like," she said as she handed him his phone. After he hung up, he told her they had a meeting set up with him tomorrow. He seemed quite pleased with himself and she felt good that he was accomplishing things one step at a time.

The meeting was set for 10 and Emily had been practicing all morning. She had to remember to call him James. Walking to the kitchen where he was waiting she said, "Well, James, let's go!" He laughed, "This is going to be daft."

The realtor was a young man but seemed to be very astute and took special care to listen to their priorities. A contract was signed, and he would show them the houses they had found that afternoon. In the meantime, Emily and Paul enjoyed a light lunch at a cafe nearby. When they had finished they got a call to go back to the realtor's office. They spent the rest of the afternoon looking at the houses plus a few more. They decided to take a day to talk it over before making any decisions. Emily believed it was good for Paul to have this diversion in the midst of his acclimation.

Chapter 16

On Monday they both rose early and dressed for the day ahead. "Are you sure you're ready for more?" Emily asked him as they pulled into the parking lot. "Yes," he answered.

She was a bit nervous, she knew Mark planned to have Paul listen to songs that were written about his death by other people, some of them his friends. She knew it would be hard on him. She dreaded it and wanted to be there with him but Mark and Sam both agreed that this immersion had to be done by Paul alone. Mark said it was important for him to be undistracted as he heard the music that was written for him and about him. Mark wanted Paul to come face to face with the reality that his replacement was felt by so many who wanted to get the truth out. He wanted Paul to know that people cared and still do.

Emily was restless not knowing what Paul was experiencing. She left her office and went to see if Sam was free. She peeked her head in his door. "I can't work, I'm worried," she said as she sat down.

Sam smiled at her, "I am too. Acclimation is rough, but especially for him with the volume of information he has to deal with." She said with a sigh, "I wish Mark would let me be there, but I have to trust that he knows what he's doing."

They chatted a while longer until there was a knock on the door. "Come in," Sam said. It was Alex, "Emily, Sam, Mark needs you," he said breathlessly.

Rushing down the hall to Mark's office, Emily stumbled a little in fear of what she would face. When she reached the door, she saw that Paul was sitting there, pale and wide-eyed. He seemed to be in almost a catatonic state. Mark was crouched in front of him trying to get his attention. "Mark, what's happening? What's going on?" she asked as she neared Paul.

Suddenly, Paul stood and looked around the room not focusing on anything or anyone, "I've got to get home," he said in a raspy voice. Turning to Sam, "I've got to get back home Sam," he repeated.

Emily stood back frightened by the look in his eyes. "Paul," she said softly as she cautiously approached him. He turned and looked at her as if he didn't know who she was. He stared for a moment longer before reaching up and stroking her cheek, "Emily, I have to go home. I'm sorry," he said before turning away from her. "Sam! Now! I've got to get back home," he said in a raised voice with his eyes wide in near panic.

Mark stepped in and gently touched Paul's arm. "Paul, sit down son, take a deep breath," he said gently. Paul just stared at him without moving a muscle. "Do you have the medication I gave you?" he asked softly, keeping eye contact with Paul.

"Yes, here," Paul said as he began to fumble with the pocket of his jacket. Mark gently reached in and took the bottle. "Paul, I'm going to give you one of these and then I want you to lay down on the couch," he said as he continued to hold Paul's eyes.

After Paul took the medication he refused to lie down, "No please. I'm fine," he said repeatedly. After a few moments of silence Paul raised his head and focused his attention on the three of them. "I'm sorry, you've all gone through so much trouble for me. I've got to get home and make it alright you see."

Emily felt as if she were frozen and unable to speak until she turned to Mark in anger. "What in the hell happened?" she demanded almost screaming. Sam took Emily's arm and began guiding her from the room. "Come on Emily. Let's let Paul rest," he said with a brotherly smile.

Emily was too stunned by what was happening to fight him. They walked to Sam's office and closed the door to any prying eyes. "What happened Sam?" she asked her voice cracking. "I don't know Em, but let's trust Mark that he can get Paul calmed down enough and then we can go back," he answered.

He picked up the phone and told Mark where they were and to let him know when Emily could see Paul. She sat down across from Sam and stared out the window. He had gotten her a cup of coffee and she wrapped her hands around it for comfort and warmth. "It's like he didn't even know who I was," she said quietly as if to herself.

Sam sat down next to her and patted her arm. "We've seen this before Emily. When the reality of acclimation hits and the realization they will never live their old life again," he said to assuage her fears.

She sipped her coffee and realized her hands were shaking. "The difference now is I'm in love and I'm scared Sam," she whispered. He smiled at her as he took the cup from her and put it on his desk. "Come

277

here," he said as he held his arms out to her. She began crying as he wrapped her in a hug while she sobbed.

He continued, "He must have become crippled with the emotion of the songs he was listening to. Imagine, hearing your friends mourning your death. I would think it's a little like going to your own funeral. He'll be fine Emily. He's tough, I promise," he finished.

His phone rang and he picked it up while Emily wiped her tears away. "Mark wants us," he said. They walked back down the hallway. Sam entered first and spoke quietly to Mark. Paul was sitting up and looked slightly better than when they had left him.

When Emily entered the room behind Sam, Paul stood and walked to her with his arms extended, "Emily, I'm sorry, I was a bloody arse," he said as he dipped his head down to look her in the eyes.

Mark and Sam left them alone.

"I had a moment of panic. I didn't mean to hurt you. I don't want to leave you. This has all been so hard. I felt a little mad for a moment," he confessed.

She looked up at him and tried to smile. "I think we should go home," she said as she kissed him. "We both need to relax," she added.

After they had gone, Mark sat down at his desk and looked over at Sam. "Well, I screwed the pooch," he said. Sam chuckled, "No Mark, you're not a miracle worker, everyone reacts differently to acclimation. Paul just has a lot more to deal with than most. Don't beat yourself up."

Once Paul and Emily got home, both of them were exhausted. "Let's lay down for a while," she said as she took his hand.

Waking hours later Paul was gone. He was in the living room standing and staring out the window as the sun began to set. "I made a fool out of meself today," he said quietly. She stroked his hair and kissed his cheek, "Stop, just stop. You have nothing to be ashamed of," she said. "If I had been through what you have and had to learn all that you have, I'm not sure how I would handle it," she finished.

"I suppose I felt a bit of panic and helplessness. I've been feeling that way quite a bit lately," he confessed.

He held her face with his hands, "I don't want to leave you Emily, I was upset you see," he said.

"I know," she said quietly. "It breaks my heart that you have to go through this. I want to be able to fix it for you," she whispered in his ear as she kissed his cheek.

He pulled back from her and held her arms as he looked deep into her eyes. "Emily, I don't enjoy feeling as if I am not in control," he said. "This situation has put me in a position that I've never been in before. I just need to work it out, I'll be fine, you'll see," he finished.

She kissed him, "Don't keep it in. If you need to scream and shout, do it. Just give me fair warning," she said smiling up at him.

He changed the subject saying, "I've been thinking it's time to buy a car. Can we go pick one out this weekend?"

"Sure, do you have an idea what you want?" she asked.

He chuckled, "Yes, I do indeed. Sam and I investigated them while I was staying there. I think I'd enjoy a Jaguar." She smiled as she gave him a kiss. "Okay, there's a Jag dealer not far from here," she said.

The next day, after spending the afternoon at the dealership, Emily was thrilled Paul had found something he loved. Arriving back home, he pulled his new Jaguar into the driveway behind her. Jumping out, he said excitedly, "This is a marvelous machine. Come, let's go for a ride and grab a bite to eat." She giggled at his excitement.

Sliding into the car, she marveled at the tan leather interior. "This is beautiful," she said. He gave her a wink and slipped his sunglasses on and started the engine with a huge smile. "God, I've missed this," he said as he began to back out. They drove a little while before stopping at a little restaurant they had been wanting to try.

Emily decided to stay home to work while Paul drove to the office to continue with Mark. Around noon Paul called her. "Emily, I needed to hear your voice," he said quietly. "How are you holding up?" she asked. There was a long pause. "Paul?"

"I'm devastated Emily, just gutted," he responded in almost a whisper.

She hesitated for a moment, "Tell Mark you've had enough honey, come home," she said as calmly as she could.

Paul looked around the courtyard, "I am feeling a bit of a fool. Mark played a song that George had done called, 'While My Guitar Gently Weeps,' near the end I could hear him calling me name," he said in a choked voice. "I could barely stop meself from weeping as well."

"Come home," she said again.

She heard him pull into the driveway as she was putting laundry away in the bedroom. She walked into the living room where he was sitting on the couch bent over as if he was nursing a sick stomach. When he looked up at her she saw such pain in his eyes that it broke her heart.

She went to him as he stood and wrapped her arms around him. "Emily, I don't think I can take much more. I've always been the one holding everyone else up. I don't know how to do this anymore," he said.

Touching his cheek with the back of her hand she smiled, "Let me talk to Sam and Mark. Your basic acclimation is complete. What you are doing now is what Mark thought would be helpful to you. If it's too much, we can stop," she said reassuringly.

"I don't want to be viewed as a quitter," he said quietly.

Emily took his hands in hers, "No one will think you're a quitter Paul. Mark thought it would show you the pain and sometimes anger at your 'death' that your friends and others felt in these songs. It was the only way they could say what they wanted to say. He wanted you to know how many people missed you and loved you," she finished.

It was late in the afternoon and she still had some work to finish up. Paul grabbed the guitar and went to the sunroom. As he strummed the tune he had been working on he would stop occasionally and look out the window feeling a sense of sadness come over him when he thought about the song George had written. It had such a beautiful haunting melody.

His mind drifted back to when they were young and still in school. He laughed to himself remembering when they went to the shore for a swim with another friend of theirs. Someone took their picture. They were shirtless and in their swimming trunks trying so hard to look tough and manly to impress the 'birds'. But they were so skinny and pale.

He sighed as he stood and leaned the guitar against the chair. He wanted a ciggie and a glass of wine. Walking to the living room he saw Emily had finished working and was in the kitchen. "How are you feeling?" she said as he walked up behind her putting his arms around her small waist.

"A bit better," he replied as he reached around her and snatched a piece of cheese she had sliced. He grabbed the wine out of the refrigerator and poured them each a glass. "I was just thinking about when George and I first met," he began. "We went to the same school and met on the bus," he chuckled as he carried a plate of cheese and crackers outside.

"We were best mates almost from the moment we met. I remember hitchhiking out of town a bit with George to learn new chords from a bloke he had heard about. Whenever we heard of something new we wanted to learn it. The bloke was on the other side of town, so we hopped on a bus and rapped on his door. I'm sure he thought we were off our nut when we asked if he could show us some new chords.

Emily smiled at him as she listened, she was glad he was remembering happier times and not dwelling on the sadness. Paul sat back and lit a cigarette as he returned her smile.

"I emailed Sam and Mark. They've agreed that your acclimation can be officially finished. Mark wants you to know that if you ever feel the need to speak with him, he will be there for you," she said.

"That's marvelous," he said. Moving his chair closer to hers, he took her hand and said, "Through all that I have lived through before and since coming here, falling in love with you has been the saving of me." She blushed slightly as she always did when he spoke so intensely of their love.

"Emily, I want our lives to be as full and happy as they can be. I once believed that I would never marry." Hesitating slightly as he took the ring out of his pocket. "But, being here with you, I now can't imagine not having you as my wife. Will you do the honor of marrying me?"

She was so taken aback at the suddenness she just stared at him in shock. He laughed as he cupped her face with his hands kissing her lips sweetly. "Paul, I, I...." She stuttered as tears came to her eyes. "Of course, I will," she finally answered. He slid the ring onto her finger. She was overwhelmed with the beauty of it. She looked at him through tears, "But when? How?"

He chuckled, "I bought it when Sam and I went out that Saturday afternoon."
She kept holding her hand up to look at it to Paul's amusement.

The next morning came and she woke up alone. It was beginning to get light out as he sat outside. He saw Emily fixing herself some coffee as she waved at him through the window and lifted the coffee pot. He nodded yes and she joined him on the patio with a kiss and filled his cup.

"You're becoming an early bird," she laughed. "I am!" he agreed. "It's a good time to write I've found," he added. "I woke with a tune in me head and wanted to work it out," he said as he put the guitar down and joined her at the table reaching for her hand. "I missed you when I woke up," she murmured. "Well, we can go back to bed if you'd like," he said with a wink.

She laughed and leaned forward as if to tell him a secret, "We will, but first play me your song." He put down his coffee and picked up the guitar and began strumming. He hadn't worked out all the words yet, but the melody was beautiful. When he finished she stood up and leaned over to kiss the top of his head. "Come with me," she said with a huskiness to her voice.

The sun was beginning to rise when they tumbled back onto the bed in each other's arms. Paul looked down at Emily and paused before kissing her. He was almost breathless with desire for her. They made love slowly, not speaking a word, but each one knowing they were telling each other about their love. Paul watched her face as he caressed her body and wondered how he had ever been with anyone else like this, he knew in his heart Emily was the last woman he would ever need, ever make love to, ever love.

Emily closed her eyes as Paul ran his hand over her hip, he had such a gentle touch. As they made love she thought to herself how two people could not be more perfect together. His lips found hers and with a sigh he kissed her softly. She had never loved like this before. She had never felt as if she were one half of someone else. Paul was her everything a small tear ran down her cheek, a tear of joy and happiness. He seemed to know, as he smiled and kissed it away murmuring his love to her.

Chapter 17

Moving to untangle herself from his arms, she slid away and turned back to him taking his hands in hers and pulling them above his head. She leaned over and kissed him lightly before gently biting his lip. He moaned and said, "Emily," she continued kissing his lips again, then her tongue around his ear blowing ever so gently. Paul closed his eyes as he moaned her name again. She wanted him so badly as she slowly moved down to delicately kiss his chest and stomach.

It was too much for Paul to bear, he needed her so desperately, he grabbed her hands and flipped her over so that he was above her. In one forceful move he was inside her, moving faster than he meant to, but he couldn't contain the passion he had for her. For a moment she was shocked at the forcefulness but soon matched his urgency until they collapsed into each other.

Falling away from her Paul laid on his back next to her trying desperately to catch his breath. "Emily, I didn't hurt you, did I?" he asked, turning towards her and realizing that he may have been too rough with her.

"Of course not," she whispered with a sly smile. "I don't break that easily," she emphasized with a seductive smile.

"Breakfast?" she asked as she started to get up. "Let me put something together for us," Paul replied. He hopped up and threw his clothes on. "You stay here love," he said as he walked out the bedroom door. Emily snuggled back under the blanket as she stretched and yawned. How is it possible to be so in love she mused as she listened to him banging around in the kitchen.

She threw on her robe and went out to join him. Before heading to the kitchen, she put some music on the stereo. He was standing at the stove turning the eggs when she slid her arms around his waist. "I couldn't stay away from you," she whispered in his ear. He turned around cupping her face in his hands and kissed her. "I want you to always miss me when I'm gone," he said with a smile.

She looked into his eyes and saw a sparkle there that she hadn't seen in the past few days. She kissed him and turned away to pour their coffee. "I will, you know, miss you when you're gone," she said as she handed him his cup. He smiled, "Good," he said with a wink. That wink, the one that millions of girls would scream and cry over, was hers now. She wondered if he realized what effect a simple thing like his wink had on them.

"When you did photoshoots, would you deliberately make yourself look adorable to drive all the girls crazy?" she asked with a laugh. He turned to her very seriously and said, "Ummm…I don't know, what could you possibly mean by that Emily," with a little frown. "Yeah, I'm sure you don't," she countered with a wink of her own.

He laughed, "No, I didn't try to do anything like that at all except to get through them sometimes. You can't imagine what it's like at every turn to have a camera stuck in your face. When we all got our own cameras, we would pull them out and take pictures of people taking pictures of us." She laughed, "I can't imagine how intrusive that must have been," she said. "It was, but we also realized it was all part of what was happening for us," he countered.

"Some of those photo shoots were daft, like the shoot we did for 'Yesterday and Today," he said while rolling his eyes. "It was uncomfortable sitting about with meat and baby doll parts all over us. George really hated it, but we thought we were being Avant Garde. But, as you can imagine, we didn't always know what we were doing."

She glanced over at him as she finished looking at her phone. She pulled up an auction site which showed how much that album recently went for. "Here," she said as she handed him the phone. "What is it?" he asked before looking at what she had found. "It's what that album with that cover just sold for. They call it the butcher album cover," she told him. "$234,000! No! That's daft!" he exclaimed. He shook his head in bewilderment. "My house in London only costs 40,000 pounds."

They moved into their new home after having renovations done both inside and out. The building in the backyard was now painted white with black shutters on the windows. Paul had it fitted with state-of-the-art recording and computer equipment which he had given himself a crash course on with some help from Sam and Emily. He and Sam had worked on the studio together and a real friendship was growing there. The thought of it made Emily so happy that Paul had someone to use as a sounding board when he became overwhelmed. He was still dealing with the emotions of his past that at times were raw and painful for him.

Paul would spend countless hours working on writing and recording demos when he wasn't listening to everything he could. He often joked that catching up on 53 years of music would take him another 53 years.

Every now and then he would fall back into the pain he first felt when beginning acclimation, but Emily always pulled him through the darkness. She was worried for a while that his need to be in control was what he had a hard time letting go of. He was a perfectionist and knowing someone was using his name to create music was hard for him to deal with. He worked on and off again with Mark trying to manage his feelings of helplessness when it came to someone else living his life. She knew he realized how much everyone cared for him and wanted him to be happy here.

Emily had plenty of books to contribute to their library, but they still spent countless weekends browsing used book stores and antique shops to complete the library. Their dream house was beginning to feel like home to them. They would spend their evenings in the library, talking about their day, reading or sipping a glass of wine as they unwound from life. He marveled at all the new books that had been written since 1966.

Paul had an idea to keep a running list of those he had and those he still wanted to explore on his new computer. Emily joked that they should have made the library two stories only to have Paul look at her wide-eyed with excitement at the idea of renovating the room to include a loft section. She was always amazed at how many truly innovative ideas he had.

The patio and pool were right outside the kitchen for easy access in the evenings when cooking outside or entertaining. Paul had the stonework redone with a Tuscany rustic gray tile. He also had a brick grilling station installed. They had a pergola custom made to cover the seating area and a fireplace. It soon became their favorite spot to sit and relax. If Emily was working at home she would sometimes sit there so she could listen to Paul work in his studio.

One evening as they sat outside by the pool enjoying the pleasant weather Paul looked at Emily and said, "Let's get married right here." She was shaken out of her thoughts and smiled at his excitement. "That's a lovely idea. The sooner the better," she said with a sly grin. "Why is that love?" he asked. She reached over and stroked his hand as she said, "I'd like to do it before I get too big." Paul looked at her with confusion in his eyes, "Big?" he said. "Yes, big," she responded. She was teasing him as he didn't seem to understand what she was saying. "I don't understand Emily, are you planning on getting fat?" He asked with a laugh. "No, not technically, but women do tend to get big bellies while they are pregnant," she finished.

Paul sat for a moment without saying anything or seemingly aware of what she had just told him. Suddenly, his eyes widened as he jumped up, "Emily! Are you telling me we're going to have a baby?" She grinned up at him as she stood. "Yes, that is exactly what I'm telling you," she said. He picked her up and spun her around. He had a look of euphoria on his face as he bent down and kissed her lips.

"God Emily, I don't believe it!" He repeated as he lifted her again in a big hug. "Whoa, slow down," she said, "I've had a little morning sickness." He gently placed her down in front of him and cupped her face in his hands. "I love you," he murmured to her with a grin. "I love you too," she said as she kissed him. "Well, we better make an honest woman out of you soon!" he said. Laughing, "Honest woman, huh?" she said. "Oh Emily, let's do this up right. We'll have it here in the evening, then have a caterer serve up a big spread you see," he said as she saw him planning and plotting in his head. One thing she had learned about him was that he had very good taste from decorating to food.

"We'll be able to find out if it's a girl or a boy," she said. "What? How?" he asked. "They can do something called an ultrasound. It's basically a picture of the baby," she explained. He sat back and shook his head. "Sometimes I think I'll never catch up with all this technology," he laughed. "I have an appointment next week for one. Come with me and we'll find out together, unless you'd rather not know," she said. "Oh, no, I would love to know so we can come up with a name and decorate the nursery," he answered as his mind kept spinning with the thought of it all.

"When shall we marry?" he asked as he traced his finger along her arm. She thought for a moment, "A few weeks from now. I really don't want anything fancy," she replied. "Does that sound alright to you?" "Yes! Come here," he said as he pulled her to him. She sat on his lap as they looked at the calendar choosing a date. "June 6th?" He asked as they checked their respective schedules. "Hmmm, sounds good to me," she responded. He grinned back at her, "You don't know how happy you've made me," he said with a catch in his voice. She leaned over and kissed his cheek while looking into his eyes she saw the love she cherished so much.

The morning of June 6th came with a burst of sunlight and plenty of activity. The caterers came early to set up and prep what they could before that evening. The florist and decorator were outside getting the space ready for the ceremony. The flowers were beautiful shades of white and pink peonies with lilies of the valley tucked amongst them. They were hanging sheer white gauzy draping over the pergola, giving the space an enchanting feel. Emily watched from the kitchen as she waited for the makeup artist and hair stylist to arrive. She saw Paul come out of his studio and begin to chat with the crew. He pointed to the pergola as he instructed them as to how he wanted it to look.

He glanced up and saw Emily watching him. He smiled at her as he began walking to the house. Opening the door, he burst in, "Good morning love!" he said. "Everything looks so beautiful," she said as she gave him a kiss. "Yes, they are doing a great job," he agreed as he poured himself more coffee. He sat down at the table patting his knee for her to sit on. She snuggled his neck as she sat. "I can't believe it's our wedding day," she whispered in his ear.

He turned to her and gave her a kiss on her nose. "I can't wait for the honeymoon," he said. She pulled back a little. "What honeymoon?" she asked. He smiled slyly. "You'll see," he whispered in her ear. She gently bit his lip. "Tell me," she teased. "No, it's a surprise," he said as they heard the doorbell ring. "Saved by the bell," he said as they got up.

It was Sam, Chris and the boys who jumped around excitedly. They were going to be part of the wedding and were thrilled. Stephen would be the ring bearer and Zak would be walking down the aisle with Meghan, the daughter of one of Emily's best friends Valerie, spreading flower petals as they walked.

Sam was Paul's best man and, of course, Chris would be Emily's matron of honor. Chris and Emily hugged as they walked to the back of the house so that Emily could show her the backyard. Stephen and Zak were jumping up and down excitedly trying to get Paul's attention. Sam said, "Okay boys, remember what we talked about, your best behavior today." Paul crouched down to speak to them. "Are you lads ready for today?" he asked. "Yes, yes," they chimed in together. Stephen stepped closer to Paul and handed him a small box. "Well, what do we have here?" Paul said. "It's a present for you!" they said in unison.

Paul stood up as he took the box. "Well, let's sit down over here and I'll open it," he said as he led the boys to the couch. Sam smiled as he watched Paul with the boys. Paul opened the box to find a watch. It had a dark brown leather strap and a gold face with diamond markings. It was very thin and quite elegant. Paul looked up at Sam, "Sam, this is beautiful, thank you so much," he said as he got up and gave Sam a pat on the back.

Turning back to the boys, he picked them up, one in each arm and spun them around, "Thank you too!" he said as they giggled. Just then Emily and Chris came back in as the boys ran to Emily to pull her so she could see Paul's watch. "Wow, that's nice," she said grinning at Paul. Her heart was full that Sam and Chris had welcomed Paul into their little circle. "Well, we thought because time brought Paul to us, it would be an appropriate gift on your special day," Chris said.

As the guests began to arrive, Sam was charged with greeting them and leading them outside where they could have a glass of champagne by the pool before the ceremony. Chris and Emily were getting the final touches done on their makeup and hair when Paul knocked on the door. Chris cracked the door admonishing him not to look at Emily. He laughed, "I won't. Just letting you know everyone is here You have ten minutes."

Emily slid her dress on and stood while Chris helped her adjust it. It was a beautiful off-white silk and lace falling to her bare feet. Her hair was up in a soft bun with baby's breath tucked in here and there. Chris noticed how her eyes were shining with joy. "Paul will not be able to contain himself when he sees you," she said as she gave her friend a hug. "Ready?" Emily took a deep breath and exhaled slowly. "Yes," she whispered.

Chris signaled to Sam that they were ready so that he could get people seated. Paul stood with the officiate, Dorian, a friend of Emily's. He was dead nervous but excited to be marrying the love of his life. Sam soon joined them while music began playing. Zak and Megan were the first to appear with their baskets of petals and excited flushed faces. Stephen, looking quite serious, walked behind them with the pillow that carried their wedding rings.

Chris turned to Emily before they stepped out the door saying, "Emily, I've never been happier for anyone the way I am happy for the two of you. Paul is a wonderful man and Sam and I wish you two the best life has to offer." She gave Emily a kiss on the cheek as she squeezed her hand.

The door opened as Chris walked out first with Emily following. Paul's heart skipped a beat when he saw her. Her bright green eyes were shining as she looked at him. For a brief moment he felt his knees almost buckle as he watched her walking towards him almost as if she were floating. As they stood facing each other, neither could keep their eyes off each other. He reached up and gently stroked her cheek as he whispered, "You are so beautiful," in her ear.

Dorian began by welcoming the guests and then quietly spoke to Paul and Emily. She looked up with a smile. "Paul will begin with the vows he'd written for Emily," she stated. He cleared his throat and began:

"Emily, I knew we were meant for each other the moment our eyes met. I have been madly in love with you ever since. We have been united through time and as time goes on we will grow stronger together. I will make a home for us in my heart. I will give you all I have, all my wishes and, as your husband, all I need in return is the touch of your hand in mine as we sit and watch the sun gently set on the horizon, and whisper to each other our love every day. I can overcome every adversity and heartbreak as long as you are with me."

When he had finished Emily reached up and touched his cheek. The world fell away, and it was just the two of them standing there, lost in each other. Emily looked down at their entwined hands before catching his eyes, she began:

"Paul, it was a mysterious force that brought you to me. When I first met your eyes with mine, I knew my life would never be the same. As your wife, I will love you forever. You have overwhelmed me with your love. To you, I promise to raise you up when you are weary, to hold you and love you for the rest of time."

By the time they both had finished there wasn't a dry eye. Stephen stepped forward and handed Dorian the box on his pillow as he stepped back and took a bow. Laughing as she wiped a tear away, Dorian finished the short ceremony by pronouncing them husband and wife. Paul gently took Emily's face in his hands as he sweetly kissed her lips.

Everyone erupted in wild applause as they walked back down the aisle. Sam and Chris each held the hand of their sons as Chris leaned her head on Sam's shoulder.

Paul had arranged for a beef carving station, lobster tail, vegetables and Hasselback potatoes. The full bar was open to all. Tables had been set up all around the pool and there was a dance floor that Paul had rented. He and Sam had set up chairs and guitars and would play a few songs later in the evening.

Before long it was time for Sam to give his speech. He stood near the table where Emily and Paul sat. After getting the attention of everyone he began:

"I have known Emily for over ten years. She is not only a wonderful coworker, she's a friend to me and my lovely wife Chris. She is family," pausing, "I've always wanted a little sister," he joked. "I have had the pleasure of knowing Paul for 10 months now. He has been a joy to all of us, especially Emily. I could not wish for a kinder or more loving husband for her.

They have shown us what real love can do in times of great adversity."

He put his hand on Paul's shoulder as he continued, "We are rarely given the gift of true love and when it is found it is something to be cherished and nurtured. In watching their love bloom, I have seen their devotion to each other that can only come from deep in the heart. If there is such a thing as soulmates, Emily and Paul are just that. Two souls entwined together through time that nothing can pull apart. As they begin this journey together, I ask that all of you here always lift them in your own hearts. So, to you Emily and Paul, I lift my glass to your happiness and your love."

Emily and Paul stood and gave Sam a hug as the guests all clapped. Emily sat down as Paul continued to stand, saying, "Emily and I thank all of you for sharing this day with us. We have a bit of an announcement we'd like to make." He looked down at Emily and smiled back at her. "This beautiful woman who has consented to put up with me for the rest of her life, has also given me the greatest gift I could ever hope for." He paused for a moment, "In a few short months, we will welcome a son into our lives." There was a stunned silence for a moment before cheers of joy and gasps of happy surprise erupted.

Chris jumped up and went to hug Emily as all her friends gathered around her. Sam gave Paul a clap on the back as they hugged. Mark was the second to congratulate him with a hearty handshake. Paul was beaming as he watched the scene in front of him. Never in his life would he have dreamt he would be this happy.

After the excitement had died down Emily caught Paul's eye. He was standing with Mark and Sam seemingly deep in conversation. When he saw her, he smiled and broke away. They walked towards each other feeling the world fall away as if it were just the two of them there. They met and without speaking took each other's hands and kissed. Emily's head was spinning from the sheer joy of knowing she had married the man she loved more than anything else in the world. Paul let himself feel the ecstasy of the moment, the day and with a whisper in her ear told her of his love.

After everyone had eaten Sam and Paul disappeared for a moment into his studio. Momentarily there was music and lights surrounding the dance floor. Sam announced that the bride and groom would have their first dance as everyone gathered around. They met in the middle of the dance floor and as the music began, they smiled at each other as Paul swung Emily around gracefully. When the song ended he gave her a kiss as the music took on a different feeling meant to get everyone on the dance floor. All the children danced together in a circle as everyone looked on and clapped.

As the evening came to a close, and their guests began to leave, Emily and Paul stood and said their goodbyes. Sam and Chris were the last to leave each carrying one of the boys. As the door closed Paul turned to her and took her hand as he led her to the couch. She sat down as he left to get his surprise gift for her that he had in his office. He laid an envelope in her hands as he sat down next to her.

"What is this?" she asked. Smiling, he replied, "Open it, you'll see." She slid the flap open and took the contents out. It was an itinerary printed on heavy paper. It took her a moment to understand. "Paris," she said barely above a whisper as she looked at him. "I want to take my beautiful wife to the most romantic place I know of. We leave in two days, you see, I've already talked to Sam about you taking time off and he told me it was not a problem. Seems to me, my love, you have not taken a vacation in years!" he finished with a laugh.

Chapter 18

The next morning Emily was rushing about before Chris got there to pick her up. She was going to buy a few things for their trip and asked Paul as she peeked her head into the studio, "Do you want me to get anything for you?" He shook his head no saying, "Remember, I want to get us some things while we're there." "I know, I know, but it will be so expensive!" He laughed at her, she still hadn't gotten used to having enough money not to worry about such things. He got up, put his guitar down, and hugged her as he kissed her forehead. "You two have fun and don't forget I have that meeting this evening."

He had contacted an agent in town after being told by Sam that there was quite a bit of music coming out of Atlanta. He felt he had enough material recorded to begin the process of looking for someone to help him get it out to the public. This was something he had never had to do before as Brian had done it all. He hoped he had done enough research to not look like a fool in the meeting. Sam offered to go along for moral support before Paul had a chance to ask.

Glancing at his watch he saw that it was getting a little late. He went inside to change his clothes deciding on a black suit, white shirt and deep blue tie. As he knotted his tie the doorbell rang. He continued to straighten the tie as he walked to get the door. "Hey, you're looking mighty fine," Sam said as he opened the door. "I don't know how to dress here sometimes, but I figured a suit can never hurt," Paul laughed.

Seeing that Paul was nervous Sam said, "You'll do fine. Just remember this isn't the only agent in town." Looking in the mirror and blowing out his breath, Paul said, "Thanks, let's go!" He picked up the guitar and cd that he had made and locked the door as they left. Pulling into the parking deck, Sam glanced over at Paul and saw a change in his demeanor. Paul had enough experience to know being professional was the most important aspect of any meeting like this. He was ready as far as Sam could tell.

They both waited in the reception area as the secretary called the back offices to let them know James was waiting. She smiled coyly at Paul and asked him if he'd like a cup of coffee or water. "No, thank you," Paul said, seemingly unaware that the young lady was flirting with him.

Sam was always amazed at the way women reacted to Paul, especially when Emily and Chris were not around. Paul had a charisma about him that was hard to ignore, whether male or female. He could charm anyone with his smile. What Sam thought really showed through was Paul's humility. He had a lot that he could be arrogant about, but he never was.

Soon Paul was taken behind closed doors. Sam waited and waited, he needed to stretch his legs so asked the secretary to let James know he would be waiting for him outside. He stopped at the cafe on the ground floor and got a cup of coffee to drink as he sat in the sun waiting. After about 30 minutes he saw Paul through the glass doors walking towards him with his guitar and a grin on his face.

"Hey! Well, how did it go?" Sam asked as he tossed his coffee cup away. "I have an agent!" Paul said excitedly. He was shocked as Sam thought it might take Paul months to get someone to represent him. "Wow! That's fantastic!" He said, clapping Paul on the back, "Tell me more!" "Well, I was dead nervous ya know and when they asked me to play a couple songs my voice cracked at first," he said, laughing, "I'm out of practice! But I got it under control, and they seem to like them." As they walked to the car, Paul turned around excitedly walking backwards as he talked. "Tell you the truth Sam, I didn't think I could do it without John," he said with wonder in his voice.

"Don't mention this to Emily. I want to surprise her while we are on our honeymoon," Paul explained. "What are you going to tell her when we get home?" Sam asked. "I'll say they haven't committed yet," he answered. Paul's eyes were shining as he cheerfully talked about the meeting, "There were five of them there, an older chap and the rest were about my age. I think that may have helped." "I'm really happy for you Paul, really," Sam said sincerely. He had been worried that Paul would be lost without his music. Paul was quiet for a moment, before saying, "There is one problem. I want them to sell the songs and they want me to sing them."

Sam didn't reply at once, stopping at a red light he turned to Paul, "You know that may be a problem with Ramsgate, right? You can't be out there performing in public. It will make them nervous."

Paul thought for a moment, "I hadn't thought of that," he said softly pondering the ramifications. Pulling into the driveway, Sam turned to Paul, "Just think about it. They would have him out there being you, and then you out there being you," he laughed, "It would drive them nuts." Paul laughed, "I suppose it would. Honestly, I'd rather write for others at this point. I've had my share of touring." They saw the light go on in the house, "I guess Emily is home," Paul said with a smile. "Hey, I'll be by to take you both to the airport tomorrow. See you then." Sam said as Paul got out of the car. "Thanks Sam."

Chapter 19

They had slept some on the plane and were determined to stay awake for the rest of the evening to ward off any jet lag. After getting settled in at the hotel they decided to walk to the Champs Elysees which was not far away. They found a wonderful little cafe and stopped and had coffee and cake as they watched the passersby. "Look," Paul said pointing across the street, "Pierre Cardin! That's where we get our suits," he said. Then corrected himself, "Got our suits." She smiled at him and said, "Would you like to go?" "Yes, I could use a new suit or two," he replied with a smile. She looked at him and said, "Why? You just got yourself one." Looking back at her he took her hand in his and said, "I've got an agent Emily. I suppose there will be meetings to go to."

"Why didn't you tell me before now?" She said as she gave him a kiss. "I wanted to surprise you," he chuckled. "They seemed to like my music, but they were trying to convince me to perform them meself." Sam and I agreed that performing wouldn't be a good idea." She nodded her head, "Yes, unfortunately, there may be problems with that," she said with a smile.

"I'm so happy! What's the next step?" she asked. "Well, I need to review the contract so Sam gave me the name of a solicitor and then they will get started getting my music to their artists," he replied. She reached out and touched his hand as she watched his face. She was thrilled that he would be able to continue writing.

Standing up, he took her hand as they strolled down the street window shopping before heading back to Pierre Cardin. He bought four suits and countless shirts and ties after being fitted. She giggled as she watched him with a serious look on his face as he discussed the cut and new styles they had to offer. She knew from watching The Beatles interviews that it was Paul who helped design the matching suits they all wore along with the people at Pierre Cardin. He apparently would sketch what he had in mind and give it to the designers.

That evening after dinner they walked back to their hotel and went to the bar so Paul could have a nightcap. After Paul's drink came, he pulled a small box out of his pocket placing it in front of her. "What's this?" she asked, looking back at him. "Open it and you'll see," he countered with a grin. She slowly opened the lid and inside was a necklace, a pear-shaped emerald surrounded by diamonds. Looking back at him, "It's beautiful!" she said. "I thought it would match your eyes," he said as he took it out of the box and stood to place it around her neck. She reached up and touched it as he sat back down. "It's perfect on you," he said. "I don't know what to say," she breathed. "No need to say a thing. I saw it at Tiffany's when I bought your engagement ring and I knew it was made for you. So, I went back and got it," he responded.

There was a piano playing softly as couples swayed to the music. He stood and held out his hand to her. "Dance with me?" he asked. Taking her in his arms he led her to the dance floor. She looked up into his eyes with an overwhelming feeling of contentment feeling safe and happy, she smiled as she said, "Paul, I want you to hold me like this forever." He kissed her forehead as he whispered, "My sweet Emily, I promise I will never let you go."

The rest of their days in Paris were spent at the Louvre and many of the art galleries that dotted the city. They had chosen two paintings to purchase, one for their living room and the other for their bedroom. Emily was still hesitant about spending so much money, but Paul insisted on the painting for the living room. It was a colorful view of Paris in the spring. It was painted by an up and coming young artist Paul had read about. The cost was beyond Emily's imagination at $25,000 dollars, but she understood as she watched Paul that he really did have a keen eye for art, and she trusted his instincts.

Once he was given the green light to explore his new world, he began devouring newspapers, magazines and books written after 1966. He had been a big part of the Avant Garde movement in the 60's in London. He even helped some of his friends open a bookstore/art gallery they called Indica. He had helped to paint the gallery and build the shelves. He was their first customer before the store even opened going through the books they were storing and would leave them a note of which ones he had taken so they could put them on his account. He even designed the flyers and their logo which was used on their wrapping paper for the store. Little of this was known at the time to his rabid fans. It was something he had worked so hard on, to immerse himself in culture and new trends taking place in the turbulent times he, John, George, and Ringo had helped usher in. He had educated himself in the finer things then and it was apparent now as they roamed the galleries of Paris.

Upon landing in Atlanta, Sam, Chris and the boys were there to greet them. Snatching up Zak and Stephen in his arms, Paul spun them around before placing them back down. "Did you bring us a present?" Stephen asked. "Stephen!" Chris said before Paul interrupted, "Yes, of course we did, but you'll have to wait till we get home to see it." Paul laughed, "I could hardly keep Emily out of the toy sections of the shops we went to. I think she believes the baby will begin building with blocks the moment he's born!" Emily swatted him on the arm as she grinned up at him.

Stephen and Zak were happily playing with the electric cars they had been given as Emily and Paul told Sam and Chris stories of Paris. Chris sighed, "I was there once back when I was in college. It's such a beautiful city." Sam looked over at her and smiled, "I will take you there as soon as we get those freeloaders out of the house," he laughed as he pointed at the boys.

"We've thought of a name for the baby!" Paul said with his eyes shining. "Yes," Emily said as she smiled at Paul. "James Cooper, but we'll call him Cooper," he said with a grin. "Since James is my father's name as well as my real first name. I suppose we should keep up the tradition," he finished.

Chapter 20

After signing the contract with Jim, Paul's new agent, he and Emily were invited to a welcoming party. It was a chance to meet some of the new young artists that might be performing his music. As the day of the party came Emily went out to get her hair and makeup done and Paul worked on perfecting a song he had written that he wanted to give to Jim that evening. He had thought about letting Jim publish the song he had written when he first arrived here. It was called 'Time X 2', it was Emily's song. After thinking about it, he decided to keep it to himself for a while longer. It was too precious for him to allow someone else to sing.

He spent countless hours making sure each song was to his high standards before presenting them to Jim. Emily was impressed by his professionalism and the care he took with each composition. He was enjoying the low profile that he has now which allows him to do the things he loved the most and still have his privacy and sanity. He was toying with the idea of taking lessons to learn how to read and write music.

She was so thankful that he realized he could continue what he loved to do. At first he was very hesitant that maybe he wouldn't be able to do it without John, but he found that he had cultivated enough Avant Garde ideas back in the 60's to succeed in today's market.

Waving at him from the car, Emily gathered her bags and climbed out. "What did you get me?" he jokingly said as he took the bags from her. "I got you a whole new me," she replied. He looked at her as she spun around. Her hair was curled and hung just below her shoulders. Some of it was piled on top of her head in a deconstructed bun. Her makeup was done to perfection as far as he was concerned. He never liked women who wore tons of eye makeup. Hers was done to bring out the green in her eyes. She looked angelic. "God, you look beautiful, but then you always do," he said as he opened the door for her.

Putting the bags down on the kitchen table he turned back to her, "I want to make love to you right now," he murmured in her ear as he took her in his arms. "No way my sweet husband. I just sat for three hours to look like this!" she laughed. He pulled his face into his signature puppy dog look. "Nope, that's not gonna work on me!" she said as she kissed him gently on the cheek. "Well, I suppose I need to go take a cold shower then," was his response. "Yes, go do that or we will be late," she agreed. She went to put on the dress she had gotten. She decided on an emerald green strapless vintage dress she had found at a little shop in Buckhead. She wore her necklace and had a black clutch that went perfectly with it.

Paul put on a black Pierre Cardin suit he had gotten in Paris and matched it with a blue shirt and a purple tie. He was making sure he had everything he needed to bring that night when she walked out into the living room. He turned around as she walked in and let out a slow breath. She looked enchanting, the necklace sparkled in the light and made her eyes look even greener than they were. "You look marvelous," he said gently kissing her forehead. "Thank you," she smiled up at him, "Are you ready?" Checking that he had everything one last time, "Yes I am," he said. "I think the car is here," he added as he noticed the limo pull up in the driveway.

They arrived at the venue and Emily and Paul stood for a moment outside as she adjusted his tie. "By the way, you look beautiful too," she teased him. He took her hand as they made their way inside. Before they had barely gotten through the door, Jim was there to greet them. "James! The man of the hour!" Still getting used to his public name, Paul was somewhat taken aback. Emily squeezed his hand before letting go of it. "Jim, this is my wife, Emily," Paul said as he held his hand at her back. "Nice to meet you Jim," she said with a smile. Jim shook her hand before giving her a small kiss on her cheek. "A pleasure to meet you Emily," he answered. "James, I have some people for you to meet. Why don't you both get a drink and then the fun can begin," Jim said as he led them to the bar.

Jim ushered Paul away soon after leaving Emily to mill about the room before she found a chair to sit in. She had forgotten how much she hated wearing high heels. She smiled to herself as she watched Paul while Jim introduced him to some other guests. She found it so amusing how people who meet him for the first time with a look of distant recognition. Lost in her thoughts she hadn't noticed a man that had sat down near her. His clothes were rather out of place and he had an edgy hard demeanor. He was staring at her as she turned to look at him.

His eyes moved from her face to her body lingering on her breasts. She thought right away he was quite blatant and felt slightly uncomfortable. She began to get up to go get another sparkling water. "Don't leave baby I just got here," the man said. Resisting the urge to roll her eyes at him she responded with a smile as she tipped her glass, "Need a refill." As she stood he reached out and stroked her arm with his finger. She silently cringed at his touch but without saying a word she walked away as he chuckled.

She stood at the bar as the bartender got her drink ready and could feel someone standing near her. The man had followed her to the bar. "Double vodka on the rocks," he said to the bartender before turning to her. "You should have a real drink, it might loosen you up," he said to her with a sneer. She looked at the young man pouring the vodka for him before replying, "I'm sorry, you seem to think I am interested in talking to you. Let me clear that up, I'm not." She said as she turned away. He laughed as she walked away. She was a little shaken thinking he was a rude, cocky man and she wanted to get away from him.

She looked around the room for Paul before a young lady struck up a conversation with her. "Are you a performer?" the girl asked with a hopeful look on her face. Emily smiled at her, "No, I'm here with my husband. Do you sing?" she asked. The girl looked down before answering, "Yes, I was hoping my agent would hook me up with some new material tonight. He said he had a guy who writes songs, but I haven't met him yet." Emily smiled warmly at her, "I'm sure you will," she reassured her. "I don't like these kinds of parties. I get so nervous and never know who I should talk to," the girl said in a small voice.

Emily thought for a moment, "What type of music do you sing?" she asked. "Oh, I can sing just about anything, but I do like ballads and love songs," she replied. Emily smiled at her when she noticed the man headed their way with a leer on his face. Sighing to herself she thought how odd it was that some men just didn't seem to know when to back off.

She patted the girl on the arm before saying, "My husband writes music," she whispered as she pointed to Paul across the room. "I've got to find the powder room. I'm trying to escape from someone who seems to be a relentless nuisance," she said with a smile and a wink. She turned and walked away just as the man was almost near them. Sitting down in the powder room she freshened up her makeup and made sure her hair was still looking presentable, she sighed as she got up to go find Paul.

She opened the door to find the man standing there waiting for her. She was angry now, as she tried to get past him he blocked her way. "Hey, I'm just trying to get to know you better baby," he said with a sly grin. "Please just leave me alone," she said as she once again began walking away. He grabbed her arm, causing her to drop her clutch. "I'm going to say this again. Leave me alone," she said as she pulled away and reached down to pick it up. "Why are you being such a bitch?" he asked.

He reached for her again as Emily felt an arm around her waist. "I've been looking for you love," Paul said as he glared at the man. "Is there a problem here?" Paul asked never taking his eyes off the man's face.

Paul gently moved Emily behind him. "No, no, I…" the man stammered. "It seems you have a problem with taking no for an answer," Paul said as he continued to block the man from leaving. Emily touched Paul on the back hoping he would just let the man pass by and not make a scene. "Emily, Jim would like us to join him for a bit," Paul said, still glaring at the man.

He turned and took Emily's hand leading her away. She could feel him shaking with anger. He leaned over to her and whispered in her ear as he pointed to the young girl she had been speaking with, "She had the good sense to let me know what was happening," he said as he squeezed her hand. "Thank you," she said, "He was really beginning to scare me." He stopped and looked at her before kissing her forehead, "I'm sorry, I should have been more attentive," he said as he touched her cheek with the back of his hand.

Jim was standing with the young girl as he searched the room for some of the other artists who were there to meet with Paul. "This way everyone," Jim said as Paul and Emily neared the group huddled around him. "I can't find Brad," Jim said under his breath as he led the group to a room off the main area. Filing in everyone took a seat or stood near the back of the room, "I'll be right back," Jim said, "I'm missing someone."

The group all chatted with each other as they waited for Jim to return. The door opened and Jim came back in with Brad at his side, it was the man who had been bothering Emily. As he scanned the room his eyes came to rest on her and Paul. Brad's face went ashen when he realized what was happening. Jim cleared his throat and held his hand out to Paul, "Everyone, this is James Mohin and his wife Emily. He is a fantastic songwriter and I believe that each of you may benefit from his considerable talent."

Emily was trying very hard to stifle her giggle when she looked at Brad, he was gulping his vodka like it was water. Paul glanced down at her with a knowing smile before saying, "Hello everyone. I do hope to get to know each of you a little better as time goes on so we can work together to find the best material that suits you." His eyes landed on Brad as he finished by adding, "Well, most of you." This made Emily turn around to keep from laughing out loud. Luckily, as she did, the girl she had talked to earlier was standing right behind her. Emily whispered to her, "I'm Emily. Thank you for letting my husband know what was happening. What's your name?" The girl looked at her with beaming eyes, "Rylee Taylor, and you're welcome."

As Jim took Paul around the room to introduce him, Emily stood and waited for them to get to Rylee. Jim said, as they drew closer, "James, this is Rylee. She is a fantastic singer and I believe your material would work very well for her." Paul put out his hand to her, "Yes, I believe we spoke briefly. It's very nice to meet you Rylee." "Nice meeting you too," she said as she looked at Paul and then back at Emily.

As Jim turned to introduce Paul to Brad, Emily and Rylee stood watching, glancing at each other trying to stifle laughter. "James, this is Brad. He is the lead singer in a band called 'Chaos Gods.' They have been performing around Atlanta for about two years now." Paul eyed Brad as he offered his hand, "Ah, interesting name," he said with a smirk before turning away.

Emily touched Rylee's shoulder and gave her a wink as Paul led her away to the other side of the room. Brad sat down and sulked with a sneer on his face as Paul made the rounds talking to all the performers with a smile on his face. After everyone had met him, Jim asked Paul to sing a few of his songs for everyone. Paul settled in on a chair as they all gathered around. He sang two beautiful ballads that he had just finished writing. His smooth, mellow voice filled the room as people stood transfixed. When he finished everyone applauded as he put down the guitar and smiled back at the group. Emily was so proud of him as he gave them all a shy smile.

After chatting with everyone for a while, Paul nodded at her across the room. She smiled back as she walked towards him past Brad who continued to sulk in the corner. Jim walked with Paul towards Emily nearing Brad, Jim stopped and said to Brad, "Did you get a chance to talk to James, Brad?" Brad looked up at

Paul and said, "Yeah, we talked earlier." Jim stood waiting for him to continue but Brad got up and walked towards the bar for another vodka. Jim shook his head and said, "he's got talent and too much attitude." Paul nodded with a smile and said, "I've always thought a little attitude was a good thing, but he seems to have a chip on his shoulder as well." Jim nodded in agreement. Paul took Jim aside before they left as Emily waited in the limo watching them talk as they stood by the door.

"Jim, I don't want Brad to use my material. He was incredibly aggressive with Emily earlier. He followed her to the restroom and grabbed her as she tried to leave," Paul said sternly. Jim was taken aback, "I know he can be a loose cannon but that is unfortunate. I am sorry James," he said. Paul nodded as he paused for a moment. "I am impressed with Ms. Taylor. Emily spoke with her quite a lot this evening and she was also taken with her. I have a couple of tunes that I think would work for her. Can you set up a meeting?" "Yes, of course, she's a good kid and has raw talent." "Good, I look forward to working with her, thanks. And thanks for the entire evening. We had a great time," he said as he shook Jim's hand.

Getting into the limo, Paul sat back with a sigh as he loosened his tie, I forgot how much I dislike those things," he said. Emily laughed, "You're out of practice is all." "I made sure Brad was out and Rylee was in," he said with a sly smile. "Oh good!" Emily exclaimed, "I really like her, and she did have the insight to get you when she saw what Brad was up to." Paul took her hand in his, "I'm sorry I was distracted and didn't see what you were dealing with. I am a shoddy husband," he said with a frown. Emily leaned over and kissed his lips softly. "You are the best husband, he was an ass," she finished. Paul laughed, "Emily, such language!" Just as he had said the first day they had met.

Chapter 21

Months later, Paul and Rylee were working closely together refining the songs he had written for her. She would come over and rehearse in the studio with Paul and her back up band. Emily would make lunch and they would all eat around the pool, joking and laughing. Emily was counting the days until Cooper decided to make his appearance. He was already late according to her due date and she felt as if she would burst at any moment.

Late one afternoon Paul was working alone out in the studio when Emily's water broke. She immediately felt the first real pain. She had been having small contractions all morning, but she hadn't mentioned them to Paul. She did not want him to worry. She cleaned up and changed her clothes before walking out to the studio. She was near a lounge chair as a contraction hit her that made her double over. Paul saw her and rushed outside, "Emily, are you alright?" He asked as he helped her sit down. "It's time," was all she could manage to get out before another pain hit. He carefully guided her to the car and ran into the house to grab the bag they had packed.

Getting into the car, he started the engine and quickly backed out as she had another contraction. "Oh God, Emily, how far apart are they?" he asked. She took a deep breath as the pain passed, "I feel like they are less than four minutes," she answered weakly. He reached over and held her hand, telling her to squeeze it if she needed to when the next one hit. "I'm sorry, did I hurt you?" she laughed slightly when she noticed his fingers were turning white. "No, I'm fine," he said as he shook his hand laughing. Thankfully, the hospital was close and there was very little traffic. As they wheeled Emily into the ER, Paul grabbed the bag and ran to catch up.

James Cooper Mohin was born February 3, 2021, weighing 8 pounds and 11 ounces. With a full head of dark brown hair and huge brown eyes, like his father. On the day they brought Cooper home Paul entertained Emily, Sam and Chris with a story about when he was born. "Me Da had given an interview that went like this. 'Paul was all red like a piece of raw meat, he just kept squawking and could only open one eye.' He said he had gone home and just cried and cried because I was so ugly. But then Da said, 'He looked better the next day and turned out to be quite a lovely baby boy.'" This made everyone roar with laughter at the thought of 'The cute Beatle', having been an ugly baby.

Cooper had a sweet disposition and began sleeping through the night very early. He was their joy. Paul began playing music or would sing to him early on. It seemed to calm him when he was in a rare fussy mood. Emily was amazed that Paul pitched in from the beginning, changing diapers, feeding and dressing him. He didn't seem to mind the 24-hour feeding schedule. He would get up and bring Cooper to Emily in the night while she was breastfeeding. He'd then soothe him back to sleep before putting him back down in his crib. Just as she had told him when they met little Johnny on their walk by the playground, he was a good father and he adored Cooper beyond words.

After Cooper was born she took time off and began working part-time until he got a little older. They were lucky enough to have the money and time to raise him without having to employ a nanny or send him to a daycare center. Paul was horrified at the thought of all those babies being looked after by just a few caretakers. Paul would often sneak off to check on Cooper as he slept, watching him closely, lightly touching his back with a gentle stroke. She would watch him with Cooper and was amazed at the love in his eyes when he looked at his son.

As Cooper grew up one of his favorite activities was to 'sneak' away from Emily and dash to Paul's studio. Paul would always pretend he didn't see him as Cooper would giggle and hide in plain sight. "I know Coop must be around here somewhere," Paul would say as he pretended to search for him. When Paul would finally 'discover' him hiding behind an amp or under the desk, Cooper would keel over in fits of laughter. Paul would pick him up, throw him over his shoulder and carry him back to the house passed the pool where he always threatened to throw him in. They would have lunch together before Cooper's nap and then while the house was quiet Paul and Emily would spend the afternoon together.

Cooper not only looked just like his father, but he had the same bright happy personality as Paul. Emily often jokingly said the only thing about Cooper that was any part of her were his feet. He could charm the socks off anyone which was apparent anytime they all went out in public. Little girls at the park would run up to him and hug him or God forbid, give him a kiss on his cheek. He would run crying to Paul or Emily that the girls were biting his face. Paul would have to stifle his laughter as Cooper would explain to him in his tiny voice the horrors of girls kissing him.

Women in the grocery store would ooh and aah over Cooper's long eyelashes until looking at Paul and realizing where they came from. Then more often than not, would begin flirting with him, sometimes right in front of Emily. She would stand back and make silly faces at Paul as women would fawn over him.

"You shouldn't do that," he chuckled as they left the store after one such encounter. "And why is that?" she asked with a smile. "Because, you may make me laugh and those women will think I'm laughing at them!" he replied with a grin. "Good!" she retorted. "The nerve of them flirting with you while I'm standing right there!" she joked. Another woman may have been jealous or insecure with the attention he sometimes received, but she knew how strong their love was.

Chapter 22

As they sat out by the pool one morning while Cooper was splashing in the shallow end Paul received a phone call. He answered and stood to walk back to his studio. Emily watched him through the window as he seemed to become more and more agitated. Seeing him disconnect the call, he stood for a moment before rejoining them outside. "Who was that?" she asked. He didn't answer right away but looked at her across the table as he said, "Jim." "Well, what did he say?" she asked when he hadn't continued.

"He wants me to meet with someone, he wouldn't tell me who it was at first, then he said it was," he continued as he looked over at her, "Richie." Her eyes widened as she realized what he was saying. "What?" was all she said. "He said that Ritchie had heard some of me songs and wanted to meet me," he replied.

"Da! Watch me," Cooper shouted as he put his face in the water. "Wow! Coop, what a big lad," Paul praised him. He looked back at her shaking his head, "He said Richie felt a connection to me music," he finished. A shadow fell across his face as he sat back still shocked by the call.

"Mommy, Da come swim!" Cooper shouted them out of their thoughts. "It's time for you to eat breakfast my little man," Emily said in response. Cooper climbed out of the pool and she wrapped him in a large towel before he sat down. "I want a nana," Cooper said as he grabbed a banana and handed it to Paul to peel for him. Emily smiled to herself as she watched the two of them chat as Cooper ate his banana. "Da, I play with Zak we made a fort and we hided from Stephen!" "You did?" Paul responded as he tickled Cooper's tummy. "I done," Cooper said as he put the banana down on his plate. "No, you're not I still see a banana!" Paul teased.

She could watch the two of them for hours. "Coop, come here," she said as he climbed down from the chair. She pulled him up on her lap as she broke off a piece of the banana for him. "Mommy, I done," he said again. "One more bite," she whispered in his ear. "Da, we swim now! He said with his mouth full of banana." "Okay, Da will go put on his suit," Paul answered as he leaned over and kissed Emily.

After taking a shower and dressing she walked into the kitchen. Looking out the window she saw Paul laying in one of the lounge chairs with Cooper on his chest, both were fast asleep. She quietly slipped out the door and took a picture, it was perfect. Paul had his finger to his mouth the habit he still had, and Cooper was sucking his thumb as his other arm was wrapped around Paul's waist. The love between the two of them was beyond what she could have hoped for. That picture would eventually hang in Paul's studio.

Waking to Cooper squirming to get down Paul kissed the top of his head and said, "Where's Mummy?" "I find her!" Cooper answered gleefully as he ran to the house. Emily was reading in the living room when she heard the door open and Cooper yelling for her, "Mommy, Mommy, we awake!" She laughed, "I see that!" Paul stood smiling at them. "Come here Coop, let's get you into some clothes," Paul said as he took his little hand in his. "I'll do that sweetheart, you go shower," she said as she kissed him and snatched Cooper up in her arms.

Paul was thinking about the phone call he had received earlier as he remembered his need to see Richie and his brother Michael when he first arrived here. He knew he could never see them, but he wished he could speak to his old friend one last time. He would call Jim back later and let him know about his decision. Emily looked worried when he told her about the call, she didn't say anything, but he knew he couldn't put his family in danger to satisfy himself. He also wanted to let Sam know what had occurred as it was best to be up front about these things.

After lunch when Cooper went down for his nap and Emily had gone to the grocery store Paul called Sam. "Sam, I have something to discuss with you. Are you free to stop by?" "Yes, give me a few minutes and I'll be there. Can I ask what it's about?" Sam said. "We can talk when you get here, it will be easier to explain," Paul answered. Emily pulled her car into the driveway as Paul went out to help her carry the bags in. "Sam's coming by. I wanted to let him know about the call this morning," Paul said as they walked into the kitchen.

She was happy that he was reaching out to Sam. She went to him pulling him close to her, "I love you," she whispered in his ear as she kissed his cheek making her way to his lips. "Mmmm, I love you too, do we have time?" He asked in a husky voice as he nibbled her earlobe. Just then they heard Sam pull into the driveway. Snapping his fingers, "Later," he said with his wink. She smiled to herself after he walked outside. She still got goosebumps every time he touched her.

"What's up?" Sam said as they walked to Paul's studio. "I got a call from Jim this morning. He's had a request from Ringo's people to set up a meeting with me," Paul answered quietly. Sam looked at him, "Why? Did he give a reason?" "He only said Richie fancied my music. And that he'd like to meet me that's all I know," Paul answered. "Well, you know we've already explained…." Sam began. "I know, I turned it down, but I wanted you to know. I won't do anything to endanger my family," he said adding with a shrug, "Jim is not at all happy with me."

Sam stood up as he thought about all they had done to be incredibly careful about keeping Paul's picture out of the public eye which was not an easy task in this day and age. Especially with the pressure from Paul's agent. Jim had wanted to use social media to promote Paul's work. "I find it curious. I think I'll look into this if you don't mind," he said. "No, I don't. Please do," Paul responded. Just then Emily knocked on the door, "I'm taking Cooper for a haircut," she said adding, "Everything Okay?"

"Yes love, Sam's going to dig a little deeper, but not to worry," Paul responded as she leaned down and kissed him goodbye.

Sam looked over at Paul after Emily and Cooper left. Paul was gazing out the window when he turned to Sam, "I'm thinking about writing a score for a new show on the telly," he remarked. "They tell me it's about the 60's. I suppose I have an inside track on that," he laughed. Sam looked at him and agreed with a nod, "Yes, I would suppose so. Do you know what it's called?" he asked. "I've got it written down here, let me see," he said as he looked at the notes strewn over his desk. "London Life," he answered. "Hmm, interesting they would choose you," Sam said as he made a mental note to look into that as well.

Sam smiled as he said, "I'm being promoted to Director next month." "Sam, that's wonderful news. Congratulations!" Paul said as he gave him a slap on the back. "I think Emily should take my position when she finishes her jump coming up," Sam added. Paul looked over at Sam, "What jump is that?" he asked. "Oh, she hasn't mentioned it yet, sorry," Sam replied. "No, she hasn't," Paul said with a frown. "When is it?" Paul asked.

"I shouldn't have said anything, I'm sure she'll tell you all about it. It's still a couple of weeks away. She's probably just waiting for the final analysis to be completed," Sam said. Paul took a sip of his beer as he asked, "What is the jump for?" Sam looking slightly uncomfortable said, "Why don't you let her tell you about it Paul. I'm sure she will when it's all finalized."

They chatted a while as they sat by the pool sipping their beers. Sam had introduced Paul to craft beer and now when they got together, one or the other had a new one to try. Emily pulled in and Cooper was beside himself to show off his haircut. "Da, Da, look at me!" He yelled as he jumped out of the car running towards Paul and Sam. Paul got up and scooped him up in his arms and swung him around. "You look very handsome," Sam said as he patted Cooper's head. "Da, I got sucker!" "Well that's nice," Paul responded with a laugh.

"He got the sucker for sitting still long enough for her to make some sense out of all that hair," she said as she gave Sam a hug. "I had better head home. Chris is going to a meeting tonight so I'm in charge of the boys," Sam said as he stood and stretched his legs. "Paul, I'll look into that call and let you know," he said as he walked towards his car.

Turning his attention to Cooper, Paul said, "Alright Coop let's go inside and make dinner." When Paul would cook dinner, he liked to have Cooper there to 'help' him. Cooper was very good at sitting on the counter next to Paul and being in charge of wiping up any spills that Paul made. Emily laughed as she watched Paul 'accidently' spill the milk so Cooper could clean it up. "Da, you so messy," Cooper said with a giggle. Paul looked over at Emily and winked. "I know, that's why I need you here!" Paul said. These were the moments Emily held on to.

After Emily got Cooper to bed she walked out to the living room to find Paul sitting on the couch having a drink looking preoccupied. "Emily, why haven't you told me you're going to do a jump?" he asked as he looked up at her. She sat down next to him picking up the wine he had poured for her. "Sam told you?" she asked quietly. "Yes, I think he was a bit taken aback that you hadn't mentioned it to me," Paul replied, adding, "and so am I."

She sighed and touched his arm as she said, "It's not finalized yet I was planning on telling you when I finished the analysis. With Sam's promotion, I feel like I need one more jump before I apply for the position he's leaving." Paul, slightly exasperated, said, "You didn't tell me that either." "I'm sorry baby, things have been so busy lately. I really wasn't meaning to keep it from you," she answered.

He stood and began pacing, "Emily, I'm not sure I'm comfortable with you jumping any longer. Especially now that we have Cooper." She looked up at him and said, "Paul, it's my job. I can't stop working because we have a child." He looked back at her before he refilled his glass. "I don't want you to be in danger, you see. Where are you going for this jump?" She took a deep breath, "New York on 9/11," she answered in a whisper. Paul had read and watched documentaries about that day commenting often how horrific it was.

He stood for a moment in shock. Fear clamped his heart as he remembered watching the films from that day. He was agitated as he sat down in the chair across from her, "Are you bloody kidding me Emily?" "Paul, it's alright…" He interrupted, "No, it's not! God, what are you bloody thinking?" She looked over at him, "I have to do this jump Paul. I'll be fine," she said quietly trying to counter the anger she could see rising in him.

Exasperated he said under his breath, "That's rubbish Emily," he got up and walked outside for a smoke.

Emily waited for him to come back in but when he didn't she looked out and realized he was in his studio. Waiting a while longer as she straightened up the kitchen, she decided to head off to the bedroom hoping he would be more understanding when he came back inside.

She checked on Cooper before changing into her nightgown. After a while when Paul hadn't come back inside, she made her way to the studio. She could hear him playing the piano as she opened the door. Watching him for a minute before she went and sat down on the bench next to him.

She put her hand gently on his knee as he continued to play for a moment longer. He stopped as he lay his hand on hers. Turning to her, "Do you remember when I was acclimating, and we had our disagreement?" He asked. "Yes," she said quietly. "I was lost without you then. I was terrified. I can't lose you. I don't think I would be able to carry on," he finished in a whisper.

"You have to trust me sweetheart. I wouldn't do it if I thought I'd be in danger," she said gently. "I'm sorry I didn't mention it before. I was afraid you'd be upset, and I was right," she said trying to cajole him out of his serious mood. When he didn't return her smile, she took his chin and kissed him gently on the lips. "It's my job, and I really want this promotion," she said. "But Emily, we don't need the money and…" She stopped him by placing her fingers on his lips, "It's not about the money. I need to work. I love my job," she countered.

"But Emily, why 9/11?" he asked. She began, "It's a contracted jump. I don't know the reason why, but we are doing everything we can to make sure I am well away from the destruction…" He interrupted, "*That* does not make me feel any better," he said. She smiled and kissed him gently saying, "Come to bed, it's late."

After locking up the house he closed the bedroom door quietly. She walked towards him slowly and began to take his t-shirt off over his head. She ran her fingers over his chest as she kissed him. "You're trying to distract me aren't you?" he murmured. "Yes," she answered with a smile as she unzipped his jeans. "It's not going to work, but we can give it a go," he whispered.

Afterwards, she snuggled close to him, placing her hand on his chest. "I promise I will be safe. You must trust me, and Sam. We know what we're doing," she said quietly. He sighed, "I do trust you both, but I am allowed to worry, aren't I? You would, wouldn't you?" he said as he kissed her forehead. "Yes, I suppose I would," she admitted. He wrapped his arms around her as they fell asleep.

The next evening Paul was at a rehearsal downtown with Rylee, it was getting late and Cooper was beginning to get grumpy from sleepiness. Emily read him a story as he sucked his thumb, taking it out of his mouth every now and then sleepily asking for his Da. Finally, she laid down with him on their bed to get him to go to sleep. She gently stroked his forehead as his eyes finally fluttered closed. She was exhausted and closed her eyes for a moment.

She woke to Paul picking up Cooper to put him in his room. Dragging herself off the bed, she changed into her nightgown. Paul was standing in the bathroom unbuttoning his shirt as she came up behind him and put her arms around his waist. He turned around and jokingly said, "I'm not sure how I feel about coming home to you in bed with another man." She said as she yawned, "It was the only way to get him to sleep." Paul laughed, "He wore you out, did he?" "Yes," she replied with a tired smile.

She asked, "How was rehearsal?" "It was good actually, they are going to record tomorrow," he answered as he spread kisses across her face. Paul had been working closely with Rylee, especially after she exploded onto the charts with one of his songs a year ago. He continued, "I couldn't concentrate though. I just wanted to be home making love to my beautiful wife." She looked at him seductively, "Is that right?" "Yes ma'am," he said huskily as he led her to their bed.

They held each other afterward and talked about their plans for the next day. "I don't have to be at the studio tomorrow. I want to give Rylee space without me hovering about," he laughed, "We can take Cooper out for the day."

As the sun crept into their room, Cooper came along with it. He climbed onto the bed as they both moved away from each other to make room for him. "Da, I hungry," he said as he poked Paul's eye with his finger. Paul pretended to still be asleep as Emily stifled a giggle. "Da! Da! Wake up, I hungry," Cooper said again. Paul suddenly opened his eyes and began tickling Cooper. "Da, stop!" He squealed in delight. Emily reached over to protect him from the tickling, "Mommy, Da tickling me," Cooper said as he tried to catch his breath. Laughing, she said, "Da needs his tummy tickled, let's get him!" Both Cooper and Emily attacked Paul until they all fell back on the pillows gasping for breath.

Paul got up grabbing Cooper and lifted him up high before he dropped him back on the bed. He scrambled back up into Paul's arms saying, "Again Da, again!" Emily got out of bed before Paul picked him up, again throwing him in the air before Cooper landed on the bed in a fit of laughter. "Alright you two, come on, let's go have breakfast," Emily said as she walked out the door. As she made the coffee and fixed breakfast she smiled at the joy she felt in her heart. Paul and Cooper joined her as Cooper stood on Paul's feet as Paul took big steps into the kitchen, Cooper giggling away. She gave Paul a kiss as she passed by them.

"Coop, do you want to go to the zoo today?" Paul asked as they all sat down. "You can see lots of animals!" "Can we see monkey?" Cooper asked. Emily looked at Paul with a smile, maybe we can ride the Ferris wheel at Centennial Park." "What Ferris wheel, Mommy?" Cooper asked. Paul said, "It's a surprise!"

After a day of elephants, giraffes, monkeys and Ferris wheel rides, they stopped to get dinner on the way home. Cooper fell asleep in the car, so Paul carried him into the house and put him to bed. Coming out of his room, Paul saw Emily sitting on the couch looking slightly ill. "My love, are you okay?" He asked as he sat down next to her. "Yes, I think so, just too much junk food I guess," she replied.

He gave her a hug and kissed her forehead. "Come here," he said quietly as she laid her head on his chest. Taking a deep breath, she sat up and looked at him. "What is it love?" he said. "Actually," pausing for a moment, "I think I might be pregnant," she said softly. "What?! Really! Oh, Emily!" He exclaimed as he held her tightly. "I'm not sure yet, but I can get a test tomorrow to find out," she replied with a smile. "Are you happy?" she asked as she kissed him. "I'm dead chuffed!" he answered.

The next morning while Paul and Cooper were swimming, Emily went to the drug store to pick up a pregnancy test. As she stood in the aisle deciding which one to get, she felt someone next to her. Glancing up, she saw it was Rylee. "Emily! Are you?" Rylee said with a huge grin.

Emily gave her a hug, "We'll see, but I sure feel like it," she said. Rylee was beaming with happiness, "Oh!, I hope so, Cooper needs a playmate!" She exclaimed. "James tells me you're recording today!" Emily said. "Yes, I just needed to pick up a few things. I'm on my way there now!" Rylee replied. "Good luck honey!" Emily said as she picked up one of the test kits. "Thanks, Em. Let me know how the test turns out!" Rylee said as she turned to leave.

She pulled into the driveway and watched as she saw Paul and Cooper heading into the house. Paul stopped as Cooper yelled, "Mommy!" As he wiggled out of Paul's arms running to Emily. "My baby!" Emily yelled back at Cooper with a laugh. He jumped into Emily's arms saying, "I big boy Mommy!" Giggling, she replied as she hugged him close, "Yes, you are!" Paul walked up to them and snatched Cooper away. "Time to get dressed Coop," he said as he winked at Emily. "And you go do the test because I can barely stand the suspense!"

Paul and Cooper were still in Cooper's room when she finished the test. She walked down the hallway and stood in the doorway watching them as they played with Cooper's car collection. Paul looked up at her, "Well?" he said. She grinned at him and nodded yes.

He was up off the floor in a flash, he picked her up swinging around, "I love you, I love you, I love you!" he repeated. "Well, you helped," she gasped. "Da, why you dancing with Mommy?" he laughed as he ran to them. Paul scooped him up as he continued to hold Emily in his other arm.

Walking to the bed, they all sat down as Paul put Cooper on his lap. "Coop, how would you like to be a big brother?" Paul asked. Cooper looked up at his father with his big brown eyes as he sucked his thumb. Paul continued, "You know that Stephen is Zak's big brother? Well, you are going to be a big brother too!" Cooper thought for a moment before saying, "Stephen boss Zak and me around when we playing." Emily and Paul laughed, "Yes, he does, but now you get to be the boss," Emily said. Cooper wiggled off of Paul's lap and began dancing around the room, "Yea, I be boss!"

Paul turned to Emily taking her face into his hands, "God, I love you, Emily. I am so happy!" He said with tears in his eyes. "I love you too," she said as she wiped a tear away from his cheek and kissed him gently.

After lunch Cooper went down for his nap and Emily sat outside under the pergola sipping an iced tea and reading while she listened to Paul in his studio. He was finishing up a song for Rylee and as usual was fine tuning it to perfection. She glanced up from her book as she heard him come near. He sat down and looked over at her with a smile, "Emily, I don't want to keep bringing this up, but since you are going to have a baby, do you think it is wise to do this jump?"

She looked at him and considered her answer, "Paul, in this time, women have to do everything men do, and more, in order to get ahead or even stay in the game. If I back out because I'm pregnant, well, that just wouldn't look good. And besides if I get a promotion, I won't be jumping anymore."

He sat back with a heavy sigh, "I'm going on record here. I'm not happy about this," he said. She reached over and took his hand in hers, "I know you're not, but I promise you nothing will happen to me. I'll be in a safe place for a short period of time," she finished.

She fully understood his viewpoint, she had to constantly remind herself that he came from a very different time where women usually only worked when they needed to just like his mother had done.

She smiled as she leaned over and kissed his cheek. He looked back at her and said, "I'm really trying to be understanding Emily, but this jump to that place terrifies me." She watched his face and saw the concern there, "I wouldn't do it if I thought I'd be in danger," she said.

They heard Cooper rustling about in his room. Emily stood up, "I'll go get him. You know he'll want you to swim with him," she said with a smile as she touched his shoulder. He looked up at her and held her hand briefly before kissing it, "Ah, you're right, I'll go get me swimsuit on," he replied. Cooper was already up and trying to get the back door open when they got there. Paul scooped him up in his arms and said, "Lets swim!" Cooper squealed with delight as he wiggled down and ran to his room to change. "Wait for me!" Emily called as she ran after him.

Paul pulled his phone out of his pocket and laid it on the counter noticing a message from Sam. 'Call me when you get a chance.' He punched in Sam's number and waited, "Hey Paul, do you have a minute to talk?" Sam said as he answered. "Yes, what's up?" "I've been feeling bad about letting it slip that Emily was going to do a jump. I hope I didn't create any problems there," Sam said.

"No Sam, we've talked about it. She insists it will be safe. And she told me she would like to take over your position," Paul said. "Yes, I don't think she has to worry about it too much though. Word through the grapevine is she'll be the next Supervisor," Sam replied. Paul smiled, "Does she know that?" he asked. Sam answered, "Not officially. She is working by the book making this jump. She will have it in the bag when she does."

Paul trusted Sam and of course Emily, but knowing Sam was behind the jump made him feel better about it and vowed to himself to try to stop worrying. "We are about to take a swim, are you all free tonight? Come on over and we can grill out some burgers," Paul said. "Will do!" replied Sam.

Walking into Cooper's room, he said, "I've invited Sam, Chris and the boys over for dinner. Do we have meat to make burgers?" he asked. "Emily looked up and nodded, "I think so, I'll check," she answered. "I thought we could tell them about the baby," he said smiling as he left the room to change. He heard Cooper running down the hall as Emily called after him, "Wait, Coop, Da's not ready yet."

Emily checked the freezer and took out the meat. "Cooper, do you want some juice?" she asked. "Yeah, yeah, yeah, apple!" he sang imitating the way his Da would sing it. Just then Paul walked in and picked up Cooper as he took the juice box from Emily.

"I think I'll run to the store and pick up some corn on the cob to go with the burgers, and ice cream for the boys," Emily said as she continued searching the refrigerator.

With Cooper still in one arm, Paul reached over and gave Emily a kiss as he turned to head out the door. Emily felt a little dizzy and sat down at the kitchen table. She remembered feeling this way when she was pregnant with Cooper. Clearing her head, she got up and went outside. "I'll be right back," she called, "Do you need anything?" she asked Paul. "No, love," he replied as he picked Cooper up and threw him in the air again, catching him before Cooper's head went under water.

When she got home, Paul and Cooper were sitting on a lounge chair. It looked to her like Cooper was telling Paul a very long involved story she thought with a chuckle. Paul would nod his head every now and then as they realized she was home, Cooper jumped up and ran towards the car, "Mommy, I tell Da story!" Cooper said as he reached her and tugged her hand, "Come sit Mommy, I tell you story too!"

She smiled at him as she asked, "What's your story about?" as she sat down next to Paul as he pulled Cooper onto his lap. "It about a bad man who take Da away," he said breathlessly. She looked over at Paul with a frown. "Oh, that sounds like a sad story," she said. "It Okay Mommy, you get him back from bad man," Cooper said as he squirmed down from the chair. "I hungry!" he said as he ran to the door.

She turned to Paul as he got up to get the bags out of the car, "What in the world was that all about?" she asked. "I don't know, he said he had a dream and then told me that story," he replied, shaking his head.

Emily held the door for Paul and found Cooper sitting at the kitchen table, "I hungry Mommy!" he said again. "Okay, what do you want for lunch?" she asked him as she ruffled his hair. "Pealow bullow and jelly," he answered. She smiled at the way he said, 'peanut butter' and began making the sandwich while Paul put the groceries away.

"Sweetie, what do you want?" she asked Paul. "I'll have pealow bullow and jelly too!" he answered with a chuckle. After she got Cooper down for his nap, they sat outside and had their coffee by the pool. Paul reached over and touched her hand, "How are you feeling?" She smiled at him, "Not too bad, hopefully I'll breeze through this one like I did with Cooper," she replied. He returned her smile, "I hope so my love," he said.

They sat quietly, holding hands enjoying the soft breeze rustling through the trees. They heard the door creak open and out came Cooper holding his blanket and sucking his thumb. "Well, hello there," Paul said as he gathered Cooper up into his arms. "I awake," Cooper announced sleepily as he snuggled into Paul. "Yes, you are," Emily said reaching over and smoothing out his hair. She smiled at her two loves before she got up and went to the kitchen to get ready for this evening.

Chapter 23

A few weeks later, Emily was waiting for Paul to get home from his meeting. It was getting late and she was beginning to worry. She dialed his number, but it kept going to voicemail. She fed Cooper and read him a story before putting him to bed. He cried for his Da, but she promised he would come say goodnight when he got home.

She had just covered his dinner when she heard the doorbell. She opened the door to see two police officers standing there. "Are you Mrs. James Mohin?" The female officer asked. Emily stared at her and barely whispered, "Yes."

"Is there anyone here with you?" The other officer asked her quietly. "My son, he's asleep in the other room. What's going on?" she asked. "May we come in?" Emily opened the door slightly to allow them in. "Please sit-down Mrs. Mohin," the officer said. "Please! No, I don't want to sit down," she said with panic creeping into her voice. "Where is he? Oh God, where's my husband?" She almost screamed.

"I'm sorry ma'am, your husband was in an accident tonight. I am sorry to tell you he did not survive," the female said. Her world fell away as she fainted. Waking to the two of them hovered over her, speaking gently to her. "Is there anyone we can call?" they asked. Somehow she found her phone and found Sam's number before handing it to one of them. She got up with the help of the other officer and sat on the couch. He had gotten her a glass of water.

"My son, my son," she moaned softly. The female officer finished the call to Sam and crouched down in front of her. "My name is Shannon, I just checked on him and he is still asleep. Your friend is on the way. Can I get you anything?" she asked. Emily just stared at her thinking this was some kind of terrible dream and she just needed to wake up, "No," she whispered.

Sam arrived and ran into the house. He spoke first with the other officer as he approached Emily and sat down next to her. "Paul," was all she said before she began sobbing convulsively. He cried with her unable to control the pain he felt watching Emily realize the love of her life was gone. Chris soon arrived after having gotten someone to watch the boys. Upon seeing her dear friend, she thought she had never seen such anguish in a human being.

Emily stopped sobbing after a long while, long enough for Chris to gather some of Cooper's things and take him home with her. Sam sat with Emily for the rest of the night into the morning. Emily was weak from grief, horror, and confusion. One minute to the next she expected Paul to walk in only to realize she would never see him again. She felt as though she were dying herself. She didn't know how she would go on living without him.

Suddenly, she felt faint again as a terrible pain ripped through her. She woke up hours later in the hospital. Chris and Sam hovered over her as she blinked her eyes open. She could see they had both been crying. She turned her head away from them gazing out the window into the darkness. "The baby?" she whispered. Chris began crying again as Sam took Emily's hand, "I'm sorry Em," he said quietly. She couldn't feel anything as she turned her head back to her dear friends. She felt as if she were dead as well. "Where's Cooper?" she asked. "He's with the boys at my Mom's," Chris replied as she held Emily's hand.

She started to get out of the bed, "I need to see him," she said as she struggled to sit up. Sam stopped her, "Emily, please, you need to stay in bed." "No Sam, I need to see my son!" she said as she began to get hysterical. Chris slipped out of the room and got a nurse to help. By the time the nurse arrived, Emily was beyond reasoning, as she continued to struggle to free herself from Sam. She was given a sedative through her IV before she settled down long enough for the nurse to take her vitals and call the doctor. Every time she woke up, she insisted on leaving so she could go see Cooper. Sam eventually pleaded with the doctor to let her be discharged so she could see her son. He promised she would be taken care of by them and have her son nearby. That is what she needed now.

She and Cooper stayed with them long enough for her to be able to manage Cooper without any problems physically. Sam and Chris didn't want her to be alone as she dealt with Paul's death and the loss of their child. It was a good distraction for Cooper, and they all knew once they got home, he would miss his Da more than ever.

Chapter 24

Emily woke with a start feeling the emptiness of their bed without him there. She lay there for a moment lost in her memories longing for her love and the realization that he is gone forever. She moved to get up when she heard a crash in the kitchen. Rushing to see what had happened, she stumbled slightly at the weight of her sorrow.

Cooper was there sprawled on the floor where he had landed. "Cooper! What happened baby?" she exclaimed as she rushed to him. "I fall Mommy, I saw angel at the window, and I play with it and I fall down," he said seriously with a little frown on his face. She picked him up and put him on her lap. "Are you Okay? Do you have a boo-boo?" she asked, kissing his head. "No Mommy, I fine," he said bravely.

She smiled and ruffled his hair, "Well, that's good," she said as she hugged him close. "Mommy the angel talk to me!" Cooper exclaimed. "She did?" Emily replied. Cooper looked up at her with his huge brown eyes and said earnestly, "Silly Mommy the angel wasn't girl, it Da." Her heart skipped a beat as she looked at him. "Angel Da said I can play with him anytime I want," Cooper said excitedly. "He say I music man too!" He finished as he wiggled down off her lap.

She sat there stunned, unable to move as Cooper danced about the kitchen pretending to play a guitar just like he had done with Paul. For a moment she believed she wouldn't be able to breathe again. But as she sat and watched him she smiled at his joy, her heart lightened a little. His little voice could be a cross between her and Paul. He would sometimes sound as Liverpudlian as Paul and in the next breath he could sound as American as her. She smiled at the thought of Paul and Cooper.

How about pancakes for breakfast?" she said. "Yeah, yeah, yeah," he repeated as he continued to dance out of the room. Paul had introduced Cooper to The Beatles early on and anytime Cooper would answer a question it would be with a 'yeah, yeah, yeah," while shaking his little head just like Paul taught him. She laughed and remembered the two of them dancing around as if Paul had a little shadow. They were so alike.

"Cooper! Come eat your pancakes!" she called from the kitchen. In a second she heard his little feet running towards her. She stood in the doorway of the kitchen and when he got to her she snatched him up and spun him around sending him into fits of giggles. "I want cup of milk," he said as she put him down. "It's right there, honey," she pointed to his place at the table.

She sat down sipping her coffee as he climbed up into his chair. "Mommy, where your pancakes?" He asked when he saw just one plate for him. "Mommy's not hungry," she said. "You have one of mine," he said seriously as he carefully lifted one off his plate handing it to her. She took it and dunked the edge into the syrup on his plate. "Thank you!" she said as he grinned back at her.

After breakfast Cooper asked Emily if he could watch cartoons. She flipped the TV on and went back to cleaning the kitchen. Her phone rang as she finished. It was Chris asking if they could stop by for the afternoon so the boys could play. She knew it was because Chris was worried about her. She tried to be as strong as she could for Cooper's sake, but grief is a terrible burden that at times robbed her of the ability to remember that life is still carrying on. She often felt that she couldn't bear to leave the house but having Cooper with her made her push past her yearning to hide away. She believed she would will herself to fade away into the shadows if it weren't for him.

That afternoon, as the boys played in the pool, Chris and Emily sat sipping iced tea as they chatted. "How are you doing honey?" Chris asked as she touched Emily's hand. Emily looked at her answering, "Oh, you know, some days are better than others. I need to tell you what Cooper said this morning."
Emily relayed what had happened in the kitchen that morning. Chris sat back while she shook her head, "Emily, Paul and Cooper loved each other so much. I wouldn't be surprised at all if he's not here right now watching out for both of you." "So, you don't think I should worry?" Emily asked. "No, if it's his imagination, it's his way of dealing with losing his Da. If it's true, well then it's a wonderful blessing, isn't it?" Chris finished.

The three boys were climbing out of the pool playfully splashing each other. "Here you go Coop," Emily said as she got up and wrapped him in a towel. She smiled as he tried to squirm away, "Come back here, you!" she said as he giggled. "Are you boys all done swimming?" Chris asked. A chorus of yeses was heard as they all jumped up and down saying, "We're hungry!" "Alright, go get changed. I have pizza for your lunch!" Emily said.

She and Chris hugged each other as they walked to the kitchen door. "How is Sam?" Emily asked. "Busy, as usual," Chris replied with a smile. He wants to take the boys to Disney World next month. Why don't you and Cooper come with us?" "Oh, I don't know Chris, I'm not sure I'd have the energy," Emily said softly. "Well, we can talk about it later. Don't say anything to the boys, it's a surprise," Chris said.

Later that evening after she had read Cooper a goodnight story and he was tucked in asleep in his bed, Emily poured a glass of wine and sat outside by the pool. She thought about Chris' offer to take them to Florida. She knew Cooper would love it and so she began thinking that maybe they should go. She picked up her phone and said, "Hey Sam! I was thinking…" Before she could continue her thought Sam interrupted her. "We made the reservations tonight you're going," he said with a laugh. "Well then I guess I am," she responded. After chatting for a bit, she sat back and closed her eyes thinking that Paul would have loved to have seen Disney World with Cooper. A tear slid down her cheek as she sighed and looked up at the stars. Saying quietly, "I miss you so much."

Before heading off to bed she peeked in on Cooper. He lay there with his arms thrown up over his head, just like Paul had slept. She smiled as she pulled his blanket up around him and kissed his forehead. She went to her room and sat on the edge of the bed, so overwhelmed with grief that she could barely breathe. She never imagined this kind of pain was possible. The horror of the night Paul died came back to her as she sat there. She tried to push it out of her mind but feared she would relive that night over and over and over again for the rest of her life.

She woke up in the morning to Cooper climbing into her bed to snuggle. Emily smiled at him as he looked up at her with his big brown eyes. "Morning sweetie," she murmured to him. "Mommy, I go see Zak today?" "Maybe. Let me call Miss Chris and see if you two can play," she answered. She hugged him close to her for a moment before he squirmed away to go watch cartoons. She poured him some cereal while she called Chris. "Hey! Are you free today? I've got someone here bursting at the seams to see his best friend," she said. "Of course, we're free. Here or there?" Chris asked. "I'll bring Coop over there if you don't mind. I need to get out of the house," Emily responded.

Chris and Emily made the boys lunch while the boys
played in the pool. Chris looked closely at her dear
friend. She could see the pain etched on her face and a
hollow look in her eyes. She hugged Emily and said,
"You can talk to me you know. It's not a burden for
me. I love you and Cooper, and I loved Paul." Emily
lowered her eyes trying to fight back the tears that
seemed to flow endlessly. "I don't want to cry in front
of the boys," she said with a weak smile. Chris
finished putting the sandwiches on a plate and turned
around to face Emily. Knowing how much Emily and
Paul loved each other she could not imagine the pain
Emily was feeling. "Come on, let's feed those
munchkins," Chris said trying to lighten the mood.

Afterwards Emily had stopped at the store and when
she got home she put Cooper down for a nap. He was
always exhausted after playing with Zak and Stephen.
She sat down in the kitchen to look through the mail.
She hadn't had it in her to take care of some of the
basic things like paying bills and answering inquiries
Paul was still receiving.

She was looking through the envelopes when one fell
out of the pile. It's rare to get a handwritten letter so
when she saw this one was written in a beautiful
calligraphy it caught her eye. She slid the flap open

and took out a sheet of heavy parchment paper. She sat stunned as she opened the folded paper. It was the lyrics to the first song Paul wrote for her when he arrived here. It had never been recorded and to her knowledge Paul had never submitted it to his agent Jim. She thought the only people who knew about it were her and Paul. The song was called 'Time X 2.'

She sat back in her chair and her head started spinning. She picked up the envelope to examine it closer and noticed her hands were shaking. She came out of her shock when she heard Cooper rustling in his room through the monitor on her phone. Taking a deep breath she gathered up the letter and the rest of the mail and went inside.

"Mommy, I fly in my dream," he said sleepily as she entered his room and turned the blinds open. "You did? That sounds like fun!" she said as she smiled at him. Cooper yawned and continued, "I fly with Da," he said with a smile. She sat on the bed and kissed the top of his little head with tears springing to her eyes. "You must have had good dream Coop. Come on, do you want a snack?" "Yeah, yeah, yeah," he said as he slid down from the bed.

She sat for a moment before she could make herself stand and follow him into the kitchen. Cooper was trying to open the refrigerator when she got there. "Here you go," she said as she helped him open it. "I want yo-yo," he said as she giggled every time he asked for yogurt. She loved him so much and she knew these little moments would someday be gone when he grew out of this cute toddler phase. "Strawberry?" she asked. "Yes, Mommy," he said seriously as he sat down at the table.

As she sat next to him she was struck again by how much he looked like Paul, more and more every day. He ate a spoonful of yogurt before looking up at her with a smile, "Da say Mommy have song," he said before he went back to his yogurt. She didn't think she heard him right, "What honey?" she asked. "In my dream, Da say Mommy have song," he said again. Her heart pounded in her chest and she felt as if she may faint. Trying not to sound alarmed she asked him, "Did he say anything else honey?" Cooper put his spoon down, "I done. He say, I good boy," he said with a short little nod of his head. Still trying to calm her heart she smiled at him as she leaned over and wiped his mouth, "You are a good boy. Do you want to watch a movie?"

After she got him settled in front of the TV, she went outside to call Chris. "Hey, what's up?" Chris said as she answered the call. "Chris, you won't believe what happened," she began. After relaying the whole story Chris was silent. "Maybe we need to let Sam know about all of this," Chris said. "Write everything down, including what you told me the other day. I'll call Sam and have him stop by this afternoon," she finished. "Alright, thank you," Emily replied as she hung up the phone. She looked in on Cooper who sat sucking his thumb wrapped in his favorite blanket bobbing his head along to the song in the movie.

She sat down in the kitchen and began writing. When she finished she set it with the letter she had received that morning and went to join Cooper for the end of the movie. She gathered him up in her arms and hugged him tight as he looked up at her with a smile. Her phone buzzed with a text from Sam, 'on my way.' She turned off the TV as Cooper ran to his room to play. Sam was about to knock on the door when it swung open. "Hi Sam, thanks for coming," she said. Cooper had heard Sam's voice and bolted out of his room, "Sam," he squealed as he leapt into Sam's arms.

"I asked Chris to come by with the boys so we can talk without interruption," he said as he put him down. She looked at him as he continued to talk to Cooper. Just then Chris pulled up with Stephen and Zak. The boys went to play in Cooper's room while the three of them sat down to make sense of everything.

Emily explained to Sam what happened this morning in the kitchen, the letter she received in the mail and Cooper's dreams that he'd been having. She then handed him the letter and envelope. He carefully examined it, being careful not to touch it too much. "Can I take this to get tested?" he asked. Emily didn't see what good that would do but agreed. "Of course, you can," she stated.

"I also think Mark should talk to Cooper. Would that be alright with you?" he asked. She was a little taken aback but agreed to it only if there would be no pressure or strain put on him. "I'll let you know if I find anything out about the letter and when Mark can see Coop," he said as they all stood up to leave. She trusted Mark since he had helped Paul so much with his acclimation when he first arrived in this time and then later he helped her work through her own grief from the loss of Paul.

"Why don't you stay for dinner? We can order pizza," Emily said after noticing it was getting close to dinner time. "Sure, my treat," Sam said. After dinner they all had a glass of wine as the boys played nearby. Suddenly they heard the boys fussing, "Hey guys! what's going on?" Sam said as he got up to walk towards them. "Cooper thinks his Daddy talks to him!" Stephen said. "Da talk to me," Cooper stated calmly while he nodded his head. "He can't talk to you, Cooper…," Stephen began before Sam stopped him. "Stephen, that's enough," Sam said firmly before turning to Cooper. "Come here, Coop," he said as he picked him up. Chris got up and had the boys start putting away the cars they were playing with. Sam carried Cooper outside and sat down.

Emily watched Sam and Cooper from the window. Chris came and stood by her giving her a hug. Tears sprung into Emily's eyes as she remembered watching Paul and Cooper talk with their heads together just as Sam was doing with him now. "Hey, do you want us to take Coop home with us for the night? The boys would love it," she asked. Emily thought for a moment, "Maybe that would be a good idea. I'm a little shaky tonight. I think he can sense when I'm upset," she replied with a small smile. Sam was walking back into the house holding Cooper's hand,

"Honey, we are going to take Coop home tonight with us so the boys can have a sleepover," Chris said to Sam. "Sounds like a plan!" Sam said as he went to tell the boys.

Emily took a bath and had a glass of wine after they all left. She sat in the living room trying to gain control over herself and her emotions after what was quite an unusual day. She heard a text come in and read what Sam wrote. 'Did you notice the return address on the envelope?' She was confused by this as she didn't seem to remember that there was one, but her mind had been a little scattered lately. She replied to Sam, 'No, what is it?' '1966 Studio Alley, London, UK IX27XI' was his reply. She looked at it for a long time before she realized what it meant. 'Come to the office tomorrow morning before you pick up Cooper.' He had texted her back.

Chapter 25

She poured herself more wine and stood looking out the window as the sun began to set behind the trees. Brutally, her grief overwhelmed her as she began to sob. She had held it in for so long and now as she sat in the nearest chair as she screamed and cried with all the pain she had bottled up inside of her. When she finished crying, she sat down on the couch hugging her knees to her chest and rocked herself back and forth. As the house began to darken she got up and turned on the light. She let out a sigh as she sat back down. She missed him terribly that she thought she would never get over the pain she was feeling. She prayed she would for Cooper's sake.

The next morning, she got dressed to meet Sam and pick up Cooper. Sam was waiting for her when she got there. "Good morning," he said as he gave her a hug. "How's my little man?" she asked. "I haven't been home. I've been here the entire time since leaving your house," he answered solemnly. "What is it Sam? What's going on?" she asked anxiously. He went to his desk and picked up the phone and told whomever he was calling to come to his office. He still hadn't responded to her when there was a knock on the door. "Come in Alex," Sam said. She was confused as to why Alex was being asked to join them, until Sam began.

"Alex has a story to tell you Emily," Sam said harshly. Looking back at Sam, Alex hung his head refusing to meet her eyes. "Alex, what is it?" she asked softly. He finally raised his eyes to her and began. "I was approached by Ramsgate. They said they wanted me to watch Paul." He stopped for a moment, clearing his throat as he faltered. "I, I didn't want to do it, but they said they would kill me if I didn't," he said as he tried to hold back his tears.

"Didn't want to do what Alex?" she asked him with panic in her voice. "I didn't want to watch him or, or..." "Or what Alex?" she questioned looking from Sam to Alex. "He was forced by Ramsgate to bring Paul here and send him back," Sam began to explain. "The body in the car wasn't Paul, Emily. Paul is alive in 1966," he finished. "I'm so sorry Emily, Sam, they threatened to kill me. I had to do it," Alex cried.

Emily was bewildered, enraged and excited at the same time. "Why?" She demanded. "Why did they want him sent back?" she pressed Alex to answer. Sam jumped in and began explaining. "It was their fear that Paul would meet with Ringo. They couldn't let that happen and so they had to stop it." "But, the letter. I don't understand," she said weakly. "It was a clue for you Emily. I sent it," Alex said, "I wanted to tell you what I had done, but I was afraid. I broke into Paul's studio one night when you and Cooper were gone. I found the lyrics to the song and sent it to you so you would know he is alive."

"You were playing God, Alex," Sam said tersely, "You should have come to one of us immediately upon being contacted by Ramsgate." Emily was too stunned to think but abruptly jumped up, "Sam we have to go get him. We have to go get him now!" She was almost screaming with shock and excitement. "Alex, you can go. I'll speak with you later," Sam said.

After Alex left Sam sat down facing her, "Emily, if we jump back to get him, he may not remember you, or Cooper. You do understand that don't you?" "He will know us Sam. Our love is too strong for him not to," she replied while calming herself. "Have you done the analysis yet?" she asked in a whisper. "Yes, we can jump tonight," he replied.

Trying to tamp down Emily's excitement, Sam began again, "I think I should go, if he remembers me, then..." Emily interrupted him, "Sam, I need to be the one. He listened to me before and he will listen to me again. If he doesn't remember me I will be alright. I promise. I need to be the one to go. He's my husband Sam," she finished as she looked back at him with hope in her eyes. "He's my husband," she repeated quietly.

The rest of the afternoon was spent confirming the data they had, making sure that later that night it would be safe for everyone. Emily went to her office to double check the data when someone knocked on Sam's door. "Yeah," he said as the door opened. It was Alex. "Sam, I know I've done unspeakable harm to Emily. I just wanted to say I'm sorry again and give you my letter of resignation. I've already cleaned out my desk," he said solemnly. Sam sat back and looked at the young man. Alex, it's not me you need to apologize to, it's Emily," Sam said firmly. "I know," Alex said softly as he opened the door. "Come back and see me before you leave the building," Sam said curtly.

Emily called Chris to check on how Cooper was doing. Chris called for Coop and put him on the phone. "Hi honey, Mommy misses you. Are you having fun?" she asked. "We playing in the pool," he said as he giggled. "Well, Mommy has to work for a while. You have fun and be a good boy, Okay?" "I good boy," he said in his little voice. She wanted to hold him so badly. Chris got back on the phone, "Be careful, Emily. I'm praying everything works out tonight," she said. "Thanks, I've gotta go," she said as she hung up.

Sam was standing in the doorway to her office. "Ready?" he asked. She took a deep breath and replied, "Yes, let's go." Sam gave her a hug as they prepared for the jump. Emily closed her eyes as it began, opening them as she landed.

She looked around a little disoriented. She had landed on the sidewalk near the bench where she and Paul had sat the night they met. She looked up at the door of the studio. Looking back at her watch, it was almost 5:00. Her heart pounded in her chest as she waited with anticipation for the door to open. She walked across the street so that she could speak with him as he came down the stairs just as she had before.

Minutes passed and she became more anxious as she waited. She prayed that he would remember her. She heard the door open and Paul was talking to someone. She assumed it was Brian. Taking a deep breath, she slowly looked up at him, her heart leapt as he turned to take the stairs.

As he reached the sidewalk he slowly turned towards her and looked into her eyes. She felt as if time itself stood still in that moment. She looked back at him and said, "Paul, I'm Em…" Before she could finish he reached up and stroked her cheek, "Is it you?" he whispered as he wrapped his arms around her tightly. "Oh God, Emily, I knew you'd come," he said with tears in his eyes as he held her tighter.

She had believed for so long that he was lost to her forever, but now she was in his arms again. She pulled away and through her own tears said, "Let's go home." She pushed the transporter and they landed in the lab still holding each other but each with tears of joy streaming down their cheeks.

Sam was shocked when he saw the signs that they were coming back so soon. He hoped that meant it was a good sign. Then unexpectedly Emily and Paul, still wrapped in each other's arms, landed. He couldn't control himself as he yelled out, "YES!" He yelled as they both stood grinning at him. Paul walked over to

Sam and grabbed him up in a big bear hug. "Sam, I've never been so happy to see your face!" Paul said as he put him down. "Where's Cooper? I need to see me boy," Paul said excitedly as he went back to hold Emily in his arms while kissing her hair. "He's at our place. I'll let Chris know you're home," Sam said while picking up his phone.

Emily and Paul stood there holding on to each other each afraid to let go of the other. "How did you know to come back," he whispered to her. "Alex left me a clue," she responded, "Then he confessed." He frowned at the mention of Alex's name. She reached up and touched his face still not believing he was there with her.

"They told me you died," she whispered as she wrapped her arms around his waist. "They said you had a car accident," she continued. He pulled back from her to look into her eyes, "Oh God, Emily, I'm sorry you had to go through that," he said quietly, "I'm here now it's over," he finished. Sam got off the phone and came back into the room, "He's asleep but she'll get his things together," he said with a smile.

"We still have a lot of unanswered questions, but all of that can wait until tomorrow. Let's get you home," he said. They arrived at Sam and Chris' place just as Chris was opening the door. She ran out to the car and caught Paul up in a hug with tears in her eyes, "Thank God. Thank God," was all she could say. Paul smiled down at her and then back at Sam and Emily, "It's good to be home," he said.

They all walked quietly into the house when Paul stopped as he saw his son. Cooper was asleep on the couch sucking his thumb and curled up on his side. Paul crouched down and brushed the hair away from Cooper's eyes as he ran his finger over his little chubby cheek. Emily couldn't hold back her tears as she watched Paul with his son again.

Cooper stirred as he felt Paul's caress on his cheek. He opened his eyes and just stared at Paul blinking his eyes awake. Taking his thumb out of his mouth he reached up and touched Paul's cheek. "Da, we playing in my dream?" He asked sleepily. "No, I'm here Coop. I'm here," is all Paul could say as he tried to hold back his tears. He gathered Cooper in his arms and hugged him tightly. "Da, you squishing me," Cooper said with a sleepy giggle. "I'm sorry Coop. I'm just so happy to see you," he laughed as he wiped away a tear. "Let's go home." "Okay Da," Cooper said as he reached up to wrap his arms around Paul's neck. Everyone had tears in their eyes as they watched. Emily was trembling with joy as she realized the enormity of what was happening before her eyes. Her family was whole again.

As they pulled into the driveway the sensor lights came on and Paul looked at Emily and smiled. He was remembering when he first arrived here and leaned over and kissed her gently. "I will never leave you again. I promise you that with all my heart," he said.

Emily grabbed the bag as Paul gently lifted Cooper out of the car. Once Cooper was in his bed, Paul joined Emily in the living room where they stood facing each other from across the room. Both were so overwhelmed with emotion and disbelief that they were together again. Paul walked slowly to Emily and lifted her chin kissing her gently, neither spoke, words would never begin to describe what they were experiencing. Words were Paul's lifeblood, but he had none to offer. His joy at being back with her and Cooper left him speechless.

Emily looked up at him with glistening eyes. "I missed you so much," she whispered. They stood and held on to each other for what seemed like forever. He gently touched her cheek, devouring her with his eyes. He took her hand and led her to their bedroom where he slowly undressed her as he showered her with kisses. As they made love, the words were still hard to find but they needed no words as they took each other in. He rested his head on his hand as he smiled down at her. "I thought I'd never see you again, never be with you like this again, never see our child again," he murmured. He placed his hand on her belly and looked at her.

Quietly she began, "Paul, the night they told me you died," she paused. "I lost the baby," she whispered as she tried to hold back her tears. They began to flow despite her best efforts. He cupped her face in his hands and kissed her softly on the lips. "I'm so sorry," she said with tears in her eyes.

He interrupted her as tears filled his eyes, "Oh God, Emily, never apologize. It saddens me that you had to go through that without me. We have a lifetime ahead of us. We can try again." She saw the tears spring into his eyes as she wiped away her own. She reached out and drew her finger along his jaw still not believing he was there. She smiled when he caught her eye, bringing a small smile to his lips.

They fell asleep holding on tightly to each other. Waking up to Cooper climbing into their bed and pushing his way in between them. Paul moved over to make room for his little body, then wrapped his arms around him as he breathed in the smell of his hair and skin. "Da come home Mommy," Cooper said as he poked her cheek with his little finger. "I know baby. We are so happy, aren't we?" She gave each of them a kiss. Cooper smiled with a big grin and said, "I want pancakes." "Oh, that sounds good," Paul responded as he tickled Cooper's tummy. Emily laughed as she got up. "You two stay here while I go get them started."

"Da, I play with you when you an Angel!" Cooper exclaimed as he grinned at his father. "I know, I remember," Paul responded. Cooper snuggled into the crook of Paul's arm and sucked his thumb. "I music man too," he said sleepily. Paul felt the tears spring to his eyes again. "Yes, you are," he said as he held his little boy tightly.

"Breakfast!" They heard Emily call from the kitchen. Cooper untangled himself from Paul and the blanket and ran out to take his seat at the table. Paul slowly moved to get up and stopped as he sat on the edge of bed for a moment he shook his head in disbelief that he was back home and gave thanks. He got dressed and joined his family in the kitchen. Leaning against the doorway watching them he smiled as Emily beamed up at him. "My God, I can't believe you are here," she said breathlessly.

Cooper stuffed a big bite of pancake in his mouth and began trying to talk. "Swallow your food first sweetie," Emily said as she patted his arm. "Angel Da say he come home soon," he said after he finished chewing. Paul looked at her feigning wide-eyed innocence.

Chapter 26

When Cooper was about to turn sixteen, he began hinting that he would like a Gretsch guitar for his upcoming birthday. He and his friends imagined themselves in a band. Emily assumed they wanted to impress the girls. He had always spent time out in the studio with Paul and could already play almost as well as Paul. He didn't mind using his father's guitars but wanted one he could call his own. Paul thought to himself, what a good choice that was.

George had used the same guitar and Paul remembered the feel of it in his hands. He began searching for one that he knew Cooper would like but that could be tossed around as a teen would do. Cooper was constantly coming into his studio and grabbing up a guitar to take to a friend's house. Paul would silently cringe to himself each and every time. Not that he didn't trust Cooper, but he worried the other lads may not understand how expensive they were.

They were having dinner with Sam, Chris and Zak at their place one evening. Stephen was away at his first semester of college. Cooper said he'd like to make an announcement. Emily leaned forward and smiled at her son as Paul leaned back in his chair. "What's that mate?" Paul said. Emily looked over to Paul, thinking how handsome he looked with a touch of gray beginning to show at his temples. She smiled at him when he caught her eye and gave her a wink. Oh, that wink she thought as she turned her attention back to her son as Cooper began by dramatically clearing his throat, "I have decided not to go to college. I want to play music."

Emily looked at Cooper and said, "Why don't we talk about this when we get home honey." Cooper glanced at his father hoping for an ally. "Coop, you're Mum's right, let us think about this a bit and we can talk about it later." Sam, trying to defuse the situation as he spoke up saying, "Hey Zak, help me with these dishes." Zak groaned as he rose to clear the table. Cooper was determined to get his father's reaction, "Da?" Paul leaned closer to Cooper. "Later son, we don't want your Mum getting mad at the both of us," he said with a chuckle. Emily swatted at Paul. "I'm not mad at anyone, just surprised," she said.

She and Chris got up to get the coffee ready leaving Paul and Cooper at the table. "Da, you understand, don't you?" Cooper pled. "You know I understand. At about your age I left home and went off to another country to play. It's not me you need to convince," Paul whispered conspiratorially. Cooper rolled his eyes but smiled as his mother and Chris walked back into the dining room with a tray full of coffee and cake. After dessert, Zak and Cooper went upstairs to hang out while the adults filed into the living room.

"What in the world is he thinking?" Emily said to Chris as they all sat down. Sam looked at Paul with a knowing smile. He didn't envy Paul when the three of them sat down to talk about Cooper's announcement. Chris replied to Emily, "Don't you remember last year when Stephen announced he was going to join the Navy instead of going to college? I almost had a heart attack," she laughed. "Thankfully, my lovely husband here talked sense into him before he went off and signed up." Sam laughed, "Hey, I just laid it all out for him, basic training, getting up at 5:00 am for duty and so on."

After a while the boys came clomping down the stairs laughing and punching playfully at each other. Cooper grabbed his jacket as he yelled, "I'm driving!" He had just gotten his driving permit and as teenagers will do, thought he should drive everywhere. This, of course, made Paul cringe, "Hey Coop, it's getting dark and it looks like it may start raining. I'll drive home tonight, and you can have the wheel on the way to school tomorrow." Emily giggled to herself at Paul's adept way of not showing Cooper he was terrified at the thought of being a passenger in a car with a 16-year-old. Even after all these years and driving in Atlanta traffic, Paul still hated not being the one behind the wheel. Cooper looked at Emily pleadingly. "You heard your Da," she said, giving him a hug.

When they all got home, Cooper insisted on finishing the conversation he had started at dinner. Emily began, "Cooper, you need to be sensible. It's different than it was when your Da and the other boys started playing." Paul watched Cooper's face as Emily continued. "What if you don't make it in the business, then where will you be, what will you fall back on?" she asked. Cooper looked again to Paul for help. "Coop, I was the only one out of the four of us who had any chance at going on to Uni," he paused, "I was young and headstrong, but believe me, me own Da was not happy about me decision to play instead of becoming a teacher."

Cooper interrupted, "But Da, you made it and you didn't go to college." He looked at Paul trying to avoid

Emily's eyes. "Maybe I need to be clearer," Paul continued, "If we hadn't made it I would have lost the chance to go on to Uni. I would have ended up working as a clerk in some factory or on the docks in Liverpool. I think what your Mom is trying to say is that you need to look at everything before you make a rash decision about the rest of your life," he finished.

Cooper stood up and stretched saying, "I'm beat, I'm going to bed. But, Da and Mom, please think about it. I think I can do it." He bent down and gave Emily a kiss before he wandered off to his room. Paul stood up and poured a glass of wine for each of them. He sat down next to Emily as he looked at her from under his lush lashes. "He is good ya know," he said. She nodded saying, "I know he is. He's your son in every way, but you see how different things are now in the music business. Do you believe he can make it?" she asked.

He sat back thinking, "I suppose with the right guidance and material, he would, if he worked very hard. I just don't know where he would get sound advice and material to sing." She ran her fingers up his arm as she smiled at him. "You know, I think he's counting on your help. The question my dear husband is, are you ready for that?"

He sighed as he sipped his wine and looked at her. "I think I am, but will our son listen, that is the question," he said with a grin. She replied, "Oh Paul, you know he adores you to the moon and back. I think he would. But I was sort of hoping he'd find physics interesting," she finished with a pout. Paul laughed, "My dear wife. He is 16 years old. I do believe the only things that are interesting to him right now are music and girls, but probably not in that order."

Paul pulled her closer to him. The love he had for her had only grown stronger through the years, something he never thought possible. He hated being away from her whenever he had to travel or work away from home. He thought about when Cooper was small, and he had been sent back to 1966 by Alex and Ramsgate. The dreams Cooper had about Paul were created by Paul through meditation. He had come to understand that there are some things that cannot be explained, better left just to experience them and accept them as the universe laid them before you.

George had encouraged Paul to learn it and as he practiced it, he found he could communicate with Cooper. It was as if his experiences of traveling through time and his incredibly strong bond with his son gave him insights into the future. He didn't talk much about it to Emily because he didn't want to bring up the pain she had experienced during that time, but he knew in his heart, if Cooper chose to make music his life, it would be a good decision.

He took Emily's hand, and led her to their bedroom. He needed her tonight just as he needed her every night. She was the light that showed him the way in his darkest hours. She was the gift that time could not take away from him. She was above all else the part of him that made him whole.

Chapter 27

Cooper finished his set and was walking off stage when he saw Paul and Emily. "Oh my God, when, how...?" He said as he gave Emily a bear hug. Laughing Emily said, "We wanted to surprise you!" This was the last concert of his tour. He had expected a long night in airports and down time. He was thrilled they were here saying, "This is great. Let me catch a quick shower and we can go get something to eat." Emily and Paul followed him to his dressing room where there were people milling about giving him fist bumps and pats on the back as they walked down the hall.

They stood waiting for him to finish speaking with someone. "Where is Zak?" Paul asked when they got to the dressing room and Cooper responded, "He's around here somewhere. I'll text him and have him join us." Zak and Cooper have been close all their lives and when Cooper's career took off, Zak was right there helping him. He now handles all of Cooper's business as well as providing a sane sounding board when things get too crazy.

There was a knock on the door before it opened, "Uncle Paul, Aunt Emily! It's so great to see you!" Zak gave Emily a hug and a kiss on the cheek. Cooper was in the shower as they all sat down to visit while he got dressed. "How are Mom and Dad?" Zak asked. "They are both fine keeping busy with the grandbabies," she said laughing. Stephen and his wife had twins who kept Chris and Sam on their toes when they watched them from time to time. Paul said smiling, "Your Dad is fine. I think he's still trying to get used to retirement." Zak laughed, "I know, I still can't believe he retired. I thought he'd work forever."

Emily was always amazed at how much Cooper looked like Paul. As he grew older he became the spitting image of Paul. His eyes and smile were identical to his father's. She got up and gave him a quick kiss on the cheek. "I've missed you," she said as she stood in front of him and fixed his collar. "I've missed you too. I'm glad this tour is over. We're all exhausted," he responded.

Zak stood as he got a call and went outside to finish the conversation. When he came back he said, "Good news. The receipts are in. Record breaking numbers Coop! Congratulations!" Cooper smiled at Paul, "Because of you Da," Cooper said as he gave his father a hug. "No, Coop, because of you," Paul said with a wink.

Paul had written some of Cooper's biggest hits early in his career until the two of them began writing together. As Cooper would practice or begin learning a new song they would sing it together. It amazed Emily how alike they sounded. Cooper could sing a ballad just as well as Paul ever had, and like Paul, could belt out a rock and roll classic just as easily with that gritty soulful sound that you never thought would come out of that face. After a while, Cooper tried his hand at writing alone, but he always sought out Paul's opinion and blessing before he finished each song.

Cooper knew who his father really was as did Stephen and Zak. It would always amuse Cooper when girls would swoon over The Beatles, especially Paul, while they were all in high school. Unbelievably, no one ever seemed to make the connection between Paul and Cooper even after having met Cooper's father. He always thought of the line from the song John wrote, 'living is easy with eyes closed, misunderstanding all you see.' He learned early on to always publicly refer to Paul as James, but in the privacy of their home and with their trusted friends, Sam and Chris, he was always Paul.

His decision not to go on to college had weighed on Emily. She feared if he didn't make it in the music business he wouldn't have anything to fall back on. But with a lot of hard work and professionalism drilled into him by his father, he became a successful performer. Paul always made sure that Cooper understood that when he was on tour he was working. It wasn't a time for site seeing or partying. Paul would tell Cooper stories of the countless interviews The Beatles had to endure and show him the videos on YouTube. Always being asked in every city they played in what they thought of that particular place and their fans there. He told Cooper what John's stock answer was. 'If we're alive when we're 40 we will come back and visit all the places that looked interesting.' Unfortunately, as fate had it, John died when he was 40, never seeing some of those places again.

They all left the venue and got into the limo and Paul suggested they eat at Anthony's, a beautiful restaurant on the harbor, that he'd eaten at before. The bar was a boat moored next to the restaurant. They settled into a booth in the bar to relax before eating. As the waitress came to their table she quickly realized who Cooper was. She blushed slightly and was a little flustered as she stood by the table to take their drink order. Paul spoke up, "Will you bring us two bottles of your best champagne please." She nodded and asked if they would like anything else. Although they didn't order an appetizer, she brought them one of Anthony's specialties, oysters on the half shell, on the house.

Their table was ready by the time they had finished the champagne. Paul made sure everyone tried the popovers, another one of the specialties at Anthony's. After dinner they went back to the bar for a nightcap. "I'm so happy you came tonight," Cooper said as he kissed Emily and gave Paul a hug. "We are too Coop. It was a great show, we are very proud of you and we love you very much," Paul said as he ruffled his son's hair.

"Oh, I've been wanting to tell you before the internet gets ahold of it," Cooper started. "I've met someone, and I think she's the one," he finished. Emily squealed with joy as Paul smiled. "What's her name?" Emily asked. "Here, I've got a picture of us," he said as he took his phone out. Showing them a picture of him with a beautiful woman. "Her name is Ali," Cooper said with a grin on his face. Zak said, "She's really fantastic. You'll like her." "How did you meet?" Emily asked as she looked at the picture.

Ali was a beautiful girl with long blond hair and bright blue eyes. In the picture she was smiling up at Cooper with a sparkle in her eyes. "She works at the record company. We met about four months ago," Cooper answered. Paul looked a little closer at the picture and said, "She's beautiful, Coop. I'm really happy for you." Emily gave Zak a hug and kiss before she stood in front of Cooper again saying, "We can't wait to meet her, honey."

After saying their goodbyes, Paul and Emily got a cab to the airport to take the jet that Paul had rented to fly back home to Atlanta. Although Cooper was done with the tour he and Zak had to make a quick trip to New York for business before heading home for a much-needed rest. He planned to bring Ali with him to meet his parents.

Cooper and Zak decided to stay in Boston overnight and fly to New York the next morning. In the middle of the night, Cooper's phone began ringing. He ignored it out of exhaustion. But soon he heard a knock on the door. "Coop, it's me Zak, open the door." He dragged himself out of bed and opened the door, letting Zak in. "What's up man, it's 3:00 in the morning," Cooper said sleepily. Zak stood there white

as a ghost, "Jesus, Zak what is it you look like hell."
"Cooper come here, sit down," Zak said shakily.

"Coop, your parents plane went down, they were
killed," Zak said quietly as he watched his friend's
face. Cooper stared back at Zak, "Damn Zak, what a
sick joke, what's the matter with y…" but looking
back at Zak with tears running down his face, Cooper
knew it was true.

"How? What happened?" He asked barely above a
whisper. "It happened near the airport, there was a
storm in Atlanta," he said. "We'll know more later,
Dad's looking into it," he said as he got up. "Let's get
you packed," Zak said, opening Cooper's suitcase.
Cooper couldn't move, couldn't think, couldn't
breathe. Zak turned to look at his friend, his heart
breaking at the horror on Cooper's face. Cooper
stood, "I'm so sorry Coop," Zak said as he went to
hug him. They stood there crying in each other's arms.
No one knew Cooper better than he did, he knew it
would take everything he had to keep him from falling
over the edge.

The flight home seemed to take an eternity. Sam,
Chris, Stephen and Ali were waiting for them when
they landed. Zak had called Ali before they had left

Boston to let her know what had happened and she immediately flew to Atlanta to be with Cooper. Zak was pulled into a hug by his family as Ali held Cooper and talked to him quietly. They all waited as Cooper and Ali held each other as he sobbed in her arms.

They heard Cooper telling Ali it was his fault. Sam stepped forward to give him a hug. "Cooper, it's no one's fault. They were so excited to see you perform. Don't do that to yourself. It's not your fault." Chris reached out to hug him. "Honey, your parents adored you, you know that. They wanted to be there for you. Sam is right, it's not your fault" she said through her own tears. Ali took his hand in hers as they left to go home. Cooper gave her a small smile and held her close to him, thinking to himself how he wouldn't make it through this without her by his side.

Chapter 28

Cooper stood and slowly walked to the front of the small chapel. His hands shook as he glanced down at the paper he held. Looking up, he scanned the room. It was a small gathering of very close friends who had come to honor his parents. He caught Ali's eyes as she smiled and nodded, encouraging him. He was thankful he had found her in the craziness that his world had become. He began speaking as he held her eyes for a moment.

"Thank you all for coming today to honor and remember my parents, Paul and Emily. I am grateful for the kindness you have shown me these past few days." He cleared his throat before continuing. "I was born during a time in their lives that was magical, miraculous and mysterious." He smiled a small smile, "Most of you know the story, and for those that don't, it is a beautiful story. They came together as the universe spun and dropped them into a world that they in turn made joyful for everyone who knew them, especially me. I was born to two people whose love for each other was timeless, never fading but only grew stronger as the years carried them through life."

He felt tears spring into his eyes as he tried to compose himself enough to continue. "When I was younger, I believe I was 16," he chuckled, "I made the grand announcement that I didn't want to go to college, that I wanted to sing." The crowd smiled and nodded as he began again. "My mother, being a doctor of physics was not all that thrilled, but she understood because she knew where my heart was. My Da, I believe, was secretly a little nervous for me, but without his guidance, advice and patience, especially when I thought I knew better, I wouldn't be the man I am standing here now."

"My parents raised me in a home so filled with love that I never felt lonely. I never felt afraid that one or the other would not be there for me when I needed them. I never saw them have cross words with each other. I never saw them look at each other without feeling their love fill the room. I don't remember a time when there wasn't laughter in our home. I don't remember a time when there wasn't music and joy in our home. And, I don't remember a time when I wasn't proud that they were my parents."

He looked out and smiled that smile that was his father's. "I was given only 24 years with them, but I will carry their love in my heart for the rest of my life. I find it very hard to comprehend that I won't see them again. I still can't make myself believe they won't walk in the door and wrap their arms around me one more time. I'm going to miss my Mother's loving hugs and the way she always knew what I needed. I'm going to miss sitting with my Da, as he would say 'bash out,' another song together.

I'm going to miss the way they looked at each other or the way my Da would wink at her," he said with a soft chuckle. "But," he faltered a bit as the tears came to his eyes again. "But, I know deep in my heart that it is fitting they are still together. I don't think either would have survived without the other. I don't think either one would have wanted to." he finished. He stepped away and was wrapped in the arms of his love as he sat back down and let the tears finally flow.

Cooper brushed his hands off on his jeans as he stood looking down at the flowers he had placed on the headstone. Looking up at the cloudless sky, two birds flew in tandem on the wind. He smiled as he watched them soar higher and higher. He waved as they disappeared out of sight. Getting into his car, he leaned over and gave Ali a kiss as he flipped on the radio and sat for a moment as they heard his father's voice singing 'Here, There and Everywhere'.

Chapter 1

Cooper slid the key into the lock and let the door slowly swing open. He had put this day off for too long. His girlfriend Ali had wanted to come with him, but he needed to do this alone.

He stood in the foyer and looked around the living room. He fully expected to hear his mother's laughter, or a melody coming from his Da's guitar. He moved quietly around the house, expecting them to appear with a smile and a hug. But there was only stillness.

Walking to the kitchen and looked out the window past the pool at his father's studio. As he stood there he let the memories flood back. He thought of all the times when he was small that he and Paul would swim before Emily would call them in for lunch. The hours of practicing in the studio with Paul when he got home from school. He felt the tears begin to well up in his eyes as he stood there feeling as if he was a young boy again. He yearned to see his parents just one more time.

Lately, he had let his anger replace the deadening sadness in his heart. At least he was able to feel something as the anger ran through him. He knew once or twice lately he had scared Ali with his dark moods. He vowed to himself to work harder at fighting off the urge to give into despair.

Cooper heard a light knock on the door before it opened. Zak stood there with a grin on his face. "Hey man, Ali said you were gonna stop by here," he said as he entered the room. Cooper gave him a half smile as he replied, "I don't know where to begin." He waved his arm, "How do I pack up a lifetime of memories?"

Zak and Cooper knew each other inside and out. He and Ali knew he shouldn't be alone today. He had promised Ali he would come over and check on Cooper. Zak could tell she was worried about him when he wouldn't let her go with him to his parent's house.

Looking over at Cooper, "Have you thought about keeping the house? Moving back in?" he asked. Cooper sighed as he thought, "I did, but I'm not sure it's the right thing to do. I'm not sure it would be fair to Ali." Ali had transferred to Atlanta after the accident that killed his parents. She and Cooper were looking for a house to move into after finding his apartment was too small for the two of them.

Zak walked into the kitchen and glanced out the window. Looking back at Cooper he saw a shadow fall across his friends' features. "Hey, if you're not up to being here, why don't we go grab some lunch," he said, trying to lighten his friend's mood. Cooper sat down at the kitchen table shaking his head. "There is so much I need to do," he said as if to himself.

Zak grabbed a chair turning it around and plopped down. "Yeah, but there's no rush and besides, if you haven't talked to Ali about moving here, maybe you should before you do anything. She might like it."

Cooper looked at Zak and smiled. "Yeah, you may be right, I'll talk to her tonight." He stood and waved his hand at his friend, "Come on, let's go down to the pub, then I gotta head home." He stopped halfway to the door, "Oh wait, I've got to get something out of Da's studio."

Watching Cooper walk past the pool and unlocked the studio door. He wasn't gone that long when he reappeared with a big notebook under his arm. Zak smiled, he knew what it was. Paul had kept all his compositions in that notebook. From the time he was writing with John in Liverpool until he died. He thought about how valuable that notebook would be now. But he also knew it was going to be Cooper's most prized and cherished possession.

Sliding into the booth Zak said, "Stephen got promoted to supervisor last week." Cooper smiled, "That's Mom's old position isn't it?" "Yeah, it is. And Dad's before he became the Director," Zak replied. "It's been really hard for everyone there. Losing your Mom left a big hole in the company. She was Stephen's mentor and sounding board, he is lost without her," he remarked.

Cooper lifted his eyes to meet his friend's, "I know the feeling," he said with a half-smile. Zak reached over and patted his arm as the waitress brought them their menus. Suddenly realizing who Cooper was, she became very flustered and spilled a little of his beer as she set it down in front of him.

Zak chuckled to himself as she wiped it up blushing furiously. After she took their orders and walked away. Zak laughed, "I love watching women around you, cracks me up." Cooper made a face at him as he sipped his beer. "How are your Mom and Dad?" he asked.

Leaning back as he answered, "They are fine, planning a trip to Paris in the spring," he hesitated, "Finally." Cooper smiled, "Good for them! I was thinking of taking Ali away somewhere. I need to unplug before getting back into the studio. Suggestions?"

He thought for a moment, "Why don't you go down to the islands?" Cooper shrugged, "I don't know, that's so cliche," he said with a laugh. "Actually, I was thinking about London. Then heading up to Liverpool. What do you think?"

"I don't know Coop, maybe that's a trip you should put off for a while." Cooper thought for a minute, "I want to see where he lived, where he grew up, ya know." He nodded as he replied, "I understand, but for now maybe it would be
better for you to just go somewhere to relax and concentrate on you and Ali."

Ali had just gotten back from the store when she heard Cooper opened the door. "Hey baby, I'm back," he said. He placed the notebook down on the coffee table before heading to the kitchen. Cooper gathered her in his arms and kissed her sweetly. "You sent Zak after me," he whispered as he pulled back to look into her deep blue eyes.

She smiled up at him, "Yes, I did," she said as she kissed him. "You need to let us help you." He broke away and began helping her put things away. "I know, I know. I just thought I could get a few things done better on my own. Turns out, I didn't get much done at all."

"Are you hungry?" she asked. "No, Zak and I went by the pub and got a burger," he answered. She nibbled on a cookie as Cooper made a pot of coffee.

"Ali, we need to talk about something," he began. "Uh oh," she laughed. He grinned at her as he placed a mug in front of her and sat down to sip his own. "Zak said something that I wanted to talk to you about," he hesitated for a moment. "How would you feel about moving into my Mom and Da's house?" She looked at him and saw he was quite sincere.

"Really? I thought you wanted to sell it," she questioned.

"Well, that was my first thought, but think about it. It's got everything we are looking for anyway with the studio and pool. And Da was maniacal about keeping it in great shape. Can I take you to see it tomorrow?"

"Of course," she replied. "It would be nice to see where you grew up." "Great," he said as he stood up. "I've got something to show you, come here."

They walked into the living room and she sat down on the couch. Cooper gently picked up the notebook and sat down next to her. "This was my Da's," he began. "Every song he ever wrote is in here," he laid his hand on the cover as he looked back at her with a smile.

She loved his smile. She was happy that he seemed to be in a better place than he had been these last few weeks.

She knew from the moment they met that they would be together. His sweet brown eyes bore right through her when they had been introduced. He had come to her office for a meeting and she happened to be in the room as her boss led the meeting. Cooper had continually tried to catch her eye and she wondered if he was even paying attention to what was being said. Zak was there as well, being the attentive manager that he was.

After the meeting ended he approached her with a smile on his face that took her breath away. "I was wondering if you'd like to go to dinner with me this evening," he asked. "I realize it's short notice so if…" She interrupted him, "I would love to," she said. "Great," he replied. "We've got another meeting across town," he said, glancing over at Zak. "Give me your number and I'll text you."

After they had gone, she tried to work but was a bundle of nerves. She knew better than to date the 'talent' as they were called around the office. But he seemed so different from the others she had met. She went to the break room to grab a cup of coffee when her phone buzzed with a text message. 'I'm looking forward to this evening. Do you have a favorite restaurant? Or would you like me to choose?'

She responded, 'I know a wonderful little Italian place in my neighborhood. You should feel comfortable there, they are not impressed by celebrities.' she followed that with a winking emoji.

He laughed when he read her message. Zak looked at him with questioning eyes. "I'm taking Ali out to dinner tonight," Cooper said. Zak gave him a smile. "She seems like a nice girl," he said.

Arriving at the restaurant, Ali greeted the bartender with a wave as she was seated at her usual table in the back of the room. She was facing the door so she could see when he got there. There was a sudden gust of wind as the door opened and he stepped in. He adjusted his eyes to the darkness and saw her there. He smiled as he began walking towards her. He actually had a few butterflies in his stomach as he greeted her with a quick hug. "This is a nice place," he commented as he sat down.

They spent hours sharing a bottle of wine and talking about their lives. He had never been with a woman before who was so easy to talk to. Someone he felt actually cared about what he was saying instead of who he was.

She had in the past never really thought of him as anything more than a pretty face with a wonderful voice. She quickly realized how wrong she was. He was intelligent, funny, talented and charming beyond words.

Pulling herself out of her memories she saw the awe in his eyes. "Cooper, are you saying he kept them all here in this notebook. All of them?" she asked. "Yes, from the very first song to the last one we wrote together." She reached over and covered his hand with hers. "I am so happy you have this, I know it means the world to you baby," she whispered as she kissed his cheek.

He had told her early on who his father really was. She had a few moments of doubt until he showed her pictures of himself and his parents when he was a little boy. Paul still had the long hair they were all famous for and that smile that Cooper now wore. Then she began looking into the replacement. She was now convinced that Paul had escaped death in 1966 and found the love of his life with Cooper's mother, Emily.

Cooper told her many stories about him as he grew up in Atlanta. How the people that wanted Paul dead, sent him back to 1966 when Cooper was just a small boy. It was a fascinating story of the strong bond between Cooper and his father that they could communicate through Cooper's dreams. Thankfully, Emily was able to jump back and bring Paul home.

"I need to go through it and see if there are pieces he never recorded. I remember hearing about one song he wrote when he first jumped into the future. It was a love song for my mom. I can't remember the name of it, I think it had the word time in it," he said with a shrug.

She reached over and touched his face, "I think you are so lucky to have this. What a wonderful gift he left you," she said with a kiss.

Putting the book on the table, he turned to her. "Ali, I know I've been a pain in the ass to live with lately. I want to apologize," he began. "I am just having a tough time with all of this and I realized I was letting anger take over. I'm going to work really hard to get back on track and I don't want you to worry," he finished.

"Cooper, I understand. You've lost the two most important people in your life. I don't blame you for being angry or upset. It would be strange if you weren't," she said. Reaching up again, she took his chin in her hand and lightly kissed his lips. "I will be there for you even if you push me away. I love you," she finished.

He smiled at her as he said, "I love you too. You are so important to me. I don't want to lose you over my bad behavior. I hope you'll put up with me a while longer."

"I'm afraid you're stuck with me. I love you too much to give up that easily," she replied with a sweet smile. She rested her head on his shoulder as he opened the notebook. "Wow," she said as she looked at the pages as he turned them gently. "I'm amazed that he was this organized," she said.

Cooper laughed, "Oh, he was! Let's see," he said as he turned back to the first page. 'You'll be Mine,' A Lennon-McCartney original. But there were others there too. "I know they had each written songs separately before they met each other," he said as he flipped through the pages.

He wanted to find the song his Da had written when he first arrived here. He knew it was written before his parents had fallen in love, or at least before his Da told his mom he loved her. He flipped through the pages and found it. It was called, 'Time X 2.' "Here

Ali, look, it's the song I was wondering about. He never let anyone sing it, but I think he made a tape of it. I want to look for it when we go to the house tomorrow."

Ali got up and took their mugs to the kitchen. She was glad that he seemed to be coping better than he had been. There were a few nights she woke to find him in the living room sitting in the dark with tears in his eyes. It breaks her heart to see him so desperately sad.

She finished in the kitchen and walked back into the living room. He stood looking out the window at the skyline of Atlanta. It was a beautiful view. She watched him as he continued to gaze out the window. "What are you thinking?" she asked.

He turned around, "Nothing really," he responded with a half-smile. She walked up to him and put her arms around his waist. "I know that look," she teased. He laughed, "I'm not always deep in thought, ya know."

He brushed her hair away from her face and leaned down to kiss her lips. "Do you want to go out tonight?" he asked. She wrinkled her nose, "Do you mind if we stay in? I still have some work to do and I

was going to make a big salad, if that's ok with you."
He smiled, "You're gonna make me eat healthy again,"
he laughed. "Yes, I am!" she said with a grin as she
turned around to head back to the kitchen where she
had her laptop.

"Hey," he said as he gently took her arm and drew her
to him again. "Have I told you lately that I love you
dearly?" She smiled as she touched his cheek. "Yes,
you have." He kissed her deeply as he moved his hand
down her back.

They were jarred out of the moment by her phone
ringing. "Oh, that will be the office. Conference call,"
she said as she rolled her eyes.

Cooper walked to the couch and picked up the
notebook. Wanting to give her privacy, he headed to
the bedroom. Laying the notebook on the bed and
taking his sweater off over his head he threw it into
the chair which held freshly washed clothes. He
grimaced as he picked it up and folded it not wanting
to appear as if he didn't appreciate Ali's efforts to
keep him organized.

He made himself comfortable leaning against the stack
of pillows. Picking up the notebook he began flipping

through it. He was amazed at the sheer number of songs and partial songs that it held. He knew his father had been prolific, but he had no idea that there were so many more songs that were never completed. He shook his head in wonder. He had always admired his Da's work ethic. But he was still continually shocked at how talented he really was.

He was still flipping through the pages reading the notes that Paul or John had written alongside the lyrics when Ali walked in. Sighing as she sat down on the bed, "They want me in New York next week," she said. "Why?" he asked.

"It's the quarterly meeting and Jon doesn't trust any of the other A & R Admin Rep's," she said as she laid down and began stroking his arm. He put the notebook on the side table next to him and turned to lay down next to her. He looked into her eyes and said, "When do you have to leave?"

"Sunday evening. The meetings begin on Monday and runs through Wednesday. I'll catch the first flight back on Thursday morning," she offered. "Do you want me to go with you?" he asked as he ran his finger up and down her arm. "Aww, that's sweet of you, but I'll be so busy and worthless at the end of each day," she said with a little pout.

"Well, I'll tell you what," he began, "I'll stay here and hang out. I want to get together with Stephen soon. He got promoted to Mom's old position." She smiled at him, "Well, from what you've told me he deserves it. I'm happy for him."

"Zak said everyone there is still pretty down, especially Stephen," he said softly. Stephen was so much like his father Sam. Hard working and tough but a softy under it all. He and his wife Tiffany have been wonderful when it came to helping him as much as they could since Paul and Emily died. Even though they had their hands full with the twins, Ben and Tim.

"I want to touch base with Sam and Chris too." he said as he turned away and lay facing the ceiling. She turned to him with her head in her hand and watched him. She could stare at him for hours, he was so handsome with his deep brown eyes and 5 o'clock shadow. "What?" he questioned as he caught her gaze.

Seductively she moved to hover over him, "Nothing, just thinking about how pretty you are," she laughed as she gently bit his lip. He shot up and began tickling her relentlessly. "Stop, stop!" She pled before he began kissing her and removing her top. "You are so naughty," she whispered as he covered her mouth again with his. "Yes, I am," he agreed.

The next morning, they drove over to Paul and Emily's house. Ali was amazed at the elegant, but homey feel it had. As Cooper showed her around she began to imagine living here. Her only worry was making it their home and not his parents place. She smiled at him when he took her hand and led her outside. The pool was beautiful, and the pergola and grilling station were warm and cozy. When he showed her the studio his face lit up with pride.

On their way back to the apartment they talked about things they could change and do to the house to make it theirs. She was a little worried about security. Having Paul and Emily live there was one thing, no one knew who Paul really was. But everyone knew Cooper.

"I'm worried about privacy," she said as they walked into the apartment. "We can't have people walking up to the door night and day," she said with a laugh. He took her in his arms and kissed her as he said, "I know, I've thought about that too. I'll look into the

HOA and see what kind of restrictions they have on fencing or gates."

She reached up and stroked his cheek, "You really want to do this, don't you?" she asked sweetly. "Yes, I do," he smiled, "It's a great house. And I promise you'll have free reign in re-decorating it." She threw her head back in laughter, "You may regret that, I'm not the interior decorator type."

Made in the USA
Las Vegas, NV
18 September 2021